Bruce B

Murder in the Fells

Detective Inspector Skelgill Investigates

LUCiUS

EVIL LIES UNDETECTED

When shepherd Jud Hope finds an American passport in a fox's earth, a connection is made to an unidentified fatality – an elderly female walker who fell to her death in a treacherous rocky gill near Ambleside.

Meanwhile, a spate of 'nighthawker' incidents sees ancient monuments desecrated under cover of darkness. The spotlight falls upon Derek Shaw, a museum curator exploring Cumbria's Roman heritage.

Onto this stage emerges a second senior American hiker, Dorothy Baum. The intrepid Dorothy is here to meet her online sweetheart, Professor Felix Stowe-Upland, an expert in classical archaeology.

But when Felix fails to materialise, Dorothy falls in with an eccentric walking companion, 'Kooky Cathy', as she comes to call her. Derek Shaw seems to be shadowing the pair. Felix remains elusive, stringing Dorothy along with promises of his arrival.

Skelgill and his team realise Dorothy is in jeopardy. But they are two steps behind and the clock is ticking. She is somewhere in the fells, but where? The chain of Roman forts that she follows stretches from Ravenglass on the southwest coast, to Penrith in the far northeast.

And Dorothy seems to be covering her tracks.

TEXT COPYRIGHT 2022 BRUCE BECKHAM

All rights reserved. Bruce Beckham asserts his right always to be identified as the author of this work. No part may be copied or transmitted without written permission from the publisher.

This is a work of fiction. Names, characters, places and incidents either are the product of the author's imagination or are used fictitiously. Any resemblance to actual persons, living or dead, events and locales is entirely coincidental.

Kindle edition first published by Lucius 2022
Paperback edition first published by Lucius 2022
Hardcover edition first published by Lucius 2022

For more details and rights enquiries contact:
Lucius-ebooks@live.com

Cover design by Moira Kay Nicol
United States editor Janet Colter

EDITOR'S NOTE

Murder in the Fells is a stand-alone mystery, the nineteenth in the series 'Detective Inspector Skelgill Investigates'. It is set in the English Lake District, in particular tracing the route of the Roman forts, between Ravenglass on the coast – via Hardknott Pass, Ambleside and High Street – and Brougham near Penrith.

Absolutely no AI (Artificial Intelligence) is used in the writing of the DI Skelgill novels.

THE DI SKELGILL SERIES

Murder in Adland
Murder in School
Murder on the Edge
Murder on the Lake
Murder by Magic
Murder in the Mind
Murder at the Wake
Murder in the Woods
Murder at the Flood
Murder at Dead Crags
Murder Mystery Weekend
Murder on the Run
Murder at Shake Holes
Murder at the Meet
Murder on the Moor
Murder Unseen
Murder in our Midst
Murder Unsolved
Murder in the Fells
Murder at the Bridge
Murder on the Farm

Glossary

SOME of the Cumbrian dialect words, abbreviations, British slang and local usage appearing in *Murder in the Fells* are as follows:

Alreet/areet – alright (often a greeting)
Aunt Sally – target for criticism
B&B – guest house providing bed and breakfast
Beck – mountain stream
Blea – dark blue (Old Norse)
Bleaberry – bilberry
Blower – telephone
Bob on – quite right
Bottle – nerve (bottle & glass, Cockney)
Break duck – score (from cricket)
Bunk up – lift on shoulders
Burn – stream (Scots)
Butcher's – look (butcher's hook, Cockney)
Caff – café
Chore – steal
Chuck – dear (person)
Chuffed – pleased
Chuffin' – in place of an expletive
Clemmed – ravenous
Corrie – post-glacial hollow, high on fellside
Crack – gossip, chat
Cricket – fair play
Coo-clap – cow dung
Cuddy wifter – left-handed
Cur dog – fell sheepdog
Deek – look
Dinner – lunch
Dod – round-topped hill
Donnat – idiot, good for nothing
Fell – hill

Fettle – health
Force – waterfall
Fret – worry
Gaan – going
Gazumping – offering more for a property than the amount agreed by an intending buyer
GBH – grievous bodily harm
Gen – information
Gill – ravine on fellside, a gully
Gooseberry – when 'two's company, three's a crowd'
GR – George Rex (referring to King George V or VI)
Happen – maybe
Hersen/hissen – herself/himself
Hey up – hello, look out
Hoying – throwing (heavy rain)
How! – cry used for driving cattle
Howay – come on
Huff – bad mood
In-bye – enclosed pasture near the farmstead
Intake – enclosed pasture reclaimed from the fellside
Int' – in the/into
Mash – tea/make tea
Marra – mate (friend)
Mind – remember
Mizzling – misty drizzle
Mowdy-tump - molehill
Neb – nose; pry
Netty – toilet
Nowt – nothing
Off've – from
Ont' – on the
Oor – our
Oven-bottom cake – bread roll
Owt – anything
Partles – sheep droppings
Pash – sudden short sharp shower of rain
Peaky – pale from illness or fatigue

Pereth – Penrith
Pike – prominent peak
Scrat – scratch
Skel – boundary, divide (Old Norse)
Summat – something
Starter for ten – clue (e.g. in a quiz)
Stotting – pelting (rain)
Syling – heavy rain
T' – the (often silent)
Tarn – mountain lake, usually in a corrie
Thee/thew/thou – you, your
Tod – fox
Trod – narrow path worn by sheep
Us – often used for me/my/our
While – until
Whitefish – flattery
Wick – fit and healthy (for one's age)
WRAF – Women's Royal Air Force
Yourn – yours
Yowe – ewe

1. OUT OF THE FRYING PAN

Hope Farm, Seathwaite – 8.10 a.m., Monday, 18th May

'So this is yon cur dog.'
'Beggars can't be choosers, Arthur.'
'Thou should've had a word wi' oor Jud – he'd have sorted you out a pup – *how!*'

The venerable farmer's exclamation, cutting short his discourse, is explained by Skelgill's letting go of the baler twine that restrains Cleopatra, and the 'Canine Cannonball' making herself acquainted with her would-be detractor. Skelgill is grinning widely.

But Arthur Hope is a hulking man, and he absorbs the well-meant impact of the sturdy Bullboxer and wrestles her down, like he has done a thousand times with wild mountain sheep that can buck and butt for England. The dog appears to relish the rough attention of the big gnarled hands.

'There, you see, Art – she don't hold it against you.'
'It weren't us that said beggars can't be choosers, lad.'
'She knows I'm only joking.'

The dog breaks away to inspect the unfamiliar surroundings. Arthur Hope rises a little stiffly. Despite his advancing years, in the gloom of the converted smithy he is an imposing figure, his head bowed by habit to avoid the exposed oak joists. Skelgill, silhouetted at the open entrance, suddenly flinches – a barn swallow arrows over his shoulder to a nest in a dark niche of the low ceiling.

'Thou comin' in for a fry.'
'You know what they say about the bear and the woods, Art.'
'Don't fret – it weren't a question.'

Skelgill gives a shrug of mea culpa. He gestures to the

motorbike that gleams on a hydraulic repair stand in the centre of the workshop.

'Nice job.'

Arthur Hope ducks out of the doorway and turns to admire his handiwork, his retirement hobby.

'Matchless. 1959. Four-stroke twin. Another week and I reckon she'll be running. I'm waiting on a copper head gasket. Come back and test drive her, if you like.'

Skelgill reacts with interest. Such is the appeal of simplicity – these machines that did not need microchips, that their owners could fix on the hoof. The man interrupts his thoughts.

'Still on your Triumph? That'll be coming up for vintage.'

'Aye, one owner since new.' Skelgill gives a sardonic moan. 'I might finish paying for it this year.'

He is prompted to stoop as Cleopatra makes a break between them. He grabs the makeshift leash and raises it illustratively.

'I came in the car.'

'Aye, I saw thee.'

Skelgill casts a reverential glance. It is no surprise that the farmer was evidently up and about before five a.m., despite that he had parked well down the lane to avoid disturbing the inhabitants.

Now Arthur Hope looks with puzzlement at Skelgill's hybrid attire.

'Training, were thee?'

Skelgill gives a growl of resignation.

'Since Jess left us for dead I've accepted my best days are behind me.'

The man seems to appreciate Skelgill's self-deprecation.

'Comes to us all, lad.'

He stretches and groans as they pick a path across the paved farmyard. A second swallow hawks for clegs, jinking this way and that. Rival house sparrows have set up an energetic chirruping from the ridges and gutters of the slate-built farmhouse, their chatter like a cascade of pebbles on the cobbles. The bright cobalt blue sky seems to resonate with the invisible bleating of lambs in-bye. Higher-pitched, a buzzard mews, rising against the sun on an early thermal.

'Nay, Arthur – you're as fit as a fiddle.'

In the hewn face, its clints and grykes chiselled out by the sharp morning light, there is a proud glint in the chalky blue eyes.

'Mind the coo-clap, lad.'

Skelgill chuckles, but does not push his point.

Arthur Hope raises oily hands.

'I'll go in via tradesman's. See what Gladis has got for t' dog. What's she called?'

'Cleopatra – she came with the name, obviously.'

He adds the rider to allay any charge of pretentiousness – but it is unnecessary; the farmer seems to take it in his stride.

'What's that, Roman?'

Skelgill looks momentarily perplexed.

'Aye, summat like that.'

They diverge, and Skelgill heads for a door marked by a rudimentary hand-painted sign that would win no prizes for advertising – but in its own way is suitably understated: that there is a rustic café and boots, bikers and Bullboxers are welcome.

*

'There we go – thou must be fair clemmed, young Daniel.'

Skelgill's stomach has been performing somersaults for some minutes, as from a serving hatch the unseen tentacles of frying bacon inveigled their way into his nostrils. But now as a great platter is set before him he restrains his animal instincts, in order to acknowledge his hostess. Gladis Hope is a well-padded indefatigable woman in her late sixties, her grey hair tied back in a neat bun. Her face is big-boned like a Herdwick sheep and in the greenish-blue eyes rests an innate kindliness.

'Gladis, it's you who's looking younger every time I see you.'

'Howay, lad – that's enough of your whitefish.'

She paws at him, dismissively, though her rosy cheeks take on a little extra colour. But she deflects his flattery with a query of her own.

'And how's your Ma? She were wick as ever, last time I saw her. Pedalling up t' Honister like the devil hissen were after her!'

'That's her guilty mind – but she's alreet, thanks – she sends her regards.'

Skelgill finds he has knife and fork poised, but he lowers them politely. That this place brings out the best of his manners is not just down to Gladis Hope's legendary Cumbrian Fry. Hope Farm was the springboard from which he and school pal Jud Hope launched their expeditions – that is, when they were not pressed into service hauling fodder to sheep, raking hay, or repairing dry stone walls. Such experience was formative in his appreciation of life in the fells. Of the unobtrusive skills handed down, epitomising the values of integrity and mutual respect, of stoicism and good honest toil. And, yes, foundation to it all was the hill-farmer's wife and her dedication to the unspoken adage: if the men are not fed the farm does not function.

'I've put you up a couple of extra sausages.'

She winks knowingly, and leans back to catch a glimpse of Cleopatra, curled up at Skelgill's feet, opining through mournful eyes that she has not been fed for – what is it, now? – it must be a week! Skelgill shakes his head – he knows mournful will become baleful if he lingers much longer.

But now Arthur Hope enters, munching upon a breakfast roll, an oven-bottom cake that looks specially home-baked for his oversize mitts. His wife regards him questioningly.

'Have thou got it?'

The farmer has his mouth full, but contrives by way of a facial contortion to convey a reply in the affirmative, and he pulls something from the hip pocket of his boiler suit and deals it onto the tablecloth beside Skelgill's plate. It is a small portrait-shaped black leather wallet, a little worse for wear, weathered, and possibly chewed. Skelgill looks up expectantly.

'He wo' gaan to put it int' lost property.' Gladis Hope is amenably chiding towards her husband.

The reprimand, however, is sufficient for Skelgill to deposit his cutlery and pick up the item.

Arthur Hope evidently feels he should offer an explanation.

'Oor Jud fount it – ower by High Street – Arthur's Pike.' He gives a little cough, as though he might be embarrassed by his own name. 'It were only yesterday he minded he had it.'

Skelgill opens the wallet. It contains a passport. The case appears to have preserved its condition. His first impression is that it is the new post-Brexit edition, ubiquitous European maroon no more, but resplendent in midnight blue. And then he realises that the embossed golden motif is not the coat of arms of the United Kingdom, but the Great Seal of the United States of America.

He opens it to the photo-ID page and stares at the details.

'Is it important, oor Daniel?'

It is Gladis Hope that breaks the silence; her words carry a note of concern. The parent-child roles have subtly shifted; now the elders defer to Skelgill; this is his area of expertise.

But if there is something of significance Skelgill either does not know or decides not to alarm the honest couple. He speaks casually.

'Easy enough for someone to drop it and not notice.'

Arthur Hope is quick to agree.

'Aye, that's what I said – didn't I, Gladis? It were in a foxhole – old tod could have carried it for miles.'

Skelgill is nodding. He glances up at the farmer.

'Have you got a flock over there?'

Now Arthur Hope responds a little more guardedly.

'Jud were doin' a recce for t' Blencathra. You'd have to ask him exactly. He's at t' sale at Pereth this morning.'

The Hopes, like many hill families, have long contributed a foxhound or two to the famous fell pack. Skelgill steers away from any conversation that may be deemed contentious.

'Aye – I saw a couple of trailers on the road – spring lambs, by the look of them.'

But he runs out of things to say – until his stomach seems to speak for itself – although the plaintive appeal in fact emanates from a slightly lower origin, of the doggy kind.

Gladis Hope tugs at her husband's sleeve.

'Howay – leave them in peace, while they've had their breakfast.'

2. PIPE DREAMS

Overnight Monday into Tuesday 19th May

From: Dorothy K. Baum
To: Professor Felix Stowe-Upland
Subject: Our adventure begins

Dear Felix, I am sorry you cannot now make the first couple of days. I entirely understand that between nursing your bad back and dealing with the financial hitches you will be otherwise detained. These things, as you say, must take priority. But what are a few days after almost a year of anticipation? And I will be fully occupied with the fascinating itinerary you have laid out for us – simply walking through the glorious Cumbrian countryside would be sufficient (I cannot wait to see the view along Wastwater that you describe), never mind the historical interest. I expect I will end up having to tear myself away from the Roman bath house at Ravenglass to keep to the schedule, and I just cannot quite imagine how it will feel to approach the extraordinary Roman fort at Hardknott Pass from across the fells, following in the footsteps of foreign legionaries almost two millennia ago. If I may digress, when during our early correspondence you wrote me that the world's largest Roman edifice is not in Italy but England, I became consumed with a hunger to learn more – and that Hadrian's Wall begins in Cumbria – and now, in the knowledge that the wall leads to the – well – to not 'the' but to 'our' cottage – I almost feel faint at the thought. In fact, I feel like my namesake Dorothy setting out upon the Yellow Brick Road!

My British Airways flight from Louis Armstrong lands at Heathrow at 9:15 p.m. your time, tomorrow. I have allowed 2 hours to clear customs and catch the express to the centre of London. My guide book tells me it is a 20-minute ride by taxi from

Paddington to Euston. The Caledonian sleeper departs at 10 minutes to midnight, and I can hop off with the mail at Carlisle at 5:07 a.m. The first train to Ravenglass does not leave until 7:10 a.m., so I am planning on a leisurely breakfast in the station buffet – my first taste of Cumberland sausage, perhaps! From there, the branch-line journey looks delightful, curving around the Solway coast, and I will alight and begin exploring shortly before 9 a.m., Wednesday.

It is so exciting to think that in just a few days' time I will literally be taking the first step of our adventure. I hope you don't mind my using the word 'adventure' – because that is how it feels to me, so much more than a journey. And also 'our' adventure – I have not dared to count my chickens, as the saying goes. But now that I have the tickets in my hand (or, at least, on my cell phone), everything is beginning to seem real.

I have my fingers and everything else crossed that the paperwork can be completed in time. I checked online and I see that Rose Cottage, Hexham is still displayed, but marked as "Under Offer". I hope that deters any other potential buyers. I believe you call it 'gazumping'! Of course, I have no comprehension of the property market in England. Over here our realtors can sell homes without the need to involve a legal expert – but I imagine that when title deeds date back over several centuries, there are bound to be complications. Oh, the idea of our living in a cottage built before the United States even had its first president is quite mind-boggling! I approved the SWIFT payment order – the electronic transfer should be activated by now, so do let me know that you receive it safely when it clears tomorrow. And please do not keep apologizing! You should not feel embarrassed in asking me. It is through no fault of yours that the buyers of your townhouse have suffered a last-minute delay. Indeed, I am honored to play my part in our joint venture – and after all, as you say, it is no more than a stopgap. (May I say, that I am sure we will be pooling our resources in our times ahead together.) I should also tell you that I have taken a hint which I believe you unintentionally dropped – and I have withdrawn $10,000 in cash, just in case there are any teething problems, such as accessing my bank accounts, or for unseen eventualities in the first month or so. I can tell you, I have never held so much money! But I was surprised how little space it takes up, just a neat stack of $100 bills. I pictured myself being stopped at immigration with a briefcase, like a secret agent or a fugitive! But it fits into my small purse. I did consider hiding it inside the wrapper of a candy bar! But it turns out that it does not exceed the limit for taking undeclared cash out of the USA, nor for bringing money into the UK. Nonetheless, I will be following your general advice, not to draw attention to myself. I would not want anything to go wrong.

On which note, poor you, how infuriating for your back injury to recur at such an inopportune moment. I pray as you say that it will come right in a day or two's time. I am sure it was the packing and lifting of your boxes of books. At least you have experience of how best to manage it. And it is encouraging to hear that walking with a backpack actually seems to help in the recuperation. On the subject of your books, I am so looking forward to reading from your historical library; it sounds as though you have a Roman collection without equal. And there is something special about antiquarian books, something about the texture and the smell, the knowledge that generations of scholars have painstakingly perused their pages. I must confess, I have put into storage for later shipping my precious collection of Dickens (I have several first editions); they transport one back in time to the bustling streets of 19th century London. But otherwise, I have divested myself of almost all of my possessions. To think that everything I own – frankly, all that I need – is already packed into my smart new backpack. And how light and comfortable and efficient they are nowadays – I remember on a student road trip struggling with a steel-framed army surplus version. And how little one actually needs when it comes to the crunch. Although I do look forward to us furnishing together our cottage; the thought fills me with a thrill, of wandering the cobbled streets of Hexham, browsing the antique shops, of stopping for afternoon tea and cake.

But I must not get ahead of myself! There is the expedition first to savor. What a wonderful idea to undertake your Roman Roamin' walking tour and finish at Rose Cottage. And I will be your sole student! I cannot quite believe that I have reached the age of 70 and yet never visited the island of Great Britain. When first we began to correspond, who could have imagined it would lead to this? That we would have so much in common. That our mutual desires for companionship would be in such true alignment. I feel we know one another so well. I understand your discretion – but, what have we possibly got to lose? We are mature enough to know that the best time of our lives stretches before us. And I know you say I have not cajoled you – but you are always too polite.

Poor Felix – I am rambling. It is late evening here in deepest Louisiana. The weather is wild and the tips of branches are tapping on my windows. Perhaps when I go to sleep a tornado will lift me up and deposit me in Cumbria! It is the early hours for you. I will go to bed and join you in dreamland. Perhaps, when I wake, there will be a reply in my inbox.

Yours in anticipation,
Dorothy.

From: Professor Felix Stowe-Upland
To: Dorothy K. Baum
Subject: Re: Our adventure begins

My dearest Dorothy, what a delight (as ever) to receive your eloquent (as ever) communication. By Jove, it is a pleasure just to read your words; honey and light in harmony; even my PhD students these days lapse into what I believe they call 'techspeak', a beastly expression in its own right. If it is not that, I receive submissions that lie at the other end of the spectrum, impenetrable screeds of tautology and circular arguments. You may hold a postgraduate degree in History, but that you are an English major shines through like a shaft of gold, when all around is dark – just as, may I say, your virtual presence does in my humble life. And to think, in a few short days I shall witness the words tumble from your lips in your 'soft Southern accent', as you call it. For identification purposes, I, of course, shall be carrying a copy of The Times and wearing a red carnation in my buttonhole!

Alas, my lumbar region, the *inferiosis dorsi*. It has a tendency to flare up a day or two after the damage is incurred, so I often have no precise idea of the cause. But – yes – I do believe it was lifting a too-heavy box. Either that, or the case of Dom Pérignon that will be waiting for us on ice when we reach our destination!

My dear, your journey will be tiring, if not tiresome. May I suggest that, on arrival at Ravenglass you find some accommodation for the night, rather than attempt the first leg of the walk on the same day? Not only may this allow extra time for my recalcitrant spine to recover, but also you will enjoy a more relaxed start. As I have explained, at this time of year, between the Easter and Whitsun holidays, the Lakes as an attraction operates at something like half capacity, so there are always lodgings to be found – in Ravenglass ranging from homely B&Bs to a jolly decent small country inn. You will be able to deposit your rucksack and take a gentle stroll to the Roman bath house. (The locals refer to it as Walls Castle.) Is it not extraordinary to think that the occupiers were taking hot baths almost two millennia ago! There were up to five hundred men stationed there between 130 AD and the end of the 4th century. The port and its fortress were effectively an extension of the Wall, the most southerly point of the coastal defence system and the western extremity of the Roman frontier, that stretched over three thousand miles to the Atlantic coast of North Africa.

Today the village itself is both quiet and quaint – still with active fishing – a marvellous location at the confluence of three rivers, the Irt, the Mite and the Esk. One may repose at the inn with a martini and savour splendid views across the estuary and marshes to the Irish Sea.

A further reason not to rush is the weather forecast. While not entirely reliable in these parts, I believe it to be more propitious for subsequent days. And indeed, might I suggest an alternative approach to the stage of the journey between Ravenglass and the Roman fort at Hardknott Pass? From Ravenglass there is a restored 19th century private railway, built originally to bring iron ore from mines high in the fells. Today it offers a passenger service, running for seven miles up into Eskdale to its terminus at

Dalegarth for Boot. The latter hamlet is appropriately named as a point from which many set off on foot! From Dalegarth station, the fort is a mere three miles of easy walking (albeit an incline) on the sheep-cropped grass verge beside the single-track lane. Onwards from Hardknott Pass – via the Wrynose Pass – and Little Langdale is reached in another seven miles, with plentiful accommodation. So, a ten-mile walk in comfortable conditions. This could be accomplished in one day, rather than taking the two-day route from Ravenglass to Wasdale Head, followed by the more arduous cross-country trek to Hardknott. However, I appreciate your desire to see the breathtaking views and towering screes of Wastwater.

But these are decisions you may make at leisure. There really is no pressing requirement to adhere to an exact timetable or route. Certainly, for my part, I should feel less anxious to know that, since you will be embarking alone, you would be in a position to summon assistance – indeed, even to hitch a lift (there is a blast from the past!). But it is true to say that at our age one cannot be too careful. I appreciate what you have told me about your extensive walking experience, and your level of fitness – but even a proficient mountaineer can twist or sprain an ankle – a minor but debilitating injury. *Contritium praecedit superbia;* pride comes before a fall! To be stranded several miles into the fells when the weather takes a turn for the worse is suddenly a serious prospect.

Either way, I should be able to join you at Little Langdale, and from there we may resume our Roman Roamin', taking in at Ambleside the marvellous fort Galava, on the shore of Windermere; thence the remarkable 'road in the sky' of High Street, which leads us to Brocavum, the fort just south of Penrith. I suggest we take the short train ride north to Carlisle (the site of Petriana, which was the largest stronghold in the district), from where we can pick up Hadrian's Wall in all its glory and begin the final homeward-bound section of our journey. Now the points of interest will come thick and fast, and you shall probably have to quell my exuberance or be subjected to a running commentary. There is so much to see between there and Hexham; I suggest we anticipate three nights of stopovers. There will be ample accommodation at the villages of Brampton, Haltwhistle and Haydon Bridge.

And then – yes! – Hexham it shall be – and Rose Cottage. I am determined to see that the legal loose ends are sewn up so that formal completion will be timeous. I am assured by my solicitor that the seized-up chain that is delaying the sale of my York property will be oiled and in motion within forty-eight hours. Although frustrating, this is a common feature over here, and nothing to lose sleep over. Notwithstanding, I am most grateful for your kind gesture to make your funds available for liquidity purposes, to underwrite my bridging loan. This means that we shall have the keys to Rose Cottage no matter what, and within the week your collateral will be returned directly by the bank. Therefore, as you say, it will really seem like 'our' cottage. It is jolly generous of you to offer to share the financial burden – although I must draw the line in entangling you in a commitment when we have not properly got to know one another. Despite our many, many communications, as I have opined on several occasions – and despite your kind protestations – you might just find me too cantankerous a companion, and a pipe-smoker at that! I am surely not worthy; I cannot quite believe that such a wonderful woman as you are wishes to – how may I put it? – team up with me. Naturally, our 'rosy' future can comprise elements such as shared ownership; that sort of thing is surely something to look forward to in the months to come, as summer unfolds, and we can enjoy exploring the district, not least the limitless tapestry of historical interest that brought us together in the first instance. And I shall certainly value your advice and good taste in furnishing Rose Cottage!

I would, however, implore you to continue to resist the temptation to mention our little venture to nearest and dearest. So far, you have been an absolute brick. I know you think I am being over-cautious – and I can assure you there is nothing I look forward to more than the day I can stand atop Scafell Pike (the highest point in England) and proclaim our union to all and sundry. Call me superstitious or irrational – but I sense that for either one of us, to be broken-hearted would be pain enough, never mind having to suffer the ignominy of a public retreat with one's tail between one's legs. And I know, dearest Dorothy, that you insist you are certain it will work out (and who am I, a mere mortal man to challenge a woman's intuition), but if you will indulge me this fancy for a little longer you will greatly allay my anxieties. And I look forward to being proved comprehensively wrong.

When you wrote I was asleep. Now it is early morning here in England, and I think of you and your sweet dreams, which I hope you are enjoying this very moment. And, I pray, not quite so tempestuous as the fictional Dorothy endured, although I am amused by your simile. When you see with your own eyes the extraordinary sight that is Hadrian's Wall, winding off beyond the smoky horizon, built with ten million pale limestone blocks, you will think it does look very like the Yellow Brick Road – and, yes, leading perhaps to the place where "the dreams that you dare to dream really do come true".

Your most humble servant and most faithful friend,
Felix.

3. FOXED

Penrith, and Arthur's Pike, High Street – 9.20 a.m., Tuesday, 19th May

'Guv, I've found a possible match.'

Skelgill and DS Leyton break off from their conversation. DS Leyton appears to be impersonating a dalek, but he retracts his arm and steps back as their younger female colleague glides into their superior's office. She has eschewed her regular sporty student get-up in favour of fashionable vintage flares and an oversized check shirt that almost might be one of Skelgill's, were it not for the lack of creases; moderate platforms that accentuate her athletic build perhaps account for the subtly altered gait. She attracts the scrutiny of her associates; both of whom seem to accept after a moment's reflection that she must know what she is doing. For their part they are in shirtsleeves; through the slats of a venetian blind snatches of birdsong drift on a balmy spring breeze.

DS Leyton looks inquiringly at his fellow sergeant, in response to her opening remark. Skelgill, at whom it was directed, seems more interested in the tray of teas that DS Jones deposits upon his desk atop a manila folder. She distributes the mugs and extracts from the file copies of a stapled two-page document, which she also hands out before taking her seat by the window. A more energetic zephyr ripples the blind and disturbs her fair hair; bands of sunlight highlight the shades of blonde and bronze. She is momentarily distracted; when she gathers herself she sees that DS Leyton is squinting with puzzlement at the dense type.

'The American passport that was handed in yesterday?'

He gives a small upward jerk of his head.

'Ah, gotcha.'

Skelgill has ignored the first page and is staring intently at the second, which comprises a gallery of images. His expression is one of distaste, a clue to the unfortunate nature of the content. DS Jones waits, until he looks up to invite her explanation.

'Remember the body that was found in the wood at Ambleside and never identified? An elderly woman? It was this time last year – the twenty-second of May.'

Skelgill nods grimly – perhaps ruefully. There is an overriding reason he would not forget. Never mind that it is always a matter of frustration to the police when a corpse remains unidentified, in this case there was the location: Skelghyll Wood. With its archaic spelling (championed by Wordsworth, it is said), other than upon his office door it is one of only two localities in the Lakes that the Old Norse compound noun appears.

DS Jones does not wait for a response.

'The passport belonged to a Patricia Carolyn Jackson. She would have been seventy-two at the time of her death. You can see there is a similarity in appearance – although I admit it's not conclusive. But there are other strands of evidence. The physical description in the lab report mentions that she was almost certainly a spectacle wearer, despite that none were found with the body. You can see in the passport photo a distinct pale line across the bridge of her nose, as though she removed them for the camera. There was also speculation that at least two items of her clothing were of North American origin – they were outdoor brands that can be bought online but from websites of US-based retailers. And, finally, the passport has a date stamp of entry into the UK – just four days prior to the discovery of her body.'

Skelgill remains pensive. It is left to DS Leyton to respond.

'It fits – the idea of her being a visitor. You've contacted the American embassy?'

He knows DS Jones well enough to imbue his question with a rhetorical inflexion.

She nods obligingly, but a small crease forms in the centre of her smooth tanned brow.

'They don't have a Patricia Jackson on their missing persons database. Nor a report of a lost passport in that name. They have forwarded my enquiry to the FBI. Unfortunately, the section in the passport where you can write your address and emergency contacts has been left blank. Her place of birth is Baton Rouge – but that might not tell us a great deal. However, it was a new passport – issued only five weeks before she travelled. As I understand it, they will have address details – I guess otherwise how would they send it out.'

'And no joy?'

DS Jones glances at her wristwatch.

'There was nothing at close of play yesterday. At the moment it's four-thirty a.m. in Washington, D.C. I'm really not sure how quickly we can expect them to respond. I feel like they have a lot on their plate right now.'

DS Leyton seems unusually perturbed.

'She'll have been someone's old granny – they must be missing her. It's not likely she took off on a jaunt to the Lakes without telling anyone.'

His logic is reasonable, but it is apparent to them all that the facts suggest otherwise, and he suffers such a second thought. He runs a hand through his tousle of dark hair and glances up to the ceiling, showing the whites of his eyes.

'I don't suppose they'll have a DNA profile – an old girl like that.'

DS Jones opens her palms, an expression of reluctant agreement. It would seem unlikely. But she reiterates her colleague's point.

'As you say – surely somebody must be missing her. Or, if not quite that, they will realise when prompted that she has gone. It would be easy enough to think a person has moved away. Especially a less-familiar neighbour. But it's puzzling, nonetheless – unless she had no relatives, or had lost touch with them.'

DS Leyton is racking his brains to be helpful.

'If she's left a property, there'll be personal effects. They'll be able to get a swab or a sample from something – a hairbrush, toothbrush, bar of soap? Then there's dental records. And don't they use private ancestry databases in the States?'

Skelgill has been listening, looking rather pessimistic. Now he rises, cupping his mug of tea as though to heat his hands –

paradoxically so given the warmth of the day. He turns to scrutinise the map of Cumbria pinned to his wall.

'What's to say Patricia Carolyn Jackson isn't merrily going about her business?'

He continues to peruse the map, swaying a little as it appears he makes some estimate of geography. It is left to DS Jones to unpick his cryptic remark.

'You mean that she simply hasn't reported the loss of her passport? That she's still here in the UK?'

Skelgill does not answer immediately; he takes a gulp of tea, keeping his eyes fixed on the map.

'It's a good stretch of the legs from Arthur's Pike down to Ambleside – the best part of High Street.'

At this, DS Leyton pipes up.

'Where is that, Guv – High Street? I've heard mention of it – the nippers' school did a history project – it was on the classroom walls for parents' evening.'

Skelgill raps a knuckle against the map. He turns and grins, a little sardonically. He raises his mug.

'More my cup of tea than yours, Leyton. Twenty-three mile. Three-and-a-half thousand foot of ascent. You'd better stick to your metal-detecting.'

*

'So, this really was a Roman road?'

DS Jones is surveying the scene. She stands a little ahead of Skelgill, looking away from him, and her expression is rather more sceptical than the careful tone of voice she employs.

Skelgill, however, seems ambivalent about the matter.

'So they say. You know how the Romans liked their beelines. If you look on the map, it's arrow-straight from Ambleside to Penrith.'

'But to build a road along a mountain ridge – it defies logic.'

Now Skelgill makes a face of disagreement.

'Think of what the dale bottoms were like. Thick forest. Swamps. Bears. Wolves. The locals.'

He produces a macabre grin, and DS Jones sees he includes himself in this latter category – though it is obvious he carries a good share of later Norse invaders' genes. She murmurs thoughtfully.

'The Carvetii.'

There is a pause before Skelgill responds.

'The what-ee?'

'The Carvetii – if I correctly recall my GCSE history. They were the Celtic tribe – the Iron Age Britons that occupied this region. We had a school trip to the site of the fort at Pooley Bridge. It was all trees and midges. A bit of a let-down.'

Now Skelgill exhibits a mild interest.

'Dunmallet?'

'Oh – maybe – I can't remember.'

Skelgill continues to be forthcoming.

'It's the name of the little fell. Wainwright wrote about it. It's called Dunmallard on the OS map.'

He points, his arm outstretched on the horizontal in a northerly direction.

'That's it there. See – the wooded dod.'

DS Jones comes to his shoulder and they both stare for a few moments. It does not take much height gain to get a good view in the Lakes, and before them the cobalt blue ribbon of Ullswater lies still in the valley like the glacier that preceded it. Emerald woods of oak and paler birch rise from the shores, giving way to intake pastures on the lower fellsides, then an irregular patchwork of bracken, mat grass and grey-brown scree. DS Jones rotates slowly on her heel, squinting reflectively as though she is making some assessment of the landscape.

'Do you think the Romans vanquished the Britons, or allowed them to coexist?'

Skelgill takes a moment to reply.

'No point sacking the workers.'

It is a somewhat oblique answer, but probably it strikes to the heart of all successful invasion strategies.

He moves on past her, and she hurries to keep up.

Against his better judgement, to locate the foxhole Skelgill is using a GPS device borrowed from his mountain rescue kit – an essential in low visibility, but a small embarrassment to him in the prevailing fine conditions. He jams it into his pocket and makes a sound of disgust.

'Jud reckons the earth's in the boulders below Whinny Crag.' They have been ascending gradually, but now he veers along the contour. 'Look – you can see where that trod runs up through the bracken.' He points to a sheep-path worn into the turf, a distinct narrow line of bare dry soil. Tod would not be averse to using the ready-made thoroughfare.

Now Skelgill skirts the junction of scree and a shelf of boulders partly grown in by fresh green bracken. A meadow pipit takes flight, its fine three-note warning call suggestive of a nest in the vicinity. He takes care to tread on the lichen-encrusted rocks, a landscape like Mars in miniature.

'There's a glove!'

It is DS Jones who exclaims.

Skelgill looks impassive.

His colleague clambers down amidst the boulders.

'And a sock!'

She hands them up. They are not in the best of order.

Skelgill glowers as he assesses the items.

'These are blokes' sizes. Fit me.' Then he smirks. 'There's not another sock, is there, lass?'

DS Jones is reaching into the tunnel – but to no avail. She takes a last look, using the torch on her mobile phone. Then she scrambles back up to squat beside Skelgill.

'Sorry – that's it.' She rubs at her sullied hands. 'They were lying outside the mouth of the hole.'

'Jud might have pulled them out. He wouldn't have thought owt of it – shepherds find this sort of stuff all the time.'

'You mean in foxholes?'

'Not necessarily – but, aye – foxes, they're like magpies. I've had running shoes took off my back step – turn up in the garden a month later. Owt that smells of human – or animal, depending what you've stood in – they'll take it for fun – for the cubs to chew and play with. This time of year, especially. Keeper I know – mind

31

Eric Hepplethwaite? – he were telling me the other night – there were a town fox that had over a hundred shoes.'

DS Jones is regarding him a little doubtfully, waiting for a punch line. Instead, Skelgill resorts to hyperbole to drive home his point.

'They'll take all sorts – they'll dig up a dead pet cat if you bury it in your garden – and never leave your grotts overnight on a low-hanging washing line.'

She cannot contain a burst of laughter – his cheeky suggestion, employing the slang term for male underwear. But she steers the conversation back around to their quest.

'So the leather case of the passport – that was the attraction to the fox?'

Now Skelgill casts about censoriously.

'I doubt it was dropped just here. Jud reckons it were a foot inside the earth.' He indicates with a jerk of his head. 'Maybe up on the summit – picnic spot. Nice flat ledge in the lee. Draws foxes at night, scavenging leftovers.'

'You don't think a fox would carry it from further afield?'

Skelgill shrugs.

'They can roam far and wide – but more likely to stay local in the breeding season. Territory hereabouts – probably a thousand acres. You're talking a couple of miles across.'

DS Jones approaches the next point tentatively.

'Skelghyll Wood – that would be too far?'

He makes brief eye contact, but quickly raises his sights to the horizon, looking due south. The fellside rises smoothly in a series of rolling bluffs with no obvious apex. If there ever were a Roman road, all traces have long gone.

'The summit of High Street's about six miles. Then Ambleside – the wood, if you went that way – you're talking the same again.'

DS Jones nods pensively.

'The time of the fall – whatever happened to her – was never conclusively established. According to the best estimates the body had been lying in situ, death having occurred, for a good two days.'

Skelgill turns to scrutinise his colleague.

'What are you angling at?'

Her response comes as a question.

'A person like that – how fast would they walk?'

Skelgill screws up his features, revealing his front teeth.

'Two miles an hour.'

'Really – is that all?'

But Skelgill wants to understand her thinking.

'Why?'

'I just wondered. Assuming she was heading south, if we knew what time she fell we could estimate what time she passed this spot. And from that make a guess at where she might have come from. The investigation took place in the Ambleside-Windermere area.' She half turns to indicate the direction from which they have approached, the opposite direction. 'Isn't it more likely she would have stayed overnight at Pooley Bridge, Penrith, even? She must have walked far enough to merit resting here. You can imagine her stopping for a snack, taking out a camera to catch the view – and the passport dropping unseen.'

Skelgill is now staring northwards, perhaps making calculations, perhaps not thinking at all.

'Guv – the passport suggests she did have her possessions with her.'

A small reaction is elicited from Skelgill. He is thinking these are fair points, albeit not conclusions he would yet wish to set much store by. At this juncture he is content to have his boots on the same ground, to absorb an intuitive grasp of the locus that may stand him in good stead if and when more pieces of the jigsaw fall into place. He feels they have learned a number of things, but he does not need to list them, nor even to know what exactly they are.

But DS Jones, characteristically, has homed in on the logical conundrum. While the incident was not recorded as a suspicious death – misadventure was the Coroner's verdict – it would not be accurate to say there were no suspicious circumstances. The hiker had been found with no form of identification, or any possessions. As DS Jones has indicated, an appeal to B&Bs, hotels and holiday accommodation, a description circulated, had proved fruitless. That the elderly female had suffered a fatal fall into a steep ravine seemed clear – as was borne out by the pathologist's report – but her identity, and the nature of her presence in the Lake District have remained a mystery.

'She might have hidden her kit.'

DS Jones seems surprised that Skelgill ventures an idea.

'What do you mean?'

He shrugs, as though he does not exactly 'mean' anything.

'For all we know she had a full pack with a tent. Wild camping. There's folk do that. It's what I do. Mainly bivvy. That could be why no hotelier reported her.'

'But what do you mean about hiding it?'

Skelgill's gaze drifts away again, this time across the lake to the Helvellyn range that separates Ullswater from Thirlmere.

'If you're ticking off summits on a route, why carry the bag to the top when you're coming back that way?'

DS Jones nods – she gets his point – but her tone remains puzzled.

'She concealed her kit and someone took it. Then they were too afraid or too crooked to own up. Do you think that's the most likely explanation?'

Skelgill looks alarmed, that his devil's advocacy would seem so definitive.

'I'm just saying.'

DS Jones regards him intently; Skelgill yawns, and stretches as if preparatory to setting off.

'I take it you want to look at the spot where she was found?'

Skelgill nods slowly, without any great enthusiasm.

It is left to DS Jones to winkle out his intentions.

'But we're not actually going to walk the twelve miles?'

He casts a sidewise glance at her; his half-closed eyes hint at mischief.

'It's thrice that by car.'

Such is the nature of Cumbrian topography. DS Jones falls in with his earlier assertion.

'No wonder the Romans went along the ridge.'

Skelgill grins wryly.

'But I'd like to know it's definitely her. No point us all barking up the wrong tree.'

She understands his logic. The identity of the woman could almost certainly hold the key to her fate – or, at very least, the explanation for what befell her. However, she is prompted to reiterate his contention.

'If she had been wild camping, Guv – say she became ill, delirious possibly, disoriented. A person's natural instinct would be to get down to safety – to have literally gravitated towards Ambleside. It could explain the absence of possessions.'

Skelgill is looking at her as though he thinks she is trying too hard – or that he thinks something else altogether, but will not say it.

'Like I say, keep an open mind.'

DS Jones concedes at this point. She gestures to the sorry-looking sock and glove.

'Should we take these?'

'Aye, we'd better.'

Skelgill has a small backpack. DS Jones bags the items and he holds it open for her to drop them inside. She looks at him inquiringly, as if something is amiss.

'No flask?'

'Don't fret, lass – there's a farm café down at Howtown – two minutes from the car.'

DS Jones chuckles. She might have guessed.

As they set off in the direction from which they arrived, she makes reference to their last moments in Skelgill's office.

'What was that about metal-detecting? Are you thinking of searching around here?'

Skelgill looks amused. He shakes his head.

'It came up last week, while you were off. Leyton's onto it – he's not greatly entertained. Nighthawkers, they call them – illegal metal detectors digging up ancient monuments without permission. Not that they'd get permission. There were two complaints from English Heritage – and then this morning another report from a member of the public at Long Meg. Looks like the culprits have come on a metal-detecting holiday. But how do you catch them? There's dozens of sites, and half of them are unfenced – no security or CCTV.'

DS Jones nods reflectively, recognising their colleague's predicament.

Skelgill makes a quip.

'They go undetected, you might say.'

He is swiftly countered.

'Unlike cafés, you mean.'

4. COAST LINE

Carlisle – 7.00 a.m., Wednesday, 20th May

'I have two lockers, thank you.'
'Certainly, madam. American, are we?'
'Is it so obvious?'
'The hat's a bit of a giveaway, if you don't mind my saying so, madam.'

The man at the left luggage counter smiles endearingly.

She raises a tentative hand to the brim.

'I thought it might help when it rains.'

Now he frowns.

'We don't get that much rain in Cumbria. Last year it only rained twice.'

'Really?'

Dorothy is genuinely puzzled. The man sounds like a local, like he would know what he is talking about. He begins to move away, squinting at the tickets that she has redeemed. He calls over his shoulder.

'First time from January to May. Second time from June to December.'

He disappears from sight before she can adjust her reaction. She is reminded of a section entitled 'British Irony' in her guide book. "Think twice before you take a Brit literally."

But when the man returns he is struggling under the weight of her backpack.

'You'll be wanting a porter for this, madam.'

'Oh, no – I will be fine, thank you, sir. I had better get used to it.'

'Going far, are we, madam?'

She wonders if she should answer with irony herself, but she is unable to think of a suitable rejoinder.

'I'm taking the train to Ravenglass. Then I'm walking to Hexham.'

Her revelation elicits a flash of alarm, and the man looks her up and down.

'What, all in one day? You'd better not miss that train.'

She realises he is joking again. Should she explain it is approximately eighty-two miles on foot and involves between seven and ten overnight stops? But he offers a guess of his own.

'I'd wager it's the thick end of a hundred miles – and that's as the crow flies – and that's a tall order in these parts.'

She finds herself offering some mitigation.

'Actually, I'm going to be following the old Roman routes – they are surprisingly straight, despite the mountainous terrain.'

But her own words have distracted her. Why has she said "I" and not "we"?

The man, however, gets on with the job at hand. He lifts a hinged section of the counter and hauls her backpack through onto the concourse.

'Sure you don't want a trolley, madam?'

'No, thank you. But I do have a question.' She wonders if she will get a straight answer. 'That building just outside the station that looks like a castle. What is it, exactly?'

He seems a little apologetic.

'It's not Roman, if that's what you're thinking. They call it the Citadel. It's not all that old – built by Henry VIII, so they say, in 1541 if I recall. Something like a fortress-gatehouse of the city wall. It's been a prison and a courthouse and council offices. Now it's summat to do with the university.'

Dorothy is momentarily diverted by the notion that something which predates almost any building in the United States can be casually dismissed as "not all that old". But, then again, she is about to embark upon a tour of relics, many intact, that date from the turn of the first millennium.

She has a two-pound coin pressed into the palm of her hand, and now she proffers it. The man is clearly surprised and tugs a non-existent forelock. (Another point in her guide book: "tipping is often not expected"). He watches, unsure of whether to help, but evidently feeling he ought – but he seems to relax when she shrugs the straps of the backpack loosely onto her shoulders and rises under her own steam.

'Much obliged, madam. Mind how you go, now.'

*

Dorothy watches as the world rattles by. She has that butterflies-feeling in the pit of her stomach like she used to get as a child, the four of them ranged along the front bench seat of her father's DeSoto Custom station wagon as they set off to the Great Smoky Mountains for their annual family vacation.

Last night, in the dark, London had seemed a little daunting, sinister, even – but in some ways not so different from, say, New York, with its late-opening shops and neon-lit restaurants and crowded streets. Of course, there were the famous black cabs and red double-decker buses – but far fewer white faces than she had expected; the majority seemed to be of Asian or Middle Eastern origin. Along Edgware Road laughing men lounged outside Lebanese cafés smoking hookah pipes, and formations of short women in black burkas patrolled the sidewalks. Yet, this morning, during her snatched early-morning search for breakfast around the centre of Carlisle she had hardly seen a person of colour. A young woman she had asked for directions had sounded Eastern European – but perhaps that was just the Cumbrian brogue of which Felix has warned her. The girl had pointed Dorothy down an alley and said something about a "ginnel".

She is aware that Carlisle is just a small city, nothing like London, which stands alongside the world's great metropolises – but, nonetheless, the railway station was like an immense Victorian exhibition hall, with its iron-framed glass superstructure and high sandstone sidewalls. When she had alighted upon the long platform and the sleeper train had slid away northbound, she had half expected a great clanking express to come thundering through, the legendary Flying Scotsman perhaps, at a hundred miles an hour filling the air with billowing clouds of smoke and steam and sound.

The station diner had been closed. That is in part what had

prompted her to visit left luggage and venture outside. Confronting her she found a surprisingly grand sight, a sort of town square, its surrounding buildings a splendid mixture of Georgian and Neoclassical, four and five storeys high, and the immense squat sandstone towers which the man had later told her comprised the Citadel. How great was the contrast to the unpretentious backstreet café to which she had been directed – it is enough to know it was called 'The Greasy Spoon' (was that more British humour at play?). A fat friendly man in a stained apron that stretched over his bulging middle whom she could not properly understand had taken her order. Felix has so often referred casually to bacon rolls – but upon her request the owner had replied with what sounded like "oven-bottom cake". But it came as a large flat bread roll with, escaping from it, a profusion of undercooked bacon; and two squeezy sauce bottles, one red, one brown; and a huge mug of scalding milky tea with the tea bag floating in the meniscus. Her early breakfasting companions had been two taciturn and burly construction workers who had conversed tersely in some obscure language (or the local dialect, again), and who had resolutely set about enormous plates of fried food (perhaps demolition was their trade), snatching wary glances in her direction, until she had eventually removed her hat, when her own meal had arrived.

If she is being honest, for the past forty-five minutes since leaving Carlisle they have been passing through slightly disappointing countryside, low-lying farmland, while not flat a gently undulating patchwork of mainly grass fields, with lots of cows and fewer sheep than she might have imagined – and the cows mainly black and white – and shorn hedgerows and occasional windblown trees, and lines of telegraph and utility poles. Sometimes a narrow highway would come alongside and there would be a glimpse of small British automobiles and trucks and occasional farm vehicles. Though green as can be, it is an attenuated landscape, and she puts it down to the salt air, for she knows the sea is not far away.

They have been stopping at series of small-town stations, the settlements themselves rather nondescript. One called Aspatria had attracted her with its unusual name – she caught sight of terraces of modest houses built from red sandstone, some stuccoed and whitewashed, others with just their window surrounds painted in garish colours, one house clashing with its neighbour – somehow not quite the quaint England she had anticipated – there is almost an industrial sense, of old mining villages.

But now her train reaches the coast. Immediately she feels her spirits rejuvenating. Across to her right, looking west, lies the shimmering Solway estuary. In the middle distance a wind farm, white blades glinting as they turn in the morning sun like a regatta with its yachts in full sail. Beyond, northwards, a long coastline fading into the distance, with misty layers of rising hills – Scotland – it looks so close! Of course, Hadrian's Wall is often referred to as the border, although she knows from what she has read that in fact it lies in its entirety in England, stretching from coast to coast, a shadow boundary at its furthest point seventy miles to the south. In Roman times the political entities of England and Scotland no more existed than did the United States of America. Only Britannia as the Romans came to call it, a great island populated by a multiplicity of Celtic tribes, most notably the aboriginal Britons.

The train is literally running along the shoreline. The tide, as it so often seems to be, is partially out and beyond sparse dunes a rough beach of pale almond pebbles slopes gently to an expanse of taupe-hued silt from which smooth rock formations protrude, marked by patches of luminous green gutweed; and unfamiliar wading birds probe with their long bills, while grey gulls hawk along the line of flotsam and jetsam and foam at the water's edge.

There are unmanned stations with no buildings or houses nearby, merely raised concrete platforms on either side of the line and a footbridge to cross between the two. Occasionally a person exercises a dog; the dog exercises nearby birds. She sees two men walking with backpacks, bent and purposeful in their manner, in single file a few yards apart, and at a halt called Flimby she is able to read a wooden signpost that stands slightly askew: it says "England Coast Path". How interesting. Perhaps it is a stretch she could suggest to Felix that they could do together someday. The gradient, she imagines, would be accommodating – at least, it looks that way. Although she feels fit, she is unsure how she is going to cope in literally crossing the entire Lake District. The dense Cumbrian mountains might not be the Rockies, but several days involve three or four thousand feet of ascent. She feels some trepidation in setting out alone; she recognises her misplaced confidence in joking with the left luggage man. Back home where she has been 'training' the terrain is relentlessly flat.

She tunes in to the rather crackly voice of the announcer. The train is scheduled to call at an extensive list of coastal towns and villages (and deserted halts, as she has seen). A number of them, like Aspatria, have peculiar names. For instance, there is Corkickle, and St Bees, and Drigg. Ravenglass is well down the list. And what does it mean? It is graphic, but its two nouns make no sense when juxtaposed. She pictures a heraldic crest on a ceremonial chalice. And St Bees – equally puzzling.

St Bees is the next stop. What she does remember, from her guide book, is that St Bees has a school that was founded in 1583. Then, when she had read it, and now – brought again to mind – she thinks of Felix in his role as Professor in Classical Archaeology, and of the cosy cloistered world of English academia, into which to settle as a companion feels so appealing. Is *companion* the word?

Now, slowing for St Bees she strains to get a glimpse of the school. And there it is across the little green valley they have entered, beyond a manicured expanse of sports pitches, artificial tennis courts and a running track – an imposing collection of old red weathered sandstone buildings, ecclesiastical in appearance, more like an abbey or convent or college of one of the ancient universities. It is just eight-thirty a.m. and she supposes the majority of pupils will be at breakfast, though a small group dressed all in white are clustered around an arrangement of nets. Could that be cricket practice?

The view becomes obscured by a stand of trees and promptly the train draws to a halt, creeping past cars that wait at a level crossing at what must be the edge of the small town. The train is comparatively empty. There are a couple of other travellers further down her coach, but she has been paying attention mainly to the environs. Now she notices a fellow hiker standing ready on the platform. A man in his mid-fifties, he is dressed in smart camouflage-style fatigues, though clearly not a military person. He attracts her attention because he has rather a lot of gear – a big backpack with a tent and sleeping roll strapped to it and another long bag that might hold a musical instrument – perhaps a guitar, or even a banjo, going by the shape of it.

She hears the external door unfastening and then its heavy clunk as he enters the little vestibule area between carriages, followed by the scraping of his luggage being stowed in the racks where she has deposited her own backpack. He appears, blinking and looking a little flustered and casts about for a suitable seat. Dorothy inadvertently catches his eye, and he smiles in a friendly manner – and she wonders if this informs his choice, for he selects the window seat at the table across the aisle, like her own, facing forward.

He drops a folded newspaper onto the table and plonks himself down with a sigh that seems to be of relief. He turns his attention to the journal, and produces a pen from a breast pocket. Dorothy realises he is doing the crossword – he has it partially completed. Perhaps he was engrossed in it in the waiting room and nearly missed his connection.

She is able to observe him without obviously turning her head. He is a little above average height, of spare build; he has large hands with long elegant fingers, and big feet in walking boots, and a strong jawline with a couple of days' growth, and a prominent straight nose, and brown hair that is turning evenly mousey but is not yet grey, cropped short at the back and sides but a little longer on top, and tweaked up at the front. She decides he is quite good looking – and for a moment she thinks of the photographs she has gleaned of Felix – Felix of course who is a good deal older – her own age – but she suppresses the little twinge of disappointment that she feels – her relationship with Felix runs much, much deeper. She doesn't even know this new man! It must be the sense of adventure that is playing tricks with her emotions.

Nonetheless, she finds herself subtly adjusting her hair. It feels rather limp and forlorn. Felix has told her that the British climate is damp and humid – that it rains on average every couple of days and nowhere is more than eighty miles from the sea. Certainly, the vegetation looks lush and vibrant in a way that she does not quite experience back home. Now it is the height of spring, Felix has said, a wonderful time to be out and about in the English countryside. But she can detect something different about the air – she is accustomed to the clinging humidity that comes with the Mississippi. She had noticed a display thermometer at a station that read "17C" – "double it and add thirty" has been Felix's advice – which she makes sixty-four degrees Fahrenheit. Maybe it will warm up as the day goes on.

She sees that the man's newspaper is The Times – the same as she has, though she has barely glanced at her copy. It is on the table, untouched. She bought it at the kiosk at Carlisle station because she knows Felix takes it. The main headline says "Canoodling Minister Resigns", which for a moment puzzles her, as if the eccentric Brits have such a government position. Casually she picks up her copy and, after a moment, lays it face down, exposing the infamous cryptic crossword.

She peruses the columns headed 'Across' and 'Down'. The clues make even less sense than the news headline. But she knows that Felix loves the crossword, he has mentioned it several times, he swears by it for relaxation, beside a crackling fire in winter – so cosy a thought – or in the shade of an apple tree in summer, with afternoon tea and scones, so quintessentially English. She would really like to learn. Perhaps this man could show her? Could she pick it up in a few minutes?

She stares intently at the first clue, one across.

"Vacate pro tem – distressed buyer's lamentation?" (6,6)

She presumes the (6,6) means it is two words, each of six letters. Felix has told her the answers, if they comprise two words or more, tend to be common phrases, like 'limited edition' or 'heavenly choir' or 'bread and butter'. She recalls an email in which he said that several of that particular day's solutions had made him think the compiler was sending him secret romantic messages about her, namely 'Southern Belle' and 'kindred spirit', and the word 'sweetheart' in one of the clues – although he had rather taken the shine off that last one by explaining that 'sweetheart' is the setter's

44

code for the letter 'e'.

She reads the first clue again, mouthing the words silently.

But nothing comes that approaches a solution. *Pro tem* – she doesn't need Felix to tell her; it means, now, for the time being. Vacate for the time being? Vacate suggests a property, or a hotel or holiday accommodation. A vacationer who should leave because they are distressed?

She steals a glance across at her new travelling companion. Although she cannot see what the man has written, he clearly has one across filled in. She strains her eyes, but it is hopeless. He notices. He looks up, and smiles, this time showing a good set of teeth.

'Going far?'

Dorothy is a little taken aback. Felix has told her not to expect the British to engage in conversation. Especially in the cities or in circumstances where both parties are strangers.

'Oh, well – just now – I get off at Ravenglass.'

'Are you taking the steam railway up into Eskdale? It's a cracking morning for it.'

She thinks he has a northern accent; he sounds friendly, reassuring. His brown eyes are trustworthy. She hesitates. Why not say it?

'Well – I, er – I'm not sure. I was supposed to be meeting – a friend' (what should she call Felix – should she have said her partner?) 'to begin a long-distance walk. But there has been a hitch. They might be delayed a day or two.' Why hasn't she said "he"?

'Ah. The coast-to-coast? The Wainwright route?' Then he frowns. 'Mind, I thought that begins at St Bees Head? Goes all the way to Robin Hood's Bay?'

Dorothy feels a little apologetic; the suggestion that she has a superior alternative.

'Er, well – not exactly. It's more of a historical thing. My friend is a professor of history who takes occasional guided tours tracing the route that links the Roman monuments, including Hadrian's Wall – we will be going just as far as Hexham.'

She notices a fleeting reaction in the man's expression – as if something strikes a chord, but then he checks himself. For her part, she suddenly experiences a welling up of emotions and she finds herself wanting to pour out her story – as if by telling him, the uncertainties that she has harboured and no doubt suppressed will be assuaged, that everything will work out. But she steels herself. Of course Felix will come.

'Sounds fascinating.'

But something has disturbed the equilibrium that was their budding conversation, and a pregnant pause begins to fill the vacuum.

She glances out of the window on her side.

'Ah – is that Ireland?'

The man squints.

'Oh, no – it's the Isle of Man – about halfway across.' He gives a chuckle that sounds a little tentative. 'It's one of ours, in a manner of speaking.'

She understands the oblique reference to her being a foreigner.

'We had some bigger ones once – Australia, New Zealand, Hong Kong – now we're down to Gibraltar and the Falklands.'

He grins self-effacingly. Dorothy wonders if she ought to mention the mixed European heritage of her own home state – but the guard's voice over the intercom pre-empts her response.

'This train is now approaching Ravenglass. Change here for all stations to Dalegarth for Boot.'

Dorothy is surprised to see the man put away his pen and fold his newspaper. He begins to rise and disentangle himself from the seating arrangement. Her heart gives a little bump.

5. MOLES

Keswick – 9.28 a.m., Wednesday, 20th May

'Leyton, these are mowdy-tumps.'
 DS Leyton scratches his head. He gazes forlornly, like a traveller who has reached an unsignposted crossroads and has no idea which way to turn. It has not helped that his superior has used the local vernacular for molehills. Skelgill takes a few paces forwards.

 They have parked in the lane known as 'Eleventrees' which runs steeply up a short distance from Keswick on the east side, and – as Skelgill had earlier bemoaned – simply passed through a gap in the hedgerow to reach the precious ancient monument of Castlerigg Stone Circle. It is as unguarded now as it has ever been in its five thousand years of existence.

 DS Leyton has come from finishing a phone call in the car.

 'The geezer from English Heritage, Guv – he was doing his nut. Reckoned there's a hole the size of a bucket been dug right in the middle.'

 He catches up to Skelgill. The stone circle lies some fifty yards ahead, and accordingly, ignoring the obvious mole-made mounds, they walk on.

 While it is no Stonehenge, the tallest of its megaliths comparable to a lofty basketball player, what Castlerigg lacks in scale it enjoys in drama. Set on raised ground and entirely encircled by mountains, no settlement visible, barely even a distant farmstead discernible, it is a scene evocative of these fells all those millennia ago, a sight that has been compared to the Ngorongoro crater of Tanzania.

 Sure enough, in its centre, they find the hole that matches DS Leyton's second-hand description.

 But Skelgill is not convinced about nighthawkers. To him this looks more like vandalism – or perhaps even someone intending to bury something – a relative's ashes maybe – and they were disturbed and took flight.

'That's been done with a shovel. I thought these detector types use little hand-trowels.'

DS Leyton is also scrutinising the hole with a critical eye.

'Could it have been an animal, Guv?'

Skelgill shrugs.

'Badgers dig latrine pits that look a bit like that. Near their sett, mind. And I doubt it would be empty, after all that trouble.'

DS Leyton makes a face that reflects he is glad it is empty.

'If it were a metal detector, what would they be looking for – a hoard of coins?'

Now Skelgill turns a sceptical eye upon his colleague.

'Leyton, this is Neolithic. They've found stone axes here. What use is a metal detector? They built this place a thousand years before the Bronze Age reached Britain.'

'How do you know all this, Guv?'

'When you're a local, you grow up with it.'

DS Leyton casts about suspiciously. He notices that close to where Skelgill was standing when he entered the enclosure there is an information board. But Skelgill continues, unperturbed.

'Besides, this land was tilled for centuries – I can't believe there'd be owt left to find.'

He glances at DS Leyton to see he appears doubtful. He points across the field.

'Look at the ridge and furrow. There's even one of the stones built into the wall yonder – see, beside that stile.'

DS Leyton remains pensive. He shakes his head, however, in an accepting manner.

'It's amazing that it's survived at all, when you think about it, Guv. All that time and no one's found a better use for the stones. Or you'd think the farmers would drag them out of the way.'

'Happen they were superstitious.'

At this suggestion, a contemplative silence enfolds the pair of them. After a few moments, DS Leyton sums up his own particular impression.

'Spooky place this, it's like we're in the middle of a giant mantrap, and it's just about to spring.'

'Pity it didn't spring when the idiot that's done this were here.'

DS Leyton sighs.

'It's flippin' thankless – trying to catch anyone at a spot like this. I reckon our best bet's to put out a public appeal – hope for a witness, some busybody who might have taken a registration number.'

Skelgill does not answer. He is gazing at the sky in the west. Unlike that portion overhead, which is clear and cerulean in its blueness, there is a mistiness, and wisps of cirrus, their tips paradoxically curled back as they advance. He is hoping to fish tonight – but he doubts that the clear spell will hold much longer.

'Here comes trouble.'

DS Leyton might almost be speaking Skelgill's thoughts, but when the latter follows his sergeant's gaze he sees that DS Jones is lightly making her way towards them. Her own car can be glimpsed through a gap in the spring green hawthorns of the hedgerow. He notes that she is more suitably attired for being out and about.

She smiles engagingly and stretches out her arms in a gesture of wonderment.

'I can't believe there aren't crowds here. What an amazing place.'

She tilts back her head and briefly closes her eyes, like a sun-worshipper enjoying the heaven-sent warmth.

DS Leyton, too, spreads his arms, palms upward.

'We've got it to ourselves, to skive off. How did you find us?'

Now DS Jones presses her index fingers to her temples, her expression one of concentration. Then she glances sideways at her colleague.

'Remember – there's been a tracker on your car, since the excitement with the boat.'

DS Leyton looks a little sheepish.

'Just don't tell my Missus how to log in.'

Skelgill is looking uncomfortable with the idea that their location has been rumbled; it is with reluctance that he even carries a mobile phone. DS Jones senses that further explanation is called for.

'I have to drop into the council offices at Keswick – there's a community liaison meeting at ten-fifteen.' The mention of this prompts an idea. 'Do you think there's a problem with local kids coming up here to hold midnight parties?'

Skelgill's response is terse, and quite likely ironic.

'Local druids, maybe.'

DS Jones looks somewhat doubtful. She notices the hole. She turns to address DS Leyton.

'Your nighthawkers' latest?'

DS Leyton makes a face of uncertainty.

'The Guvnor reckons it's badgers.'

Now Skelgill scowls.

'I never said badgers, Leyton.'

DS Jones waits patiently but cannot herself offer any inspiration. Such unseen acts of vandalism are the hardest to solve – and if an unknown item is taken, there is double the conundrum; she does not envy her colleague.

She looks at Skelgill, and speaks now with renewed energy.

'We've had some information overnight from the FBI. It's not conclusive, but it fits with our unidentified victim.'

Skelgill, who has seemed rather indifferent to DS Leyton's dilemma, settles back on a low stone, a sign that he is prepared to pay attention.

'The good news is that they feel there is something in this, so they are still working on it. The address of the passport that belonged to Patricia Jackson was in St Louis. That's Missouri – well, kind of Missouri and Illinois. Her place of birth, you'll recall was Louisiana.'

Her colleagues are looking at her blankly.

She continues.

'From her Social Security number they determined that she was a retired schoolteacher. They emailed some of our photographs to the St Louis Police Department. A local officer visited the address and there was an interesting response. The property was what the Americans call an in-law suite – it's kind of like a flat within a larger property, with its own entrance. The owner could not be certain that our woman was her tenant – not from our photo – which is understandable. But she was able to say that Patricia Jackson gave notice and moved out at a time that corresponds to her trip to the UK.'

DS Leyton is listening with interest.

'What about her gear?'

'The apartment was fully furnished. It seems she didn't have much of her own. Also, she had only been there for just over five months. Apparently she kept to herself – the landlady didn't really know her. She had told her she was a widow and had no children. Her rent was paid up to leaving. The FBI are trying to fill the gap – where did she come from – previous address, any recent part-time occupation, friends, relatives. They said they'd try a few other tricks that they have up their sleeve, but they didn't want to tell me what they were. At least – not in writing – maybe when I can speak to the agent that replied. Obviously it's hard to know what resources they're prepared to dedicate to a case like this – when she's not even a registered missing person, either in the States, or here. And that we're not able to call foul play – that she could be living happily in the UK.'

DS Jones sees that Skelgill is scrutinising her. This is, of course, what he had quipped – although she knew at the time he was merely playing devil's advocate. But she can read in his expression that he senses there is more to come from her.

'Yes – I have found something. And I believe it further corroborates the ID.' She grins wryly. 'I found her on Facebook. It's a definite match with the photo and location. But other than that, there's very little information – her account was private. How easily we can get into that – you know what these social networking companies are like for guarding privacy.'

DS Leyton makes a disdainful scoffing sound.

Skelgill, to whom pretty much all social media are anathema, folds his arms.

'But what I was able to tell is that she was a member of a private Facebook group called 'Cumbrian Confederates'. There are about two hundred members. I had a look at the public page and it's for tracing antecedents and living relatives, exchanging information and stories, and just general interest about Cumbria. It's clearly aimed at people who live in the USA – perhaps in the South – although I might be reading too much into the name.'

Skelgill does not speak. But DS Jones recognises the look in his eyes. While there is no reason to believe an injustice has occurred, she understands he is uneasy with the status quo, the unidentified elderly walker, and her lack of possessions, the passport outlier, loose ends that dangle uncomfortably over his patch.

'I'm hoping to have a call with the States this afternoon.' She checks her wristwatch. 'Meanwhile I had better go and play Aunt Sally at the council.'

DS Leyton regards her sympathetically.

'Don't let us make you late – you should have just phoned, girl.'

'I tried. Your number was going through to voicemail.'

DS Leyton hurriedly pats his pockets.

'Shoot. I left mine in the motor. I was on a call when we arrived.'

Skelgill reluctantly drags his own handset from his hip pocket.

'Mine's out of charge.' He grimaces. 'Besides, there's no signal inside this circle.'

DS Leyton looks at him in astonishment.

'Really, Guv?'

'Leyton – you donnat!'

DS Leyton slaps a hand off the top of his head in self-reproach, that he has been caught out.

Skelgill assumes a more conciliatory tone.

'I'll tell you what, though – you can't count these stones and get the same answer twice.'

His subordinates nevertheless regard him doubtfully – but after a moment they each begin silently to count, turning in opposite directions.

DS Jones is quickest.

'Thirty-eight.'

DS Leyton frowns.

'I made it thirty-nine. Hold on, let's try again. Tell you what – I'll walk round.'

But Skelgill rises from his throne and waves an imperious hand.

'Howay, Leyton – we'll be here all day. Bring the bairns up and do it. Keep them busy for a Sunday afternoon.'

6. CLUES

Ravenglass – 3.10 p.m., Wednesday, 20th May

Dorothy watches a seagull perched on the fence that surrounds the tea room garden. The gull watches her. Or, perhaps – she thinks – more accurately, the gull eyes the cracker that came with her espresso, and which she has not quite had the appetite to eat. At another table a woman is looking through binoculars – not at the gull, but across the sandy estuary. Dorothy reflects that Felix was right. She *is* tired after her journey, and to rest a day here is a pleasant relief. Although, for the time being, she does not have the martini.

He was also right about the splendid view. While not the open sea, before her – beyond a little grassy bank that must be a tidal defence – stretches a broad estuary of creeks and saltmarsh, dunes and sandbanks; a scattering of sailing boats stranded on their keels by the retreating tide; a low horizon of sand dunes topped with glaucous maritime grass, and a powder-blue afternoon sky, high and wide, with just the odd wisp of cloud.

The sun on her face makes her feel a little sleepy. She half-closes her eyes and listens to the piping and trilling of wading birds and the tinkle of rigging in the light breeze. There is the salt smell of the air; of seaweed, shoreline decay. It is such a contrast to her preconceptions of the walk – all of the photographs and videos she has studied online have been in the fells. A base camp at sea level had not occurred to her. Here, she feels a little more at home – though she doubts now that she could turn back; she really has to go through with it, though she is glad of this hiatus, despite the extended anxiety.

Over to her right, spanning one of the creeks, is a low trestle bridge and now a navy-and-white train like the one she arrived on rattles over it, leaving Ravenglass northwards on the line to Carlisle.

In a short while it will stop at St Bees, and she finds herself jolted from her reverie.

She had not banked on feeling alone, lonely, even.

Back home she lives a mainly independent life. There is always the option of company, if over time a diminishing one. But even though she knew she was coming to a different kind of company – hooking up with Felix, or whatever is the word, a sort of commitment to which she was unaccustomed – she had not really considered how she would get time to herself. Certainly, they would be in one another's pockets, for the duration of the walk, ten days or so, and then initially at the cottage. But Felix would have his academic commitments at the University of York, over two hours by train. He might be away for long days, even though he says his work is mainly part-time, that he is looking to wind down and retire, and why not, given his age. That is surely the whole premise of their friendship.

But time alone can be precious.

She shakes off these contradictory thoughts. She has her newspaper – she brought it along just in case there would be time to kill. Time to kill, with The Times. But she gnaws unproductively at the bare bones of the crossword. Still she is no closer to the solution to one across. But she believes she has a couple of answers.

Fifteen down, for instance. *No time apparently when operation starts* (4,4). "Zero hour" came quickly to mind. That is when a military operation begins. And surely zero hour is another way of saying "no time".

And twelve across. *Permission to begin, motorists go on it* (5,5). Could that be "green light?"

The crossword brings her train journey back to the forefront of her thoughts.

When the man had helped her, kindly lifting her backpack from the train and holding it so that she could slip into the shoulder straps, she had assumed he would bid her farewell and jump back on. But upon climbing aboard he left the door wide open and reappeared with his own luggage.

"Oh, do you get off here, too?"

He had grinned, his eyes shining as though he had been keeping a little secret that he somehow knew would please her – and indeed had detected in her tone that she was pleased. Or was it relieved?

"Yes. I'm booked in on the Caravan and Camping Club site for two nights. It's just a short walk from here. How about you?"

He had begun to shoulder his own pack, and had asked this without seeming unduly nosey. Dorothy had been reminded of her predicament. Should she visit the Roman bath house and set off on foot for Nether Wasdale, a seven-mile walk along easy paths to the inn – or change plans in accordance with Felix's suggestion, and spend the first night in Ravenglass? She had wavered.

"Oh, I – er – I might stay here. If I can find some accommodation."

He had glanced at her sideways and grinned a little mischievously.

"You're footloose and fancy free, eh?"

"I'm sorry?"

"Until your friend arrives – you're mistress of your own destiny?"

"Oh, well – yes, I suppose I am."

They had started walking towards the exit.

"There's a pub with rooms. A decent little hotel. And several B&Bs. All along the main street. I'll show you, if you like." He had chuckled. "Translate for you."

She had felt then – for the first time in a long while – how it was uplifting to have the companionship; in particular, that of a man.

But she had declined.

"Oh, I will manage just fine, thank you. Besides, you must have your own things to be getting on with?"

He had reacted as though he thought she had some idea of his purpose. He had raised the long flat bag.

"There's no hiding this, is there?"

By now they were passing through a parking area; Dorothy was following the man's lead, until he directed her otherwise.

"Are you a musician?"

He had laughed.

"A travelling minstrel? In which case I should set out my stall on the platform, shouldn't I?"

There was a twinkle in his eye. But he did not elaborate. Instead he had, in a manner of speaking, seized the moment.

"Look – why don't we meet up for a cuppa, say three o'clock? There's a nice café with views over the foreshore from its tea garden – you can't miss it – it's between the hotel and the pub." He had added a rider. "If you're still here, of course."

Dorothy had experienced an unexpected rush of conflicted emotions – yes, there was the reassurance, but set against it the sense of having a stranger cramp her style (just an irrational impulse, surely) – and what would Felix think. But surely Felix would be happy to know that she was feeling safe. After all, he had expressed his concern about her taking the mountain route to Hardknott.

There was a little awkward moment.

Then the man had extended his large hand.

"I'm Derek, by the way."

Her smaller hand had been gently enveloped.

"Dorothy."

*

'Tuppence for your thoughts.'

Dorothy looks up, squinting a little into the sun. She has become engrossed in the crossword, despite no further success. The man is standing roughly where the seagull was perched, on the other side of the low fence. She hurriedly folds over her paper and sets it aside.

'Don't get up, I'm not royalty.'

He seems relaxed and has the sleeves of his khaki shirt turned back at the cuffs, showing strong brown forearms covered in fine sun-bleached hairs. Slung over his shoulder is the strange-looking instrument bag, which she now notices has a folding camp shovel strapped to the outside. He carefully props it against the inside of the fence, steps over and takes a seat opposite her at the circular picnic table.

Dorothy is uncertain of what to say, but he begins before she can muster a response.

'Apologies for keeping you – I made a rather unusual find.'

Dorothy smiles pleasantly. She has no idea as to what he can be referring. He seems to know the area well enough, but before she can venture a guess and suggest the Roman ruins he inserts his long fingers into a breast pocket and holds out his hand, palm upwards.

'Know what it is?'

It is a coin – or, at least – a darkened copper disc that might almost be two inches in diameter.

'Take it.'

Dorothy obliges. The item is curiously substantial.

'When I say tuppence for your thoughts it's for a reason. That's a George III cartwheel twopenny. It needs cleaning up. But you can just make out the king's head on the obverse, and the letters of BRITANNIA on the reverse, and the date, 1797.'

Dorothy looks closer, suddenly fascinated. A little piece of history in her hand. George III was King of England and another George – George Washington – was the first President of the United States.

Meanwhile Derek elucidates.

'The cartwheel name comes from the wide raised rim. It's the largest coin in British history. Weighs two ounces. I expect that accounted for its unpopularity – it was soon withdrawn from circulation.'

Dorothy weighs it in her palm. She feels a little nervous in possession of something so precious. She gingerly hands it back. Though he casually pockets it.

'Is it very valuable?'

He makes a non-committal face.

'You can buy them from coin dealers for a couple of hundred pounds. More scarce than valuable, I'd say. Curiosity value. A satisfying find.'

Now Dorothy gets to the point that has been puzzling her.

'Did you – just, er – stumble across it? It seems amazing.'

The man laughs – but he waves a hand in a way that suggests he realises he ought to have explained himself.

'I'm a detectorist.' He gestures with a thumb over his shoulder. 'That's my metal detector.'

'Oh, I see, of course – how silly of me.'

But Dorothy must look a little alarmed, for he assumes an apologetic manner, if not exactly defensive.

'Don't worry – I shan't be digging up the Roman bath house – in my day job I'm a curator at the Castle Museum in York – it wouldn't be cricket if those of us that espouse the rules break them in their spare time.'

Within his revelation Dorothy has heard "York" and is sidetracked. York, where Felix is employed at the university. Historians alike, Felix and this man Derek might know one another. Words are almost out of her mouth when some instinct has her biting her tongue. Instead, she ventures a rather weak rejoinder.

'It's your hobby?'

The man frowns a little resignedly.

'This is something of a busman's holiday. We're planning –'

He breaks off. A vigilant waitress has identified him as a new arrival and approaches pen and pad poised. He looks at Dorothy's empty cup and responds decisively. He makes a circling gesture with a long index finger, as though he is stirring the air above the table.

'We'll have a pot of Darjeeling for two and a couple of scones with jam and cream, please, love.'

The waitress nods and begins to retreat – she hesitates for a moment when she sees that Dorothy might be about to protest – but the man intervenes, waving her away as he addresses Dorothy.

'You need building up, for what you've got in mind. Besides, I insist – my treat, as I'm in pocket'

He pats the bellows pocket where the heavy coin presses visibly against the fabric.

Dorothy smiles gracefully.

'Well, thank you, Derek.'

He smiles, too, perhaps pleased that she has used his name. Now he wags the finger, like a conductor picking up a dropped tune, engaging the musicians.

'I was saying – we're planning an exhibition next year – Roman economics and commerce.' He looks at her keenly. 'You might have noticed my ears pricked up when you mentioned your own interest. I'm doing a bit of groundwork, understanding the geographical relationship of the various Roman settlements. York, you see, was the nerve centre, so to speak, the northernmost base of the imperial army. It was called Eboracum – capital of the administrative area or province known as Britannia Inferior.'

He taps the weathered wooden surface of the picnic table.

'Do you know, they had a signalling system using milecastles and signal towers that could get a message from the garrison here in Ravenglass to York and receive orders back in a quarter of the time it would take a team of despatch riders? It would pass up the coast, along most of the length of Hadrian's Wall, and then follow the route of the road south to York.'

Dorothy finds herself frowning – this contradicts something Felix has told her. This man is a museum curator, but Felix a university professor. While she is drawn to query the statement, her good manners hold her back. She finds herself shifting the subject.

'So – the metal detecting?'

The man holds up his big hands in a supplicative manner.

'Naturally, I don't go anywhere sensitive, or where I don't have permission. We have a long-standing arrangement with local councils – so roadside verges, for example, are generally fine. Once I've dug my way through the layers of ring pulls and bottle tops that folk toss out of their cars.'

Dorothy leans a little closer, her expression sympathetic, but he grins sardonically.

'When you think about it – all the litter that's thrown away, all the pieces that fall off cars, things that get accidentally dropped in laybys – that's what folk have been doing since time immemorial. So these ancient thoroughfares have had thousands of years to accumulate lost property of all flavours. In particular the approaches to Roman forts, where men and horses would have gathered, where local settlements would have sprung up to service the inhabitants; cattle and sheep brought and penned ready for slaughter. Imagine the mud and the mire – who'd dig into that for an item they'd dropped, if they even knew it? Imagine keeping a garrison of five hundred legionaries fed and entertained. All those wages needing spending somehow!'

Dorothy is listening, enrapt in the picture he paints of order and chaos intermingled. She realises she must train herself to see beyond the piles of bare stones that she visits, that they are to be admired not for their face value, however impressive, but for the lives they once supported.

'Do you ever find Roman coins?'

'Occasionally, although they are much rarer. Naturally, I log and report every item to the authorities.' He taps the side of his nose. 'Hand it in to myself at work on a Monday!'

Dorothy smiles, understanding his little joke.

'So – will you be visiting the Roman forts in this area?'

'Certainly. I shall be going up to the Hardknott Pass, tomorrow. Kill two birds with one stone, so to speak.'

Dorothy is about to respond, but the waitress arrives bearing a laden tray. A couple of slightly awkward moments ensue, as they each try to help the other to their refreshments; Dorothy is endeared by the man's unaffected courtesy. He instructs her in the ritual of cream tea, explaining the Cornish (jam first) and Devonish (clotted cream first) alternatives for preparing a scone.

But Dorothy is eager to return to the county of their present locus.

'Will you be walking – so that you can detect en route?'

'Oh, no – it's a bit far, there and back in a day – I shall take the train. It's a cracking ride up into Eskdale.' Though he frowns knowingly skywards. 'Besides, the forecast's not too clever for tomorrow. Look at those mares' tails.'

Dorothy is confused.

'But it seems such beautiful weather.'

He points again, a brief jab with a finger.

'Cirrus cloud – it's the leading edge of a warm front.' Now he traces an imaginary line along the surface of the table, a series of ripples. 'This time of year, we're on the cusp of the warm Atlantic air and the cold Arctic air. Cyclones come spinning across from the Caribbean, along the fault line, breaking into the cold air mass. There can be a continuous sequence of fronts. A warm front brings cloud and rain. A cold front, showers and then a clear spell. It's what I call 'rainbow weather'. The Scots, they say, if you don't like it, wait twenty minutes!'

He grins.

'Your hat should come in handy, either way.'

However, he sees that Dorothy is looking pensive.

'How about you, Dorothy – have you made a plan? Have you got your friend sorted out?"

She finds herself being hesitant, though she cannot fathom why. His questions are plain and considerate and carry no hint of scheming.

'Yes – I – tomorrow I want to hike to Hardknott. Then I should press on, to Little Langdale – I hope to meet him there.'

The man looks away as though to suppress some reaction, but when he turns back to face her it is with an expression of concern.

'That's a big ask in a day. Come on the train with me. I can see you as far as the fort. Especially given the weather forecast.'

He sees that Dorothy is conflicted. He again raises his palms in his unassuming way.

'Look – I'll be going up on the ten o'clock service. The chap at the kiosk said there's plenty of seats. You can just turn up – make up your mind in the morning.'

Dorothy knows her mind has long been made up. She has not wanted to ask for company – but she wants it, all the same. Though it is not the climatic threat that drives her sentiments; indeed she finds it almost impossible to believe that such a magnificent day will not be repeated tomorrow.

While she is apparently mulling over her options, the man adds a supporting argument.

'Besides, that pack of yours – when I lifted it down on the platform, I thought, what's she got in here – American hunter, brought her own guns and ammunition!'

Dorothy smiles apologetically. Is that their reputation?

'Oh, you know us ladies – the kitchen sink and all that.'

He grins self-effacingly.

'I'm afraid I'm no expert in such things.'

He does not expand in the way she might like, and Dorothy finds herself taking the route of least resistance.

'Is there hunting in the Lake District? I thought – with it being a national park?'

A flicker of amusement seems to cross his features.

'Well – if you mean driven shooting – yes, on private farmland and estates, mainly for pheasant, and grouse on the higher moors – but it's highly regulated. You won't find anyone walking round in public with a gun slung over their shoulder. Besides, we're out of season now – so you don't have to worry.'

Dorothy indicates, pointing briefly along the narrow roadway that passes through the village.

'I noticed a warning sign beside the slipway. It said something about red flags and guns being fired out to sea?'

He looks momentarily puzzled; then an answer comes to him.

'I think that would be MOD – Ministry of Defence. Eskmeals Firing Range. I believe they test large calibre stuff. Heavy ordnance.' He laughs ironically. 'The sort of thing I dread finding. I think I've got a Roman hoard, poke in my trowel – and, boom!'

Dorothy raises a hand to her lips.

'Oh yes. I hadn't thought of that. Not so much detecting as demining.'

He grins boyishly.

'Luckily I tend to stick to sites that relate to the time before explosive devices were invented. But I dig up my share of lead musket balls, souvenirs from the English Civil War.'

Dorothy again feels inexplicably uneasy – it must be the talk of guns and weaponry. She makes light of the topic, changing its trajectory.

'You must be very handy to have around the house – when your wife mislays her car keys – or loses an earring in the back yard?'

He only shrugs helplessly as he despatches the last of his scone. As he is finishing his mouthful, she tries another tack.

'How is the campsite?'

He raises his eyebrows, swallowing and covering his mouth with his hand. But he seems more enthused by this question.

'Very good facilities. Though I'm slumming it really – you should see some of the campervans. Palaces on wheels, all mod cons. I can't believe the amount folk spend on these things. Keep them standing on their driveways for most of the year.'

Then it must strike him that he ought to reciprocate.

'How about you, Dorothy – I'm guessing you sorted out your accommodation?'

'I got a room at the hotel – they told me it would be ready for me to check in at three-thirty. I left my luggage at reception.' She picks up her napkin and dabs at her lips. There is something of finality in her action and she glances at her wristwatch. 'Actually, Derek, if you don't mind, I ought to check my emails using their Wi-Fi. I haven't been able to get a data signal on my cell phone.' She looks at him appealingly. 'My – friend, you see?'

If anything, she thinks she detects a look of relief in the man's eyes.

'Yes, of course. You must be wondering.' He gestures airily. 'You get along – I'll see to the tab.'

'Oh, no – let me, please.'

Dorothy reaches for her belt-bag, but the man swoops on the bill that is held down by the sugar bowl.

'No, no – I insist. It's nothing. I'll see if they're smart enough to accept my cartwheel twopence.' He chuckles. 'It would have just about covered it, in its day.'

He grins amenably, and then stands in gentlemanly fashion as she rises.

It is running through Dorothy's mind that he is sleeping on a campsite and she is staying in a comfortable country hotel. She ought at least to invite him for dinner. But there is still the outside possibility that Felix might arrive and surprise her. They endure a slightly stilted moment as they stand facing one another across the table.

Dorothy has her folded newspaper pressed against her midriff, and now he comments upon it.

'I see you've been having a crack at the crossword. It's not easy, The Times.'

She bows her head meekly.

'I don't know about a crack. But I've not given up yet.' She has to check herself from saying it will give her something to do tonight. 'I noticed on the train, you sailed through it.'

He waves a dismissive hand.

'Don't fret, it took me years to get the knack. Want me to give you a starter for ten?'

Although she does not understand his precise meaning, there seem to be no strings attached to his offer.

'I couldn't get past one across.'

He cocks his head to one side and squints.

'Oh, yes. Do you want me to tell you completely – or just how to interpret the clue?'

Dorothy turns up the newspaper and frowns at the folded page. *"Vacate pro tem – distressed buyer's lamentation?"* (6,6).

'Perhaps the latter would be more beneficial.' She might be able to impress Felix; he would be pleased to know she is interested in another of his pastimes.

Meanwhile the man is summoning up his advice. He rubs his unshaven jaw thoughtfully.

'When you see a word like 'distressed', it's probably telling you that the letters from the words on one side of it are an anagram. Then the words on the other side, that remain, they're the synonym – the second alternative clue to the same answer.'

Dorothy stares at the clue.

'Well – "buyer's lamentation" has more than twelve letters.'

The man winks.

'There you go, then – you're halfway there.'

Dorothy looks doubtful.

He adjusts his position.

'Well – a quarter at least. Look – why don't I give you my phone number? In case you get stuck and want a hint? Just drop me a text.'

*

From: Dorothy K. Baum

To: Professor Felix Stowe-Upland
Subject: Ravenglass

Dear Felix, there is so much to tell you. But I ought to keep it brief – you may be wondering why I have not been in touch, but until now there has hardly been a signal. I have taken a room at a quaint little hotel in Ravenglass – it comes with a faint but functioning Wi-Fi connection and a view over palm trees to the estuary! Mournful bird cries reach my ears.

I hoped you would have emailed, but I suppose you still await definite information – perhaps you are with your attorney – or chiropractor, although I sincerely wish not the latter.

As you can see, it is after 4 p.m. and I have had an eventful day. It is hard to believe that it began, all but for a few minutes, on the platform at Euston station. You were quite right when you said I would be tired. I think I could fall asleep right now and not wake until morning. But I will be ready for the Roamin', never fear!

My journey from London went smoothly – although, I must say, the Caledonian 'sleeper' is something of a misnomer. I had hoped to be gently rocked to sleep, but there was a good deal of stop-start motion, and speeding up and slowing down, when a steady pace would have been more conducive.

I ate breakfast in a rough café in Carlisle at the end of a 'ginnel'. No Cumberland sausage – but my first bacon roll! Although, if I heard correctly, the owner called it an "oven-bottom cake".

I saw herds of black-and-white cows, and the coastal scenery was spectacular. Ravenglass, as you said, is an idyllic fishing village, nestled among the sandy creeks. So different, I imagine, to the Lakeland settlements that I will soon see.

My visit to the Roman bath house was leisurely – it is just a short walk from where I am staying. Another first – my first Roman building. How amazing to think it is still standing after almost two thousand years. And the idea of a great fort manned by five hundred Roman legionaries, here in this tiny hamlet. That's a lot of bathing! Did they have a rota and a priority system? Hot water? Soap?

It has been a splendid day, but the locals tell me a 'warm front' is approaching, and that means rain. Put together with my tiredness, and Ravenglass being such a wonderful little haven, it helped make up my mind to follow your advice about the alternative route.

So, as you suggested, tomorrow morning I will ride the ten o'clock train to Dalegarth for Boot and walk from there beside the mountain road. It will be a shame not to have you to show me around the fort at Hardknott Pass, but I will take plenty of photographs and you can enlighten me in due course.

I have managed to book ahead – at a guest house in Little Langdale called 'Wetherlam View'. It will be exciting to follow the old Roman road through the fells, knowing there is a cozy welcome ahead. As a guest house rather than just a B&B I gather they serve evening meals and have some public rooms for relaxing, so it will be more like a small hotel. I will await your arrival – unless you make it there before me!

It is of course so tempting to call you, especially now that we are both in the same time zone. I am accustomed to thinking you will be fast asleep whenever I email. But I agree – let's keep that as part of the surprise of meeting in the flesh. We have managed for this long, and it would seem a shame for our first actual conversation to be about logistics! Meanwhile, though it has been tempting to tell my story when people ask me in passing, I think I like our secret even more. I might almost have the Crown Jewels smuggled in my backpack!

Well, I think that is all you need to know for the time being. Besides, your news is so much more significant than mine. I will press 'send' and wait in great anticipation for your reply.

Yours, Dorothy.

But when Dorothy presses 'send' it is not so much anticipation as apprehension that she feels.

Naturally, she tells herself, she has been eager to communicate with Felix – really since the moment she touched down at Heathrow airport. But she has not wanted to pester him with a running commentary. It has been better to hold off until she could give him a definite plan, and making the reservation at Little

Langdale is something she has only just completed. Nor has she wished to give the impression that she is needy. While Felix sounds very much the traditional English gentleman, there is a line to be drawn, and she should demonstrate that she is a self-reliant, independent woman.

She has not, therefore, raised the question of whether he might still come this evening. She has looked up the train timetable – if he were able to leave from York at seven minutes past four, he could arrive on the last connection that stops at Ravenglass at ten minutes to nine. But it is probably too late for that – surely he would have sent her an email detailing his plans, and that he was already en route. And, of course, for all he knew, she might have gone on herself, and by now be checking in at Nether Wasdale.

It struck her, too, when she reviewed her message before sending it, that she has not mentioned Derek. Despite – as she had told herself earlier – that Felix would surely be pleased that she has been taken under the wing of a competent travelling companion, something had stopped her from communicating the fact. Perhaps Felix would be a little jealous? But more likely she would make him feel guilty that he has not been there to accompany her – when the reasons are beyond his control, and concern matters that simply have to be dealt with.

Thought of Derek reminds her that she faces a long evening ahead. She has the crossword, of course. Then there is his offer of assistance. But how could she possibly begin to send him text messages, and not invite him along for a drink, at the very least? But what if she missed an important email from Felix, and was slow to respond? And what if Felix did indeed arrive, entering the bar with a bunch of roses (she can imagine it is the sort of gesture he would make), and there she is canoodling with a younger man!

Which brings her to the matter of sleeping arrangements.

As her communications, and then relationship, and then plans with Felix gradually evolved, this was something that neither of them brought up and still has not to this day. The longer it was left to lie the harder Dorothy has found it to raise. As regards the Roman Roamin' trip, Felix has simply alluded to the fact that they would be able to pick up accommodation as and when they needed it, to allow for maximum flexibility – that at the very least there would be 'vacancies' signs at farmsteads every few miles, and plenty more B&Bs in every village or hamlet. When it came to making reservations herself – finding the room here at Ravenglass, and then for tomorrow night at Wetherlam View – she had wavered when asked, and then had requested a twin room. She really was not sure if that was what she wanted – but equally it would have seemed rather rude to have to say to Felix that she had booked two singles. But a double – *hmm* – what on earth does she think about that?

It really is a bridge they will have to cross when they meet it – and ideally they should meet it together. One thing is for certain, that in discussing Rose Cottage, Felix had stated at an early stage that it is two-bedroomed, and surely that was to reassure her that they were entering into this practical relationship as the 'very good friends' that they have become in their virtual relationship.

Dorothy sighs. She puts aside her cell phone and takes up the newspaper. She settles back on the bed and tries to focus upon the crossword. But she is tired. Come on, Dorothy – one across. Now, what was it Derek said about that anagram? It must be the words "Vacate pro tem" that are to be reconfigured. She tries to picture the twelve letters, picked up by a twister, spinning and rising in a column, rearranged time and again, and one of those fleeting combinations revealing by chance the correct solution. She closes her eyes.

*

When she wakes, Dorothy realises almost two hours have passed.
Something has woken her.
She has an email.

From: Professor Felix Stowe-Upland
To: Dorothy K. Baum
Subject: Re: Ravenglass

My dearest Dorothy, what a jolly clever girl you are – I must say, I am proud of you, making it all alone in this foreign land of ginnels and oven-bottom cakes! Good show!

And I am mighty relieved to learn that you have dropped anchor at the once-great Roman port of Glannoventa; quite a contrast in its present-day incarnation as tiny Ravenglass, don't you agree?

Like you, I shall be brief, for alas versus both the intransigent transaction and my recalcitrant vertebrae I cannot yet claim victory (indeed, as regards my back an uneasy truce is the best I can hope for). But I do hold out hopes for progress tomorrow, such that I may join you at the delightful-sounding Wetherlam View. As I recall, Wetherlam is a fine-looking fell, known for its ancient copper mines. If all goes well, I shall arrive at Windermere by train, and thence sally forth by local bus.

I wholeheartedly approve of your revised plan to reach Little Langdale. You shall have quite a day to look forward to – *carpe diem*, indeed! The old steam locomotive. A splendid fort – quite extraordinary in its isolated location – unlike anything one would expect to find in England. And the remarkable roller-coaster walk crossing the two passes of Hardknott and Wrynose. Remember, you can always hitch a lift should you become excessively tired – simply stick out your thumb and stand proud!

If you do not object, I shall sign off – sitting here at my computer, my back is sending me warning twinges, and I should lie down to perform my hourly round of remedial exercises.

As the Romans put it, *festina lente* – make haste slowly – I think it applies to us both!

Until tomorrow, ever your servant,
Felix.

Alone in her room, Dorothy has no need to hide her disappointment – yet as she moves across to see her reflection in the mirror above the dresser she finds herself doing so. It is not that all hopes of Felix arriving this evening are dashed – she had already discounted that possibility – but more the nature of his reply. Of course, he explains his reasons for brevity, and in many respects there are only so many times that they can go over the same ground – the details of their walk, Rose Cottage, life thereafter. These matters must pass from the land of conjecture into the real world of the present day. It is just that today was to be that day. She notices his omission of the precise details of the property transaction, the state of play with the delayed buyers, the receipt of her own funds for the bridging loan. She can only presume that everything is in order and it is just a matter of time before the pieces fall into place. And neither still has he mentioned accommodation – namely: the sharing or otherwise of bedrooms. That she informed him she has made a reservation at Wetherlam View provided the perfect opportunity for him to broach the subject. He might have asked – does she have two rooms? As things stand, she does not feel she can question him further – when normally she might respond immediately to one of his emails, and a more informal dialogue would ensue, a quickfire exchange of quips and flirtatious humour. She has the sense that he has rather closed off the conversation for the night.

She wonders – is the walk itself going to prove too much for Felix just now? Does he perhaps not want to tackle it, given his medical condition? Is there something in his tone that suggests a rowing back from his earlier enthusiasm? Or is there a more profound issue – that he is getting cold feet about the whole enterprise? But – no – surely it is just her imagination at play. It is the insidious nature of worries, they wheedle their way into your confidences before you know they are there, and whisper to the subconscious as though they are your own thoughts, a malign deception owned by no one but the devil.

7. BOGEY MORTEMS

Bassenthwaite Lake – 9.04 p.m., Wednesday 20th May

Syling, hoying, hossing, stotting. These are all local words for rain in varying degrees of ferocity. A 'pash' is a short, sharp shower and 'mizzle' is a hybrid of mist and drizzle. But standard English pattering is probably the order of the day, Skelgill being out on the water, and the effect of the moderate downpour being amplified, both by the expanse where it lands within earshot (when upon the ground it would fall silently) and the steady tapping upon his olive-green fishing umbrella, which he has clamped in an improvised vice arrangement just forward of one of the rowlocks.

'Alreet, lass.'

His phrase is used in the reassuring context, and engenders no reply, its recipient being the Bullboxer, who has raised her head in response to a sudden movement on her master's part.

It is not yet dark, but the blanket of cloud that smothers the surrounding tops has precipitated an early and prolonged dusk, and Skelgill can see the flicker of headlights as vehicles pass along the A66, close to the wooded west bank of Bassenthwaite Lake. The fine rain in the air and its ambient sibilance cocoon him from what would be an undulant traffic hum. Only the occasional *kirruk* of a moorhen from the reeds penetrates the invisible baffle. It is humid, mild and windless, but mercifully he seems to have been spared the midges that might normally have sought him out. But there is a growing impediment: the raindrops disturbing the surface and the murky light combine to render his orange-tipped quill float only just discernible, and bites are becoming increasingly easy to imagine.

'Bogey mortems.'

Cleopatra seems to understand it is a false alarm, and resumes her napping, curled as she is on an army blanket in a plastic trug – which if the boat were to sink might leave her in her own small craft. She has heard the term before and knows it to fall into the category of 'stay' and 'wait', albeit less galling. Skelgill, musing, reflects that he still does not understand the etymology – "bogey mortems" being a phrase he heard as a very small boy, fishing bankside in the company of a wizened Glaswegian angler and fellow caravaner on a family holiday to Kinlochleven – Skelgill all eyes and ears, absorbing tips like blotting paper, and despite limited grasp of the man's dialect (probably actual Scots, now he thinks about it) gleaning from associated actions that the said bogey mortems were some kind of ghost fish that created false bites.

Skelgill stares over the water into the deepening gloom. He can still picture the loch out front, Loch Leven, mountains steepling up from the far shoreline, the distinctive Pap of Glencoe, the calls of oystercatchers, and the little "burn" at the back of them, creating the wooded isthmus on which the dozen static caravans were lined. The more or less incessant rain that kept the rest of the family pinned in the caravan. They thought it rained a lot in the Lakes!

But he also remembers a terrible feeling of dread that had descended upon the little campsite. For one morning the man's wife had come knocking on their flimsy door to announce, "Jock's rod's been lifted". The words, overheard from his shared bunk, did not at first make sense. Though he knew their gravity by the woman's troubled tone. He had seen from beneath the blankets his mother's suppressed flinch, the dread revealed in her body language that one of her offspring might have transgressed – a reaction he has witnessed countless times in his profession, knocking on the doors of miscreants.

That the man was called Jock was a minor distraction – that it actually was a real name. His elder brothers had privately nicknamed him 'Teef' for his projecting dentures, and they had ribbed young Daniel for his slavish following. Then there was "lifted" – the euphemism for stolen – neither did this make immediate sense. Then that it had been taken from where it had been kept ready beneath the neighbouring caravan had seemed impossible. Who would do such a thing? It was an isolated site with only a few fellow campers.

But Skelgill had felt the invisible hand of injustice heavy upon his shoulder. At an age when running wild in the district was part and parcel of growing up, so was being caught for minor misdemeanours, and being wrongly accused of more major ones. He had assumed that everyone must think he took the rod – after all, only he was mad on fishing – and never mind the irrational aspect: where would he hide a twelve-foot spinning rod?

They had joined in a search of the site and the environs. Teef was looking broken, but doing his best to hide it. Skelgill remembers his father kneeling to look under their own caravan – and feeling a shock of fear – what if it were there? What if Teef had put it under the wrong van in the dark, and he Daniel would get the blame? And then a worse idea struck him – what if his Dad were the thief – and was now backtracking by being the one to find it?

There was relief when his father got up and shook his head.

The man and his wife were leaving that morning. Skelgill never got his last fishing lesson. But the incident left its legacy stamped upon his subconscious. The shame it could bring upon a family. His mother's unspoken agony. The feeling of true guilt, despite doing no wrong. It was something he never wanted to endure again. And there was another thing. One day he would put right that wrong. He would get Teef his rod back.

He is still looking.

In the near darkness, his features are grim.

Then his mobile phone rings.

Skelgill does not move, but Cleopatra responds to the ringtone with a beating of her tail – *tap-tap-tap* against the plastic bowl. If she were cast adrift, she would have means of both propulsion and steering.

Skelgill clumsily answers, activating the loudspeaker.

'A packet of cheese-and-onion.'

'Sorry, Guv?'

'I'm talking to the dog. She knows your ringtone.'

DS Jones does not attempt to make sense of Skelgill's gibberish.

'It sounds like you're outdoors – I can hear raindrops.'
'Bass Lake.'
'Ah –'
She realises he ought not to be disturbed – but then again, he has answered.

Indeed, he offers a prompt.

'What's new?'

'Something I wanted to bounce off you – that I've found concerning Patricia Jackson.'

Skelgill looks at his dog; she is eyeing him optimistically.

'Partridge – half an hour?'

'Really?'

Skelgill makes a scornful scoffing noise.

'Can't disappoint Cleopatra.'

*

Skelgill tugs at the shoulders of his shirt as though it is a little damp.

'Saw a fox and a badger walking down from Peel Wyke.'

'Hand in hand?'

'Very funny.'

DS Jones sits upright from her doubled-over position, half beneath the table. She grins.

'I'm sure I've only given her crisps once before.'

'She's quick to catch on.'

'She's quick to make them disappear.'

Skelgill leans back to get a look at Cleopatra, making short work of her much-anticipated treat.

'Natural instinct. The higher the food value, the faster they eat it.'

DS Jones frowns.

'Do cheese-and-onion crisps have a high food value?'

Skelgill puts down his pint and folds his arms a little defensively.

'In the wild, a third of the wolf's diet is elk dung.'

DS Jones makes a face that corresponds to the notion.

'Is that healthy?'

'Needs must. Apparently contains carbohydrates the wolf can't access unless the grass has been processed through a herbivore's stomach.'

The quasi-scientific explanation seems to impress her.

'Did you read that?'

Skelgill, thirsty after several hours in his boat with an inadequate flask of tea, takes another pull at his ale before he responds.

'Nay. Arthur Hope told us. One day his dogs were eating partles. Me and Jud were trying to stop them. He made us leave them be.'

DS Jones knows the local word. She reprises her expression of mild distaste.

She looks at Cleopatra chidingly.

'I hope you don't do that sort of thing.'

The dog, now licking the salt clean from the foil packaging, pushing it along the floor, seems to understand and beats her tail. She gazes up with mournful Boxer eyes that could do no evil, as if to say "someone ate my crisps."

DS Jones addresses Skelgill.

'Can we change the subject, please? Can I tell you about Facebook?'

'Facebook?'

Now it is Skelgill's turn to show disapproval. His exclamation briefly attracts the attention of the girl who has served them, but she leaves, and they have the small smoke-stained wood-panelled bar to themselves.

'As I mentioned, it concerns the Patricia Jackson case.'

'Aye.'

Despite his little outburst, Skelgill seems reasonably cooperative.

'You know I found her on Facebook. I applied to join the group – Cumbrian Confederates. I was accepted promptly. It meant I could look back at the various threads – conversations.'

'She's not alive?'

Skelgill has cut to the chase.

DS Jones shakes her head.

'There's no activity since before last May. So that fits, as well.'

'Don't they shut down the account?'

'Not automatically. I suppose they have no way of knowing. It requires a family member or an executor. You have to submit a copy of the death certificate.'

Skelgill nods as he drinks.

'I have no doubt it's the Patricia Jackson of the passport. But she didn't post on her timeline. However, I found occasional comments she had left on other people's posts. Nothing really that stood out – kind, supportive remarks.' She glances at Skelgill, as if to check whether his concentration is waning. There are stuffed fish in wall-cabinets that draw his eye. 'But what I did notice, she had liked a particular member's posts, every time, dating back for almost a year. A Professor Felix Stowe-Upland from York.'

Skelgill gives an involuntary laugh.

DS Jones regards him blankly.

'Pardon me?'

Skelgill lifts his glass to inspect the remaining liquid against a light.

'A made-up name.'

DS Jones shakes her head.

'I googled it. I found a series of academic papers – admittedly about twenty years old – filed as pdfs. It seems he is – or was – a professor of ancient history. The studies were co-authored and attributed to the University of York. However, there's no mention of him on the website. I rang the university. I got put through to the Department of Archaeology – but it's past the end of term – they've just got a skeleton staff working. They couldn't help.'

'What was she liking?'

His question belies his professed ignorance of social media. DS Jones nods approvingly.

'That's the interesting thing. As far as I can see, the vast majority of the members of this group are Americans – that's who it's designed for. He is clearly not – and seems to specialise in posting photographs of ancient monuments in Cumbria. Almost like a blog, roughly one per month, with some commentary about its origins and significance. Quirky facts, like about Roman toilet habits – and eating goat dung, funnily enough. So he appears to have picked up a good number of followers.'

Skelgill drinks silently; his countenance reveals little of his thoughts.

DS Jones willingly presses on.

'It seems something more than a coincidence that Patricia Jackson – with the caveat that it is she – came to the UK and was found dead in Cumbria – when she was involved in this group and has had some contact with a local enthusiast.'

Again, Skelgill demonstrates that he is not merely sitting and savouring his cask ale.

'What contact?'

DS Jones holds up her hands in a conciliatory manner.

'Well – okay – I agree – there's nothing explicit, else obviously I would have already told you. But they could have been PMing one another.'

Now Skelgill plies his companion with a sharp sideways glance.

'Private messaging. It's a facility on Facebook. If you're friends with someone or in the same group you can interact in person, rather than post a comment on the public thread. Visually it looks a bit like text messaging, just within the Facebook system.'

'But there's no way of telling?'

'No.'

Skelgill finishes his pint. He stares pointedly at the clock above the bar. He rises.

'Come on, lass.'

Cleopatra is quickest off the mark.

'What are we doing?'

'I'll tell you in the car.'

*

'What a pleasure, young lady. I have heard a good deal about you.'

DS Jones eyes Skelgill suspiciously. He frowns in denial.

Their host seems amused by the unspoken interchange. DS Jones addresses him.

'I hope it's not too late for you, sir?'

Professor Jim Hartley gives a shake of his shock of white hair.

'Not at all – a delight to see you. You are just in time for a mug of cocoa and a slice of hot Borrowdale teabread – my latest experiment. Unless you would like something stronger – I still have a spot of that fine malt you kindly gave to me, Daniel.'

Skelgill grins wryly.

'Thanks, Jim – but I'm driving and this lass is parked at the Partridge.'

'Ah, how is Charlie? I must drop in. I tend to head over mainly to Derwentwater while it's the trout season, you know. Landed a two-pound brownie on a *Bibio* only last Friday. That was one of yours, Daniel.' The man turns to DS Jones. 'There are no limits to this young fellow's talents, I am sure you will agree?'

DS Jones looks amused – perhaps that there is a glint of alarm in Skelgill's eye at such an open invitation to take a pot at him – but she is too polite and merely makes a gesture of acquiescence. They have entered the cosy slate-walled kitchen of Skelgill's old angling mentor's Braithwaite cottage. He gets them seated at an oak table and sets to, clanking on his range.

Perhaps understanding on which side her teabread is buttered, Cleopatra has arrived without fuss or introduction, and takes up a station at Skelgill's feet. DS Jones cannot help another smile. With alert eyes and twitching noses the hound and her master have more in common than those who would muse at the superficial incongruity.

The professor calls over his shoulder.

'But there must be a reason for your impromptu visit?'

'Aye, there is, Jim.'

Skelgill indicates to DS Jones that she should speak.

'I understand that you lectured in history at the University of Durham?'

'That is correct, for my sins. But I am long retired. I can make no claim upon their recent bouquets or brickbats.'

DS Jones continues evenly.

'Actually, it's not in direct connection with Durham – at least, we don't think so. Possibly the University of York. Someone we would like to speak with – we wondered if he were familiar to you. A Professor Felix Stowe-Upland?'

'Oh, yes.' Jim Hartley's response comes without hesitation. 'I know that name. Quite unmistakeable. There can only be one Felix Stowe-Upland.'

The man pauses, however, and groans a little as he wields a bread knife.

'Excuse me – I must butter this while it is still hot.'

He turns with a tray of three mugs and a plate laden with slices of his home baking. He deals out the mugs and side plates and takes a chair, while Skelgill makes himself busy loading sugar into his cocoa.

'What is it you say, Daniel – never compete with the tea lady. A wise aphorism. There we are, tuck in. Now – yes – I know the name. Of course, as I say, I am long retired, and I should imagine he would be too. I would have us down as contemporaries – although he may have been the elder.'

DS Jones politely takes a bite and makes an expression of approval before she continues.

'Did you know him personally?'

The professor draws the fingers of one hand through his rather wild hair.

'I can't say that I did. We rubbed shoulders at the occasional conference of northern universities. And we overlapped for a short time on a steering committee – used to meet in York, as a matter of fact. But don't be fooled by the fact that we were both historians. You might think it is a small world but it grows by the minute. My field was Medieval – his was Classical, if I recall. I believe he achieved some minor renown for a paper that argued that the Romans did more for us Celts than all of the subsequent invaders put together – the Jutes, the English, the Saxons, the Vikings, the Normans. Make of that what you will.'

He gazes from one detective to the other; then with sudden alacrity darts out his hands, fingers spread, like a magician trying to make the plate of cakes disappear.

'But I digress! Have another.'

Skelgill needs no such encouragement. DS Jones is more judicious in her manners. She holds up her second slice.

'This is delicious – did you bake it to your own recipe?'

The man gives a bow of his head.

'Alas, I must confess to borrowing it from an old cookbook I stumbled across while researching in the local library.' He looks to Skelgill. 'I think I mentioned it once before, Daniel – remember, those rum nickies that you took a fancy to?'

DS Jones regards Skelgill with an expression that might translate as "why am I surprised?" – but he just keeps eating, and not at all sheepishly.

It is left to her to pick up the thread of their inquiry.

'This Professor Stowe-Upland – we were hoping to contact him.' She glances at Skelgill; he nods, the suggestion being that she can say what she wants without fear. 'We have an investigation into a missing person, and it's possible he may have had some online communication with them which may shed light upon their movements.'

Skelgill is watching her casually. It registers with him that she does not reveal the gender of their 'missing person'.

The professor looks at DS Jones earnestly.

'Naturally, you have tried the university?'

She nods gracefully.

'Yes. It appears they may have lost touch with him. That would not be surprising, I suppose – given what you say about his likely retiral being some years ago.'

Jim Hartley is munching on cake, but now he lifts an index finger to indicate he has an idea. He rises.

'One moment. I may be able to help.'

He disappears from sight and they hear the click of a door catch from the hallway. Good to his word, he reappears promptly, now brandishing a small faded booklet.

'This was the last annual report of our committee – a kind of almanac that we produced mainly for our own purposes.' He resumes his seat and begins to leaf through the pages. 'Here we are, contact details.' He makes a shushing sound as he peruses the entries. 'Yes – good old Felix!'

He presents the booklet triumphantly, its pages spread.

'No email or mobile numbers of course – but that was his home address. Must be a good chance he's still there. We're creatures of habit, we historians.'

DS Jones slides her phone from her hip pocket.

'Mind if I take a photo?'

'Be my guest – take the booklet, if you prefer.'

DS Jones waves the handset.

'This will be fine, thanks.'

While she is thus occupied, Skelgill notices that his friend's expression becomes conflicted.

'Summat up, Jim?'

'Oh – well – I was reflecting on the age of that pamphlet. I assume he is still alive?'

DS Jones glances up.

'We believe so – there is recent online activity.'

'Ah, jolly good – I should hate to be responsible for sending you on a wild-goose chase.'

DS Jones sees that Skelgill steals a glance at the wall clock. She suspects he is torn between the remaining slices of teabread and last orders at the Partridge.

He pushes back his chair.

'Jim – we'd better leave you in peace.'

DS Jones follows Skelgill's lead and begins to rise. She addresses the professor.

'It was nice to meet you. Thank you for your help with the address – and your hospitality.'

She begins to gather together the used crockery onto the tray.

'You are welcome any time, my dear. But leave the plates, do. I should imagine you have your hands full as it is.'

The man gives a little laugh, but no explanation. However, as they file out along the shadowy stone-flagged hallway, a thought plainly strikes him.

'I trust old Felix is not embroiled in this plague of illegal metal-detecting?'

When both detectives appear surprised, he elaborates.

'I heard one of your chaps – the Londoner fellow – on Radio Cumbria this afternoon. An appeal for witnesses at sites of historical import. It seems a coincidence.'

Skelgill is shaking his head. In desperation DS Leyton must

have carried out his threat to enlist the general public.

'Not that we know of. Was he into that sort of thing?'

The professor furrows his brow.

'You know – now we mention it, I have a feeling he might have been. I don't know why I think that – just something in the back of my mind. Perhaps he brought along the occasional find for an interested party. Obviously, it's a legitimate research method. Unfortunately, in the hands of amateurs it can do more harm than good. Rather like these infernal drones. I was buzzed by one on Derwentwater – it came back and forth like a giant dragonfly. Entirely spooked the fish. I didn't see a rise for a good fifteen minutes afterwards.'

He looks at his visitors as though he suddenly thinks he might be testing their patience, although it is more likely that they are both distracted by outside possibilities. Skelgill has the front door open, ready to step out.

'Wait another moment!'

The professor suddenly scurries away. Cleopatra, for the first time, gives a little whine.

Then their host reappears, holding aloft a small foil-wrapped parcel.

'I believe it's called a doggy-bag.'

8. PASSES

Wrynose Pass – 2.08 p.m., Thursday 21st May

Caveat emptor. So that was the answer. Of course, the buyer's lamentation. An anagram of *vacate pro tem*. And perhaps there was an additional hint in the wording of the clue, one Latin phrase pointing to another. Dorothy had done quite well in the end, solving perhaps half of the cryptic crossword without assistance. She had swithered over bringing it to show Felix this evening, perhaps for them to finish it together – but during moments of distraction she had doodled around the edges, including the penning of reminders of a couple of questions she thought she ought to ask him – and it would feel a little awkward for him to see that. In the end she had left her copy of The Times, correctly in the bin marked 'recycling'. Giving up at least meant she could ask Derek this morning, although she had in fact forgotten until their parting moment at Hardknott fort, and he had merely waved her away with a rendition of the solution to one across.

She had taken it to be a word of advice. Two. He had also presented her with a small tin of Kendal mint cake. That must be why he had briefly gone into the gift shop at Dalegarth station. He told her it would see her through any difficulties, as if it were the Cumbrian equivalent of Tolkein's 'lembas' or waybread. He has another night camping at Ravenglass. He did not mention what his plans were. Perhaps he will return northwards around the coast by train.

She reflects that Derek has been kind all along, and seemed a little reluctant to let her come on alone. But she insisted she would be fine. All she has to do is follow this road. And Felix was right, the sheep-cropped grass verges make pleasant going underfoot, taking care to avoid the droppings, the occasional sheep, and the very occasional vehicle.

She had watched Derek set off, looking just like a military deminer in his combat gear, with his headphones on, gently swinging his metal detector. But she had realised he could only then cover one side of the road, returning from Hardknott to Dalegarth. In chaperoning her, he had foregone the other verge. It was very unselfish of him. And he had forfeited another half hour to show her around the extensive remains of Mediobogdum, the Roman fort. She had been awed at just how knowledgeable he is – pointing out small details like the sudatorium or steam room in the bath house, and broad matters such as the strategic location of the citadel, commanding the pass and readily defensible, when to construct it lower down in the valley would have been more practical in many respects.

She almost might not need Felix's further exposition. She had, however, taken photographs to discuss with him, each time carefully excluding Derek from the frame, and had declined to pose herself in a couple of shots he suggested, lest she was quizzed about who had offered to take them.

She had thought the scene was extraordinary, the stronghold perched on a great rocky spur in the deserted fells, magical, bleak – and even the adverse weather contributed to the sensation. Derek had spoken of paganism, and how to have espied at night the fires and hear the chants of rituals far down in the afforested dale must have unnerved the Roman soldiers, conscripts from distant Croatia, yearning for their homeland and its Adriatic climate.

If she is honest, the climate – though it has not been ideal today for photography – at least is cool for walking. The ten-mile stretch from Dalegarth to Little Langdale is a rollercoaster, taking in the steep passes of Hardknott and Wrynose – the latter being her present climb. At the foot of the Hardknott Pass there were warnings: "narrow route – severe bends – unsuitable for all vehicles in winter conditions". Derek had pointed out a sign indicating a 30% grade that warned motorists to engage low gear – he said it is reputed to be the steepest road in England. With her heavy pack she could believe it. Derek – his kit being at his campsite – had chivalrously exchanged her backpack for his detector bag. Now she has to go it alone, although Derek had laughed and said not to worry, the Wrynose Pass has an incline of only 25%!

She had heard the rain during the night. Her room in the eaves was cosy and her bed comfortable. She had enjoyed the sound; it was soothing and had lulled her off to sleep – and she had not let herself think about walking in a downpour today. But thankfully, there has been none. Derek had explained that they were in the 'warm sector', the wedge of mild air between the now-passed warm front and the approaching cold front. But the moist tropical air mass means cloud, and that is what they have, a low-lying blanket of dense nimbostratus that cuts off the fell tops and forms a great dark roof. At Hardknott fort it was swirling not far overhead, and Derek had warned her that the summit of the Wrynose Pass might be completely shrouded – but at least she could stick safely to the road, and would soon descend out of it.

Earlier, the hike through Eskdale had begun in bucolic surroundings. The road, tree-lined in places, was bordered by sturdy dry-stone walls lavishly adorned with luminous green moss, separating the narrow thoroughfare from neat enclosures. Small birds with white flashes in their wings and tails that Derek identified as chaffinches sang at intervals. The gradient was gentle, as to be hardly noticeable. But almost imperceptibly there was a sense of the fellsides closing in, and the pastures becoming attenuated, invaded by encroaching moorland grasses. At the point where the signposts warned motorists, Dorothy's eye had been taken by an old red telephone kiosk, its paintwork faded and its glass panes missing – although there appeared to be a working phone inside; it had seemed poignant, a weathered sentinel, a harbinger of the difficulties that lay ahead.

From there the road had steepened alarmingly, and the reassuring walls and hedgerows had disappeared; the way was now bordered by open fellside, thick with bushy bracken. Derek had seen her eyeing the strange breed of sheep – their grey fleeces thick and grizzled, and their lambs a kind of chocolate black – he said they were Herdwicks, hardy mountain creatures brought by the Vikings.

She is used to the sheep now; they seem to roam free – every hundred yards or so a ewe grazes with its lamb in tow, sometimes twins. They allow her to approach quite closely – but only so close before they break off from their foraging and with a little gallop clamber a dozen yards up the fellside, the lamb bleating a protest that it is being left behind. They have been her only accompaniment. She has not seen a soul – other than being passed by a red Post Office van and an old dilapidated Volkswagen camper that sounded like it had something wrong with its engine and puffed black smoke from its tailpipe; she was pleased when that was gone.

The descent from the summit of Hardknott Pass had been incredibly steep. The road zigzagged in a series of improbable hairpins which, at their bends, even on skis would have been terrifying in icy conditions. She was relieved when the hill began to ease – in its own way it was almost harder than going up, and has exacted quite a toll on her knees. Entering the long barren stretch known as Wrynose Bottom, the three-mile trough between the two passes, she had felt her pace begin to slow.

And there was still the Wrynose Pass.

She estimates that she is about halfway up.

On her left, close to the road, runs a rocky stream, wide, shallow and buoyant with last night's rain; she supposes it will diminish as she ascends, and eventually peter out – a sign that she is nearing her destination – or the 'hause' at least, as Derek has called the saddle. From there, she tells herself, it is downhill all the way to Little Langdale, and just three miles further.

And it looks like Derek was right. As the hill begins to steepen, the cloud appears to descend to meet her, and swathes of mist become detached to drift down from its ragged base. The single-track road, its tarmac dry at a lower altitude, is now slick, and so is the grass of the verge, causing the grey felt toes of her walking boots to darken. The weight of her backpack seems to grow heavier with each shortened step.

The visibility is decreasing. First, the stream disappears, although its rushing seems to intensify, perhaps as the thickening mist begins to damp out sounds from further afield. Then, paradoxically, the mournful cries of sheep become more distinctive, perhaps more urgent, as the ewes and their lambs fear separation.

Dorothy wonders how Felix would ever have guided them across the boulder-ridden slopes, had they walked together and taken the original route via Wastwater and Wasdale Head. She is thankful she did not try it alone; at least she has the road to follow, despite its punishing gradient.

There was no further email from Felix this morning. And, each time she has checked since parting with Derek, she has not even had a phone signal. She will have to wait until she reaches the guest house, in order to use the Wi-Fi. But perhaps Felix will already be there!

The thought spurs her on – albeit a burst of hope that is short-lived. Despite that she knows it is getting cooler as she climbs, and as the fog thickens around her, she is not feeling the benefit. Instead there is the discomfort of overheating, and knowing she can do little about it. If only there were a headwind to soothe her brow.

She ought to drink. The stream, now invisible, sounds as if it is a little way below. But she could clamber down and fill her empty water bottle. She rues that she did not do it when it was closer, when she could see. She is dreadfully thirsty.

But she does not want to stop. Only so many steps left. If she stops, how ever will she start again? Keep going, Dorothy. Grit your teeth. Stay in the fight. Remember what Derek said – the Wrynose is nothing like as tough as the Hardknott.

The Wrynose. The name repeats itself in her head, in Derek's blunt northern accent, the stress on the 'wry', the 'nose' drawn out and pronounced 'nause'. At his first mention she had not grasped the context, and thought he was talking about actual rhinos – and that he was teasing her with the idea of there being wild animals.

A sudden clatter of hooves close at hand makes her start. It must have been a sheep, scared off by her soft-soled approach, scrambling away across the rocks. But did she detect a larger, darker shape? The lambs are dark, but small. But there are no big creatures here. She knows that – no bears, no wolves – definitely no rhinos.

Then comes the bleat of a sheep. *'Here. Here.'* It sounds like it is calling her. A siren, trying to lure her off the road. It receives no reply from its lamb. It continues. *'Here. Here.'* Perhaps Dorothy should follow – find a spot to rest for a few minutes? She is becoming exhausted.

Then she hears an engine.

It is faint at first, straining in low gear. Coming up, she thinks. She halts.

She recalls Felix's suggestion.

She is wearing her Stetson, which will surely say something about her, judging by the comments it has attracted to date.

The road is just a narrow strip of tarmac, a single car's width with half-formed passing places at irregular intervals.

The visibility is no more than twenty feet.

To be in the road would be risky.

But she is at a passing place.

It is a good spot to flag down a car.

She feels breathless, light-headed; it must be the altitude.

And a little dizzy; there is the slope under her feet, with nothing to see that might aid her balance.

She sways.

She makes a decision.

She steps out, facing downhill, arm outstretched, thumb raised.

The vehicle is nearing.

It is loud now but still invisible, one or two bends below.

And then everything happens in a kaleidoscopic blur.

Close by, the desperate cry of a ewe. *'Here!'*

A last-second warning to its stricken lamb?

Close by, lights appear. Onrushing. Headlights. Fog lights.

Behind the dazzling glare, the shape of a car, vaguely grey-green in the mist.

Dorothy raises her other hand, a half-hearted appeal.

The car accelerates.

Swerves.

She gasps.

It comes at her.

Dorothy half-turns.

An onrushing.

A great force.
The hand of a giant.
She is flying.
Falling.

*

When Dorothy regains her senses and opens her eyes, everything is green, misty.

Her entire body feels numbed.

She moves toes, then fingers.

Around and above her, ferny fronds. She is buried in bracken.

Silence.

Silence of the lambs, even.

Then a car, reversing.

Has she been knocked out? For a few seconds? An hour?

The car is getting closer.

It stops, somewhere above.

It drives forward a little.

It reverses again, and stops.

There is a pause, just the engine idling, the brakes protesting a little as they fight gravity.

Now it moves slowly forwards again, crawling.

Dorothy should get up and summon assistance from the driver.

At least shout for help – the occupants of the car must have their windows open.

Her heart is racing, her pulse loud in her ears.

Her veins are flooded with adrenaline.

Her fight-or-flight responses battle for supremacy.

But some other instinct holds sway.

The third way.

Keep still, silent. Stay hidden.

It is a strange land.

The car drives away.

She counts. A minute passes.

'Here. Here.' The Herdwicks resume their conversation.

Dorothy performs a further evaluation. She has sore shoulders and bruised armpits. It hit her backpack – flipped her.

If she had not sprung at the last split-second – if she did not have her judo to keep her spry – it could have been worse.

She gets first to her knees, and then, rising out of the deep bracken, to her feet.

She is at the foot of a steep bank.

The stream is close – she stumbles across for a drink. The damp turf wets the knees of her hiking pants. The stream water is cold, peaty. She gulps double handfuls.

Her thirst quenched, she removes her backpack and sits upon it. Then she remembers the Kendal mint cake.

Her hands shake as she wrestles with the hinged lid – but it yields to reveal slim squares that look like translucent icing.

It melts in her mouth – the mint invigorating – the sugar revitalising. She eats piece after piece – the entire first layer.

Her thoughts begin to organise themselves.

The mist is so thick, the driver perhaps hardly saw a thing.

Did they think they had struck a sheep? Swerved to miss the lamb and hit the mother?

If they had known it was a person they would have surely called out.

She was foolhardy to stand in the road.

Felix will think it was a dangerous thing to do – that she is not safe on her own. But he might also blame himself, especially as it was his idea to hitch-hike.

She will have to be careful about how she explains it – but at least there are no telltale injuries, apart from bruised pride, and she can hide that.

Dorothy resolves not to be daunted.

She is shaken, but she is also stirred.

*

'You alright, chuck? You look a bit peaky, if you don't mind my saying so.'

Dorothy looks up from her cell phone.

'Pardon me?'

'American, are you? That's nice.'

Dorothy is almost lost for words. But the woman is smiling broadly at her. Dorothy makes a self-referencing gesture with one hand touching her breastbone. The last time she was asked this question she was wearing her 'cowboy' hat.

'Is it so obvious?'

The woman, without invitation, lowers herself into the armchair opposite Dorothy. She groans and gives out a "Bloomin' 'eck". The guest house living up to its billing, Dorothy has a favourable position in a bay window of the residents' lounge with a view across the wooded dale towards Wetherlam. The woman leans forward conspiratorially.

'I overheard you when you arrived. I'd been along to the bathroom, and I was looking at the watercolours on the landing. Do you have an ensuite?'

'Er, well – yes, I do actually.'

Dorothy does not want to seem to be engaging in some sort of one-upmanship, but she can think of no alternative than to give a straight answer to the question. The woman, a complete stranger, seems to be the polar opposite of what she has been told to expect from the 'reserved' English. Although now she stares rather blankly, giving no indication of how she has received the information. Dorothy would estimate that she is in her mid-fifties. She is plainly dressed, in new-looking grey hiking pants and a pale cerise fleecy. She is of below average height, a little well-padded but not overly so. She has long thick blonde-grey hair pulled back in a band, and small grey eyes, quite wideset, in a doughy fair-skinned face that is distinctive only for its large rosy cheek-patches, without prominent cheekbones, brows, nose or lips. Her broad forehead is smooth and she holds her head tilted back in a way that gives her a startled demeanour.

'Not bad news, I hope?'

Dorothy is perplexed. The question does not quite compute, as far as their respective conveniences are concerned. She finds she repeats herself.

'Pardon me?'

Now the woman reaches to pat Dorothy's handset, which she has unconsciously placed on the occasional table that separates their armchairs.

'When I came in, just now – you looked like you'd had a shock.'

Dorothy is still lagging behind. She employs a tactic of her own to buy a few seconds. She extends a hand.

'I'm Dorothy, by the way. Louisiana.'

The woman looks surprised, but accepts the offer to shake hands. Her grip is unexpectedly limp.

'Catherine. Lancashire. Call me Cathy.'

Dorothy is just wondering what to say – whether she can move on from the subject that has been left dangling, when the woman changes it, anyway.

'New Orleans – that's Louisiana. I had an auntie moved there. Jean Shrimpton?'

She seems to be asking the question – the ridiculous question – does Dorothy know her?

'The name seems familiar.'

Dorothy waits for a response.

'She's probably dead by now – I were just a little girl when she emigrated. She were in the WRAF. Met a US airman at Lakenheath in Suffolk.' She gives a slight shake of the head and re-engages with her surprised look – which may also double as inquisitive. 'So, what are you up to? A lone voyager, like me?'

Derek had apologised, saying he was a "blunt northerner" – although Dorothy thought he was always polite. This woman – Catherine, Cathy – does seem more to fit the bill, and Dorothy supposes she should just take her candour in her stride and make conversation accordingly.

She decides to be decisive about how she refers to Felix. After all, Cathy evidently does not miss much and will surely identify the fact that they may be sharing a room.

'Well – not entirely alone. Although, I have been. If I appeared engrossed when you entered – perhaps it was because I was concentrating on my messages. I have had no signal all day.' She gestures to her phone. 'I am expecting my partner to arrive later.'

The woman seems to chortle. It is the kind of exclamation that Dorothy would interpret as meaning, "unlucky you", when perhaps the opposite sentiment might be more appropriate.

'I've abandoned my lot. Left them to fend for themselves.'

Dorothy wonders if she should inquire how many children Cathy has, what ages they are, and so on. But she has the distinct impression that the woman is not interested in talking about them.

She grasps at an alternative straw.

'Lancashire is not so far away, I believe.'

'You're bob on, there – the adjoining county.'

Dorothy indicates to the late afternoon landscape beyond the window. There is an impression that the cloud base is lifting and breaks are beginning to form; there are patches of paler light shifting across the fellsides.

'Do you have a special interest, Cathy?'

'I paint waterfalls.'

The woman looks at her a little strangely, as if Dorothy ought to know this fact. Dorothy wonders if she is a locally famous artist, and that this explains her odd manners. Perhaps she is put out at not being recognised.

'Pictures of them. Not graffiti – or cave art.'

She sounds serious. Surely she doesn't think Dorothy has misunderstood?

'Really? Is it a hobby – or more than that?'

'I sketch – take photos. Paint when I get back home. If you paint when you're here, you waste too much time in one place. I can get a year's worth of painting out of a week's holiday.'

Dorothy notices that the answer is somewhat oblique. However, she nods supportively.

'And it seems that the weather changes so quickly, that the scene at the beginning would be nothing like the scene at the end.'

The woman again looks slightly irritated, and baffled.

'Make your colours run, more like. And there's no point in an umbrella. It'll be blown into the Yorkshire Dales.'

She gives a sudden short artificial laugh, with which Dorothy tries to join in. But she is too slow, and she finds the woman looking at her with a sort of disapproving curiosity. It is as if she has unfavourable opinions of Dorothy; she is not quite ready to share them, but is unable to keep them out of her face.

Before Dorothy can think of what to say, the woman changes the subject again.

'Are you eating here – or do you fancy going down to the pub?'

Dorothy feels rather awkward. Cathy seems to be suggesting they dine together. But she has already informed the landlady that she might need a table for two.

'Oh – the pub? I didn't think of that.'

However, the woman seems satisfied with the response. She nods, and in a rather peremptory fashion rises.

'Nice to meet you, Dorothy – perhaps I'll see you at dinner, then.'

'Nice to meet you, Cathy.'

*

Dorothy is pondering.

Felix's brief email arrived a few minutes after her return to her room. His explanation for brevity being that he had just left his attorney's office and was about to ride on public transport. A longer missive will follow. But she has felt compelled to reply straightaway: the gist of his message is that the property transaction is still in abeyance and he will not be travelling to meet her this evening.

She reprises her as-yet-unsent reply.

Has she toned down sufficiently a) her disappointment and b) her misadventure?

From: Dorothy K. Baum
To: Professor Felix Stowe-Upland
Subject: Little Langdale

Dear Felix, how frustrating for you (and for me, naturally) that there is still a hitch with the legalities. I do hope it can be concluded in the morning, as you anticipate. In the meantime, do not worry about me, I have arrived in Little Langdale, and have a very comfortable room at Wetherlam View. This morning, I took the mountain train from Ravenglass, and in due course reached Mediobogdum.

I have so many photographs for you to tell me all about it. It is quite extraordinary that the ruins just sit there on the fellside, unattended, unadorned by signposts and fences and kiosks; not a trace of 'Disneyfication' as they say. It is a rival to Machu Picchu, in my opinion. And, of course, many times more ancient. Beneath the snows of winter, for the poor legionaries it must have seemed like a posting at a Tibetan monastery, so isolated and bleak – and magnificent – is the setting.

Your advice about the route was wise. The weather did indeed take a turn for the worse. Although not rainy, crossing the Wrynose Pass I found myself in dense hill fog. I do not know how one could navigate across country – although I expect you have the skills. And even this safe route was not without its dangers. Can you believe, I was almost struck by a passing automobile? It actually clipped my rucksack and sent me spinning off the road! But do not worry, it was a minor incident and I am perfectly fine! I feel sorry for the poor driver. The visibility was almost down to zero, and I suspect they think they hit a Herdwick sheep.

In the meantime, I will relax here. There are some other guests. I met a rather talkative lady artist while I was having a cup of tea in the residents' lounge. She threatens to buttonhole me at dinner, so I will not lack company, albeit I fear a mainly one-way conversation!

Then, looking at our route plan, I see that it is just five miles to Ambleside. A pleasant morning walk. It leaves the whole afternoon free to visit the Roman fort. I will find accommodation and await your arrival – hopefully we will be able to do that together.

Yours,
Dorothy.

Dorothy still hesitates before she presses 'send'.

To say she has glossed over her escapade is an understatement. But – here she is – yes, a little battered and bruised, sore in places –

but indisputably in one piece. And, the more she thinks about it, the more she could be accused of bringing it upon herself. The rejuvenating effect of the water and candy was a timely reminder – she had allowed herself to become dehydrated, which in turn had affected her blood sugar and isotonic balance. She was actually becoming a little delirious – possibly even beginning to suffer delusions. Like a walker in the desert, hallucinating at mirages, she was imagining rhinos! But, no – she should not take the suggestion too far, for she definitely did not imagine the car. She has the aches and pains to prove it. But there is no point in causing unnecessary worry to Felix. She must put it down to experience.

But she is thankful to Derek and his gift of the Kendal mint cake. She must stock up on that as soon as she arrives in Ambleside.

She hits 'send'.

It seems that hardly a minute passes before Dorothy is surprised by a response.

From: Professor Felix Stowe-Upland
To: Dorothy K. Baum
Subject: Re: Little Langdale

My dear Dorothy, *do not worry?* How awful! You make light of your 'minor incident'. A glancing blow from a car? *Cruentum infernum!* (If you will excuse my Latin.) Are you certain you are unhurt? I am mortified that I was not there to protect you, unused as you are to this country and its ways – it is such a simple thing to forget that we drive on the opposite side of the road.

I am inclined to suggest that you report it to the police. Perhaps you have already done so? Did you manage to get the registration number of the car? I deduce from your account that the driver did not stop – which is clearly an offence. Did you get a description of the car, or of the driver?

Yours concernedly,
Felix.
P.S. How did you learn of the Herdwicks?

Dorothy, conscious of her furrowed brow, types her answer.

From: Dorothy K. Baum
To: Professor Felix Stowe-Upland
Subject: Re: Little Langdale

Dear Felix, no – *really* – please do not worry, I am perfectly fine. It *was* a minor incident and, as you say, a reminder to me about which side the traffic drives! The road over the Hardknott and Wrynose Passes is of course only wide enough for one car, but I was at a passing place, and I suppose the driver naturally veered to the left, following the verge – or perhaps swerved a little, trying to avoid a poor lamb. At least I have that consolation.

I do not think it would be fair to blame the driver – even if I had a description (which I do not – not even the color of the car or the nature of its occupants – all I saw was a bank of dazzling lights). And I would rather not become embroiled with officialdom – I imagine the British police have more important cases on their hands than silly tourists wandering the fells, don't you think?

I repeat, don't worry.

Yours,

Dorothy.

P.S. It must have been someone on the train who mentioned the name of the Herdwick sheep.

Felix's reply is again swift – she wonders if he has arrived at home or is still waiting for his bus.

From: Professor Felix Stowe-Upland
To: Dorothy K. Baum
Subject: Re: Little Langdale

My dear Dorothy, I have said it before, but you are a brick. You reassure me with your fortitude and indomitable spirit. That's my girl!

You are probably right about the police. I do not wish to disparage them unduly, but they may not take an entirely favourable view of the circumstances. And, if you are sure you do not have any identifying details, I suppose their task would be next to impossible. That said, had you suffered injury, they would have been obliged to investigate.

If you find yourself walking alongside the road tomorrow morning, I suggest that you stay on the right-hand side wherever possible, so that you may see the oncoming traffic. You might even consider joining up with a party of walkers, for greater visibility, and more pairs of eyes and ears. *Vires in numeris.* The routes between the Langdales and Ambleside are more popular with ramblers, and I am sure you could enlist a couple of hearty chaps who would happily accompany you – certainly if you relate your tale of jeopardy. A wandering lamb!

Yours, until anon,
Felix.

Dorothy reproaches herself, that her first thought is of Derek. If only he had been coming this way, now it seems she would have permission to fall in with him. And he is such a gentleman, and only intrusive in a mildly flirting manner that, if she is being honest, flatters her. He does not talk about himself unless asked, and then he is both economical and self-deprecating. A decent British chap altogether.

But her mind shifts to the bigger picture. She lays her cell phone on the nightstand and settles back on her bed. The mattress is welcoming and the pillows fresh and soft. Her old bones feel like they are floating. They took a bit of a battering today. No matter how fit she keeps herself, they are enjoying the respite.

Yes, the bigger picture.

She detects no lack of enthusiasm in Felix's tone, but his messages have become shorter and scant on detail these last few days. She revisits the question of him getting cold feet. But why would he keep promising to see her at the next stage? It is perfectly reasonable and likely that the financial and legal transaction is protracted and riddled with pitfalls – after all there is a chain of buyers and each link must close simultaneously. But does Felix really have to be there to sign and seal the deal in person? He has not mentioned his back today – and could the truth lie more in that direction? Perhaps it is not healing and he does not want to admit it, and is holding off until the more arduous section of their walk is complete, his Roamin' route through the fells. It terminates at the fort near Penrith after the long descent from High Street. From there they go by train to Carlisle to pick up Hadrian's Wall Path, which she knows to be less demanding. Should she factor in a few more days of making her own way – to Penrith or Carlisle?

Dorothy flexes her spine. She has been blessed with good health, when it is such a common ailment. Even today's injuries were restricted – minor bruising above the armpits – thanks to the design of the modern backpack. With its wide straps and broad padded waistband, it acted like the harness of a parachute. When the force of the automobile caught the body of the pack, she was lifted snug in the harness. She closes her eyes and recalls the feeling. She literally was flying for a few moments! Not quite freefall, but the steep bank created some air. Thankfully, the deep bracken, four or five feet of fresh growth sprouting from years of accumulated dry foliage, made for a cushioned landing, further checked by her pack. It was perversely comfortable lying there. She might almost have dropped off to sleep.

Sleep.

'Dorothy. Dorothy!'

Dorothy opens her eyes. A hand is shaking her shoulder, a thumb pressing on the tender spot, and a cartoonish rosy-cheeked countenance is peering at her from a disconcertingly close range. Beyond, she sees that her bedroom door is wide open.

'Are you coming for your dinner, chuck?'

Dorothy tries to speak but her throat is dry. She feels a sudden sense of panic. How long has the woman been in her room? Is anything disturbed? She glances about, affecting disorientation. Her belt-bag is still on the chair where she left it; she can just see one of the straps poking out from beneath her backpack. She breathes a sigh of relief.

'Hark at you – you were out like a light. Now, powder your nose – I'll go and order us a couple of large G&Ts.'

9.
INCOMMUNICADO

Ampleforth, N. Yorks – 9.17 a.m., Friday 22nd May

'That must be him, Guv. Look – it says "The Old Manse" above the front door. *Guv?*'

That Skelgill does not immediately reply (and that DS Jones is perhaps a little short) owes its explanation to Skelgill's attention being taken by two scantily clad female joggers – although she sees in his expression a look of consternation as much as anything worthy of reproach; it could be their lack of attire given the weather; the detectives having driven through alternate sharp showers and bright rainbows, the air much cooler than recent days, despite the dazzling early-morning sunshine. Or it could be that the sight of bare limbs is simply out of context in the rustic village that nestles in the shadow of the North York Moors.

'What's that?'

'The man gardening – that must be him, don't you think?'

Skelgill engages the handbrake and follows his colleague's direction. On their side of the road, set back behind a weathered limestone wall is a long low stone property with a roof of ochre pantiles and yellow rambling roses sprawling over a narrow porch, and neat lawns divided by beds dominated by rose bushes, most yet to come into bloom, underplanted by spring bedding of pink wallflowers and late-flowering purple tulips. Alongside the roses, the other distinctive feature of the cottage garden is a series of classical ornaments, including a Three Graces bird bath, and a sundial set on a spiral column.

A straw hat is bobbing just beyond the wall.

DS Jones is first to leave the car; she appears eager to make her move.

Skelgill follows a few paces behind, delayed by the fact of being in charge of his dog, his regular dog-sitter attending a trade show in Birmingham. He has slipped a length of baler twine through her collar. He grimaces; the leash cuts into his hand as Cleopatra decides she is missing out on something up front.

'Professor Stowe-Upland?'

The man rises easily from a squatting position. He is small and wiry, and his movements quick and birdlike. He wears a loose-fitting check shirt and faded brown corduroys with makeshift kneepads fashioned from what look like old rugby socks. His skin is tanned, at once wrinkled and taut, and clear blue eyes fix upon DS Jones from beneath the brim of the hat. She estimates him to be of an age with Professor Jim Hartley, and there is a certain tribal resemblance, if one that is hard to pinpoint.

'That is correct.'

His expression is a little apprehensive, albeit not alarmed.

'I'm Detective Sergeant Jones from Cumbria CID. This is DI Skelgill.'

'Is it about my Venus?'

'I'm sorry, sir?'

The man gestures with a pair of vintage parrot-beak secateurs. There seems to be nothing at first, until DS Jones's gaze comes to rest upon an empty stone plinth at the centre of an island rose bed.

'I reported it last week. I was hoping it was sixth-formers who had escaped to the Fiddler's Arms and on their way back to their dorm had kidnapped her under the cover of darkness.' He grins ruefully. 'The head says there is no trace of her.'

DS Jones is momentarily a little bemused – perhaps by the idea that CID from another county might be investigating the theft of a garden ornament. But the man is alert to her reaction.

'No – no – it cannot be that – you must be far too busy.'

There is a questioning note in his statement. He moves a couple of paces to the wrought-iron gate and pulls it open. Cleopatra makes an unexpected lunge, almost pulling Skelgill off balance. But the man drops to his haunches to greet the animal.

'A Bullboxer. I did not realise they made good sniffer dogs.'

He looks up. In the shadows of the hat there is a twinkle in his eye. He rises, and regards DS Jones expectantly, though she smiles politely at his implied joke.

She has in one hand her electronic tablet; she turns it to illustrate her point.

'We hoped to ask about some online activity in your name, sir.'

Her tone is light – when the subject matter might potentially be somewhat sinister. The professor's expression becomes a little cryptic. He is about to speak, however, when sudden large drops of cold rain begin to strike, the range-finding artillery of the next massing spring downpour. DS Jones withdraws the tablet, pressing it against her midriff. The man takes a step back and makes a beckoning motion with his secateurs.

'We had better go inside. Can I interest you in a tea? If you have driven halfway across the country. My wife is somewhere in the back garden – azaleas are her thing – mine, roses – we have our own territories. She will probably come in, too.' He points heavenwards, referring to the precipitation. 'Bring the sniffer dog, young man.'

He turns and moves quickly down the cobbled path. The detectives exchange glances – of the nature, 'suck it and see'.

The front door is unlocked. The professor pauses only to hang his hat on a hook and reveal a mainly bald head. He gestures to a room on the left.

'There – go into my study. Make yourselves comfortable. I shall organise refreshments.'

Despite the time of year a log fire smoulders in a broad stone hearth, and the low, beamed room has an almost medieval feel to it. Motes of dust are picked out by bars of sunshine that penetrate the latticed windows, and there is a general impression of old wood and leather-bound tomes; shades of brown dominate. A clock ticks methodically and Skelgill's dog reacts nervously as a log shifts in the grate.

They settle in comfortable worn leather armchairs. Skelgill contemplates the fire, and DS Jones can see he is fighting the urge to adjust it with a cast-iron poker.

The professor takes a little longer than they might have expected, and when he does reappear he bears a tray with earthenware mugs of tea, which he sets down before them to reveal a plate of chocolate digestives.

'My apologies, she has not succumbed. A hardy old devil.'

It seems he has assembled the snack himself. Skelgill's attention has shifted to his favourite variety of biscuit; now DS Jones is wondering if he will be able to resist dunking them, or eating what he considers a requisite ration. The professor, taking a third armchair, seems to be something of a clairvoyant.

'Please help yourselves. Sorry it's all a little rudimentary. Dunk away!'

DS Jones cannot suppress a grin – but she moves promptly to pick up where the rain obliged her to leave off.

'Sir, I should first apologise that we have descended out of the blue. We couldn't get a telephone number.'

'Ah, we are ex-directory. The nuisance callers, you see?'

DS Jones nods her understanding.

'Perhaps I may show you something.'

She raises her tablet and tilts it experimentally.

'Do you have a Wi-Fi connection that I could use?'

The professor bows apologetically.

'I am afraid we don't have the internet. We don't have mobile phones. Or even television.' He pauses, and gazes reflectively into the hearth, where a flicker of flame has kindled. 'So little to go wrong. And so much to listen to on the radio or the gramophone. When one is not reading, of course. Or writing actual letters – so much more satisfying to receive, don't you think?'

DS Jones politely cuts to the chase.

'Sir, are you on Facebook?'

'I am more likely to be in the Domesday Book.' The man chuckles self-effacingly. 'Of course, I am being a little facetious. Naturally I have heard of it – I know of its existence.' He gestures to a brass scuttle at one side of the fireplace that contains newspapers. 'There was an article in yesterday's edition of The Times bemoaning their contribution to societal dysfunction. Another chapter of human history for future academics.'

The bright eyes interrogate each of the detectives in turn. DS Jones returns his gaze respectfully; Skelgill seems to be counting under his breath as he holds a biscuit dipped into his mug.

DS Jones manipulates the screen of her device.

'I think I can just about connect to the local base station.' She frowns at the screen for a couple of seconds before she achieves some success. 'Yes. Sir – there is a Facebook group called Cumbrian Confederates. One of the members goes by the name of Professor Felix Stowe-Upland. He appears to have a special interest in Roman history.'

She turns the tablet to reveal the display.

'May I?'

DS Jones hands over the device. The professor seems to need no tuition in how to scroll. He is plainly fascinated by the content, but remains calm and collected. After perhaps a minute he hands it back. He gives a shake of the head and raises his eyebrows questioningly.

'That's not you then, sir?'

He brings brown bony fingers up to his chin in a gesture of academic contemplation.

'If I may blow my own trumpet, I would have called the Roman fort Petriana by its more correct name of Uxelodunum.'

He nods conclusively.

'Do you know of another person who shares your name, sir?'

DS Jones asks the question without expectation in her tone; nevertheless, the professor plies her with an old-fashioned look.

'I am the last of the nominal Stowe-Uplands. The double-barrelled name only came into existence in the 1940s – at the marriage of my parents. I am an only child. It would be quite a coincidence if another Stowe and another Upland had become united in matrimony. Not to mention my title and Christian name.'

His logic is compelling.

'Sir – do you have children?'

'Oh, yes – a daughter.'

DS Jones hesitates before she indicates to the screen.

'This couldn't be her?'

'I somehow doubt it. Apart from the fact that she goes by her married name of Aldrin, she lives in Florida. She is an astrophysicist. She works at the Kennedy Space Centre.'

DS Jones nods acceptingly, but does not excuse herself from protocol.

'Would you mind if I took a contact number or address?'

'Certainly not. Any help I can be.' He regards DS Jones with a look of some determination. 'After all, I should rather like to know who is trading on my brand, as they say.'

He rises and crosses to a drop-leaf bureau that faces the window. He flicks through the pages of an address book and writes with a fountain pen upon a sheet of notepaper picked from a leather holder. He uses a traditional rocker blotter to finish.

DS Jones has been interrogating her device, but she sets it aside when their host returns. She thanks him and sees that the letterhead is entitled, "Dr F. I. Stowe-Upland & Dr E. F. Stowe-Upland".

She waves the sheet pensively.

'Do you have any suspicions, sir – of who it might be?'

The professor remains standing. He cocks his head on one side, the intelligent eyes raised for a moment to the beamed ceiling.

'What I would say is, for a person to know my name and specialism – it would suggest someone up against whom I rubbed in a professional capacity – some time ago. But there would be hundreds of academics ... and thousands of students.' He raises an index finger. 'If anything springs to mind, I shall certainly let you know.'

There is some aspect of finality about his manner, and this appears to suit DS Jones. She rises, and hands over a calling card.

'My number is on there, sir.'

Cleopatra is quick to detect signs of departure, and is on her feet with a skittering of claws on the floorboards.

'A well-behaved dog you have there, Inspector.'

Skelgill raises a cynical eyebrow. Quite likely Cleopatra could smell the chocolate, a confection she knows to be off limits; although a lesson taught for not entirely altruistic reasons.

Skelgill has presented a stolid presence during the interview, but now he rises and steps across directly to a low bookcase on which are arranged several glass-topped specimen cases. They contain coins.

'Are you a metal detector, sir?'

The man looks a little surprised – and amused, but in a pleased kind of way – perhaps that some interest has been generated by his collection.

'I own a metal detector, certainly. Indeed, you remind me that I must dust it off. I have not had it out this year. I have permission to prospect in the grounds of both the abbey and the school.'

Skelgill's response is a rather peremptory nod and he turns to duck under the low doorway that leads back into the hall, although he can be excused for wanting to keep an eye on his four-legged charge.

DS Jones moves to follow, but she speaks conversationally to the professor at the same time.

'Did you ever teach at Ampleforth College, sir?'

Now the man looks at her in alarm.

'Good heavens, no. In my day I believe it would have involved becoming a monk.'

They spill out into the garden. The air is fresh and damp, and raindrops on roses glisten beguilingly. A blackbird takes advantage of the resonant air to project a melody. Beneath a cloud in the west a vivid rainbow arcs as the next shower advances.

Though the scene distracts them all, the professor evidently still has the local private school in mind. His eyes fall upon the vacant plinth.

'Besides, there would be those infernal pupils.'

DS Jones smiles sympathetically.

'Good luck with your Venus, sir.'

*

DS Jones is eager to speak, but Skelgill is driving and simultaneously looking in his rear-view mirror. She feels responsible for navigation. However, somehow they round a bend and he looks forwards. Though he is a little grim-faced.

The elderly man, having donned his straw hat, had stood scarecrow-like, stock still, watching them out of sight.

DS Jones lets go of the breath she has been holding and inhales again to speak. But Skelgill pre-empts her.

'Do you believe him?'

She is surprised by Skelgill's question. He seems to be placing an unnecessary hurdle for the sake of devil's advocacy. She pats the pocket into which she slipped the notepaper.

'On the letterhead there is no mobile number or email address – just a landline. I checked with my tablet – there was no Wi-Fi signal in the cottage, and the only mobile phones that my Bluetooth detected were ours. You would think if he had a computer, it would be in his study – but there was nothing – no printer, no cables. They could have a plug-in modem in another room, but I somehow doubt it.'

Skelgill is frowning, but not in a manner that suggests disagreement. He did note there was no external television aerial affixed to the cottage chimney stack.

'Like he said, nowt to go wrong.'

DS Jones shoots Skelgill a sideways glance and a wry grin – she knows well enough that Skelgill would consider there to be other more profound benefits of being unconnected.

'He could obviously go somewhere else to post on Facebook – but since he's not at work, I'm not sure where that would be.'

'Looks like an imposter, eh, lass?'

Skelgill, however, intones teasingly, as if he does not quite take seriously his own suggestion.

DS Jones hesitates, her expression pensive.

'He said it would have to be someone that formerly knew of him. But it would also have to be someone that knows that he wouldn't twig to what is going on – that he is being impersonated. Don't you think?'

There is a delay before Skelgill responds.

'I think there's a burger van in about ten minutes.'

'I don't believe this.'

Despite his colleague's exclamation, delivered with restraint but for all that with intensity, Skelgill does not immediately react; he is occupied with biting into a large Yorkshire bread-cake stuffed with crispy bacon and soft, cooked tomatoes that he is struggling to contain. DS Jones gives up her napkin.

Skelgill gestures with his eyebrows that she should elaborate.

She raises her mobile phone as though it were an exhibit to be auctioned.

She looks at him a little wild-eyed.

'I've had a private message from Professor Felix Stowe-Upland.'

Skelgill munches, seemingly unperturbed. When he can, he responds casually.

'What – has he just remembered summat?'

DS Jones shakes her head in an exaggerated fashion, dislodging strands of hair that fall across her eyes.

'No, Guv – not the real one – the *fake* one!'

Skelgill makes a face that exhorts further explanation on his colleague's behalf. DS Jones has not even begun to unwrap her roll and now she places it on the dashboard. Skelgill appears a little bemused by her choice of priorities.

She raises the handset again.

'I joined the Facebook group, right?' (Skelgill nods.) 'I thought I'd kind of mirror Patricia Jackson – so I went through the posts by Stowe-Upland and "liked" them. Now he's messaged me. It must have come through while we were in the queue.'

She stares for a moment at her watch.

'At best it's five a.m. in the States. That supports the idea that he's based in Britain.'

Skelgill shrugs, as if they thought that to be the case anyway. Indeed, he is processing the obvious connections.

'Is your photograph on your profile?'

DS Jones looks at him with what might be a mixture of alarm and a hint of awkwardness.

'Oh, no – I invented an entire persona. Most of the group members seem to be retired women – so I just copied that. Quite a few of them have their pets – I used a photo from my phone of Cleopatra.'

The dog raises her head from the back seat. Skelgill glances over.

'He saw her.'

'He did, Guv – but I really don't think it's him. I mean, honestly, do you?'

Skelgill sighs resignedly.

'What name did you use?'

Now DS Jones definitely looks a little sheepish.

'I made up a nickname. Cumberland Lass.' Skelgill is frowning, but she continues quickly. 'I put my location down as Lakeland, Florida. I wanted to give the impression of being an ex-pat with pride in my roots. I stated my interests as British history, pets and home baking. I put my age as sixty-five. Occupation, retired detective.'

Skelgill performs a double-take. There are several aspects of her statement that might wrongfoot him – but it is the final word that really does the trick. But DS Jones cannot contain a laugh.

'Very funny.' He clicks his tongue in frustration. 'Only stupid criminals need apply.'

DS Jones returns her attention to the screen.

'Don't you want to know what he's said?'

Skelgill re-engages with his bacon-and-tomato roll, which she takes as an affirmative response.

'It's quite short. He welcomes me to the group and thanks me for liking his posts. Invites me to be his friend, so I can follow him. He says he makes regular visits to sites in Cumbria as part of his studies of the Romans in Britain. Then he asks whether I still have relatives in Cumbria.'

Skelgill finishes his snack and wipes his hands and mouth with the tissue. He clanks the car into gear and accelerates dynamically from the layby onto the main carriageway.

'What will you say?'

DS Jones speaks slowly. 'I need to think about it. I mean – we need to discuss it. What would be the natural thing to do? Maybe not immediately – I feel.'

Skelgill nods slowly.

'Aye.'

When he offers no further advice, she picks up the discussion.

'It's weird – I mean, we've just seen the real Professor – and now the imposter is speaking to us. I feel more like an undercover agent than a police detective.'

Skelgill has his foot down and is staring ahead, intermittently checking his rear-view mirror. They are heading more or less due north on the A1, the Great North Road – in places the Roman Dere Street lies beneath the tarmacadam. The North York Moors are visible as a dark wooded ridge some miles to their right. Tall white shower-clouds sail the open blue skies. The spring hedgerows are burgeoning with the intense cream blossom of the may, and great van-Gogh-yellow fields of oilseed rape startle the eye.

When he does not answer, DS Jones knows better than to ask him the question that circles them; instead she grabs down the proposition.

'There's something in this, isn't there?' She gives Skelgill the chance to react, but he is unblinking, treating the question as a statement. 'An elderly American – we think – dies in inadequately explained circumstances. She has an interest in Cumbria. She has a Facebook connection to a Professor Felix Stowe-Upland. He is apparently operating behind a fake profile.'

Skelgill, of course, is notoriously resistant to jumping to conclusions.

'When do you reckon you'll hear from the FBI?'

'Maybe later today. But I'll send this new information, and hopefully have a conversation this afternoon. It might just add to their appreciation of there being cause for suspicion.'

'We need to nail this ID. Jackson's a common local name. Find out if it's her maiden name. She might have been visiting relatives. Trouble is, there's a lot of Jacksons in Cumbria. I had two in my class most of the way through school.'

DS Jones nods somewhat broodingly. It is becoming a pressing matter. If the ID does not match up, where would that leave them? A still-unidentified body buried in an unmarked South Lakeland District Council grave. And a missing American who may or may not have visited Cumbria.

She redoubles her determination.

'I'll contact the FBI at the earliest. What time do you think we'll arrive back at Penrith?'

Skelgill is already testing the legal limits. He glances at his tachometer and then at the clock in the central console.

'I promised I'd meet Leyton for a bite in Keswick.'

DS Jones knows this to be code for not sparing the gas. They are approaching a road sign that tells them it is fifteen miles to Scotch Corner. Then another fifty across the North Pennines.

She feels the car speed up a little more. He has probably done the same calculation. Now he seems to be humming a Beatles tune.

DS Jones grins.

'Will you last until lunchtime?'

Skelgill's humming ceases.

'Good point. That teabread's in the glove box.'

DS Jones shakes her head in mock exasperation.

'Wasn't that intended for Cleopatra? A doggy-bag.'

'I reckon that's what you call a figure of speech.'

'What do you call it?'

'Elevenses.'

10. HANG OVER

Bleaberry Nook, Ambleside – 2.14 p.m., Friday 22nd May

From: Dorothy K. Baum
To: Professor Felix Stowe-Upland
Subject: Awaiting your arrival?

Dear Felix, I am rather breathless, having just checked in to a quaint B&B overlooking the northern reaches of Windermere (see – I have remembered not to sound like a tourist, and call it "Lake" Windermere). I have hauled my pack to a room in the eaves on the third floor (that's the British third floor, one higher than in the USA). And I await your arrival!

I must confess, my head is thumping – more of that when I see you – but for the time being I put it down to the steep stairs and the sense of anticipation. The B&B is called Bleaberry Nook and by good fortune is just two minutes' walk from the Roman fort – so you should have no difficulty whatsoever in finding me. The landlord informs me that there is a bus stop almost directly outside, on the route from Windermere railway station.

I say 'good fortune' because I took your advice about finding a walking companion. The pushy lady I mentioned – her name is Cathy, from Lancashire – is also travelling alone, and she is familiar with the Lake District. She, too, was heading for Ambleside and had made a booking ahead. When I told her something of our trip, she kindly rang to inquire if there were vacancies. Along with the ideal location, it avoided a 'hit and miss' choice – you know how there are so many fake reviews these days. Just wait until you see the vista! What a wonderful scene Windermere makes, her wandering banks cloaked in oaks and the fells rising gently all around. I cannot wait to explore Galava, which seems to be situated on a small flood plain at the very northern tip of the lake.

Cathy has gone off to sketch and photograph a waterfall just on the east side of the town – Stock Ghyll Force I believe she called it. It seems that waterfalls are her big thing. I was thinking it might make a pleasant walk for us this evening after dinner. I would like to see if it lives up to Cathy's billing.

I wonder at this moment where you are – and whether you have a signal?

I will send this now – perhaps you are almost here!

Yours,

Dorothy.

Dorothy presses 'send' and waits for the little *whoosh* before she puts down her cell phone and rises from her armchair. The Wi-Fi signal seems weak this far up in the house. She crosses to the dormer window. The view is indeed captivating. Britain might not be very big by American standards, but there is something about the model-village quality of its dense countryside that she has experienced nowhere else in the world. Could anywhere look more beguiling than the English Lake District on a late spring day? She sees a boat leaving and wonders if they will have time to take a lake cruise. Perhaps there are dinner cruises? It hardly gets dark until eleven p.m.; the scenery would be magical in the long dusk, and, after a morning of sharp but invigorating showers, the weather seems set fair for the rest of the day. No doubt it will change tomorrow!

Thought of this 'rainbow weather' brings to mind Derek – and she has to admit to a slight pang of longing. How much more enjoyable would his company have been than 'Kooky Cathy' (as she has, to her own slight guilt, secretly nicknamed the woman). But she ought to count her blessings. Face the fact, like Derek, Cathy has filled a little gap – and, in her own eccentric way, added colour to Dorothy's trip – to her 'adventure', as she had described it to Felix. If Felix had not been delayed she would not have met either of them. Soon enough Felix will be here, and Cathy can be consigned to the past.

But will Felix be here?

Her cell phone sounds an alert.

She does not turn immediately.

Like that last letter from hospital. It could bear good news. But it might not. She had set it aside for days. But here she does not have the same luxury.

She returns to her armchair and takes up the handset.

From: Professor Felix Stowe-Upland
To: Dorothy K. Baum
Subject: Re: Awaiting your arrival?

My dearest Dorothy, oh, what a bother! And so frustrating, now that you are so perfectly ensconced beside Galava. I cannot tell you how I itch to be there and for us to wander around those timeless remains together. It seems as though the Gods conspire to keep us apart! *Numquam duo conveniant!*

Yes – you have probably guessed, another hurdle erected in my path. I am only this minute off the telephone from my solicitor, who in turn has heard from the bank. Apparently they are insisting upon security for not just the bridging loan but also the Stamp Duty. This is an entirely separate payment that must be made up front. Think of it as an English property tax.

It seems to me something more like a 'bail bond' – but I am afraid they have us over a barrel. I have sent my lawyer off with a flea in his ear – to negotiate some alternative – but he is doing so under protest, and does not sound optimistic. Frankly, the simple way out of it would be to come up with the money – like the initial guarantee, it would be literally for a few days until the logjam is freed and all the cash transactions cascade through in rapid succession.

I wondered therefore if we may make a final temporary call upon your resources? I feel terribly guilty in asking – but my hands are tied, my capital frozen in my York property – if only I could dig out some of the bricks and mortar and take them along in a wheelbarrow and dump them on the steps of the Tax Office, I gladly would! I think twenty-five thousand should do the trick. That could make all the difference, and break us out of this infernal chain. Everything will quickly come out in the wash, and you will be fully reimbursed, along of course for any penalty charges.

Dorothy, do let me know, and I shall put the necessary wheels in motion. As soon as that can be accomplished, I shall set off to intercept you – I shall study the maps and calculate our possible point of confluence. We are like two great rivers meandering in the wilderness; soon we shall find our Khartoum.

Yours, until anon,
Felix.

P.S. For the avoidance of doubt, that is twenty-five thousand, sterling.

Dorothy finds herself typing rather robotically.

From: Dorothy K. Baum
To: Professor Felix Stowe-Upland
Subject: Re: Awaiting your arrival?

Dear Felix, oh – such a shame – I was just gazing out of the window and picturing our walk amongst the ancient ruins. But I will not dwell on what cannot be – it seems action is called for. Leave it with me to contact my bank. If I cannot get funds released quickly, perhaps they will facilitate a short-term loan against my deposits as security. I also have some funds invested in stocks, but of course there is the matter of the settlement date, usually two days after the sale. I will let you know the moment I hear.

Yours,
Dorothy.

Dorothy stares at her screen for a few moments after she has pressed 'send'. She glances up, and catches sight of herself in the long mirror on the back of her door. The person she sees looks … how does she look? Worried? Deflated? Determined? Older than she feels? That is hardly possible!

She forces a grin and the person returns it.

She rises and crosses again to the window. She stares pensively, this time not seeing the view. Then she turns decisively and straps on her belt-bag and zips her mobile into it. Opening the door, however, she hesitates – and darts back for her cagoule. She has remembered Derek's words. Maybe these showers have not finished for the day.

*

From: Dorothy K. Baum
To: Professor Felix Stowe-Upland
Subject: Re: Awaiting your arrival?

Dear Felix, despite the disappointment I am feeling better. I ventured out to clear my head – sorry, this sounds like I am a little distressed, and I know you would not want me to feel any such thing.

What a remarkable location for Galava, literally on the shores of Windermere. Not so much to see above ground as Mediobogdum, but impressive nonetheless. I imagine the Romans made good use of the lake as a means of transport – the longest in England, I understand.

I was equally enchanted by a quaint little shop that seemed to be given over entirely to the sale of Kendal mint cake. I had not realised just what a popular local delicacy this is! I gather it has been carried by generations of mountaineers, including to the top of Everest on the very first ascent – and, having sampled it, I can see exactly why. Indeed, I feel quite pepped up!

There is also good news concerning the money. I did not expect my bank to be so forthcoming – but they are prepared to make an advance against the sale of stocks. A transaction should go through overnight British time, so please check your account in the morning. Let us hope – as you say – that this will do the trick.

I thought I would be brief and let you know, so that you can make preparations for leaving tomorrow. Please let me know what you think I should do – should I plan to spend an extra night here in Ambleside? I know from your Roamin' itinerary that there are several options at this point. Naturally I would rather be in the best place for you to meet me.

I will await your response.

With fingers crossed!
Dorothy.
P.S. How is your back – you have not mentioned it?

Dorothy checks the time. It is approaching five p.m. and she is expecting a knock from Cathy at any moment. But a reply comes quickly.

From: Professor Felix Stowe-Upland
To: Dorothy K. Baum
Subject: Re: Awaiting your arrival?

My dearest Dorothy, splendid stuff! I knew I could rely upon you! But you understand how we Brits find this sort of thing embarrassing. You Americans are such straight talkers and straight actors. My back is feeling better already! *Miracula numquam desinunt!* As for Roamin' – I rather feel you should not look a gift horse in the mouth. While there remains a little doubt over my timings, I suggest you stick with your companion – Cathy, I believe you called her? Obviously, given what you say about her interests, she may have her own plans – but there are several waterfalls worth seeing along the route from Ambleside up to the southern end of High Street. Indeed, I had very much wanted to show you these myself. There is Stencher Beck in Skelghyll Wood, and more falls above High Skelghyll. It would mean you are again not alone – frankly, better for the safety of you both, should either of you turn an ankle. Your next port of call could then be in the vicinity of the hamlet of Troutbeck, whence the eponymous stream forms a possible route up to the beginning of High Street (and more spectacular waterfalls on the way). If I am unable to meet you at Troutbeck, then a descent from High Street to Hartsop would be the logical move, and I should come down from Penrith via Ullswater. From there we could return to High Street for the final stretch to Brocavum. What an intrepid wayfarer you are becoming! And do not despair. There will be plenty left for us to see and do. Hadrian's Wall, with its forts, milecastles and signal towers is like no other ancient monument on this earth! Just imagine if the perimeter of the

Colosseum or even the streets of Pompeii took a week to walk around!

I shall leave you to reflect upon this, while I break off and compose an email to my solicitors, so that they are primed and ready first thing tomorrow morning.

With deepest gratitude for your indomitable fortitude,
Felix.

Dorothy finds herself mulling over mixed feelings. She tries to put to the back of her mind any ideas of doubt or indecision. There is no point. She is in too deeply. Here she is, a nomad in the middle of the Cumbrian fells, most of her worldly possessions close to hand, most of her ties to home severed. There is no turning around. She must push on – make what she can of the circumstances as they unfold. Take Felix at his word – and perhaps she will look back at these, what feel like great fissures in the fellsides, as mere wrinkles upon the map when it is proudly mounted on the wall as a souvenir and her little red line traced across it from Ravenglass to Hexham, all one hundred miles of it.

But there is the question of Cathy.

She has not been entirely candid with Felix – nor herself, come to that. Not only is she unsure whether Cathy is the sort of person she will enjoy spending much more time with – as opposed to being alone – but there is an associated nagging annoyance that she was rather too forthcoming in her conversations with her, which she now rather regrets. The trouble had been that first gin and tonic. Dorothy had not admitted to herself how the incident in the Wrynose Pass had left her traumatised. The alcohol, she *is* forced to admit, came as a welcome stress-reliever. Far from a regular drinker, it had gone straight to her head, and onward – to wherever sits the gatekeeper to one's inhibitions. Accordingly, she had overindulged – they had almost finished a second bottle of wine with their dinner, which, now she recalls – of what she can recall – she had last seen Cathy wielding as she disappeared into her room. In payment, Dorothy, sore from her close encounter with the car, and weighed down by her pack, had spent much of this morning's walk beneath the extra burden of a thumping hangover, listening painfully to Cathy's inane and disjointed chatter – something that cannot be called a conversation – she never seems to stick for any length of time to one subject; she mixes odd comments about herself with peculiar observations about anything ranging from their surroundings to politics – and then, out of the blue, the occasional personal question that she just does not seem to sense might be embarrassing to answer.

In consequence, Dorothy had found herself – after dinner in particular (more so than this morning, when she was necessarily more taciturn) – relating something of her story. She had disclosed rather more of her circumstances than she perhaps ought. She was drawn at times into a little one-upmanship, Cathy being somewhat doubting. She is blunt and to the point. Although, in many ways, she only poses the questions that must occur to most people, but they are too polite to ask. Such matters as concern Dorothy's personal, domestic and financial situation. After all – it is natural to be inquisitive when one hears that an American senior has uprooted, sold up, emigrated – to come and live with a comparative stranger. Dorothy found herself having to ride to Felix's defence. At times it made her a little uneasy. Perhaps the woman was right. She seems to have a sceptical take on most people. She does not have a lot of good things to say about her own husband, or even her children. She seems to resent them taking advantage of her. It does not seem fair, however, to assign others' meaner motives to Felix, when she does not know him.

But perhaps Cathy is the sort of devil's advocate to whom everyone should expose themselves when faced by an important series of decisions. Someone who will not be polite just because they know you, someone who sees it from the outside, not the inside, hampered by the same scales that cover one's own eyes. Although she thinks, no matter how well Cathy gets to know her, she doubts whether the avoidance of being rude will ever come into her calculations. In her obdurate way, at one point she had declaimed, "I reckon he's stood you up, chuck".

She will have to think carefully about how she deals with the situation. As things stand, she has told Cathy that Felix is coming to Ambleside. Of course, Cathy had pooh-poohed this and she will no doubt say she told her so when Dorothy has to admit he is now not. And, as Felix mentioned – Cathy might have her own plans to head in a different direction – Dorothy has avoided such a conversation in case there were the risk of her tagging along with them when Felix did arrive; a recalcitrant 'gooseberry', as the Brits say! Dorothy might have to play her cards carefully at dinner, and sleep on the decision tonight.

That said, perhaps Cathy will be pleased to wave her goodbye?

11. BELOW

Skelghyll Wood – 11.17 a.m., Saturday 23rd May

'Sure you don't want to come and see these *humpty-dumps* – whatever you call 'em, Guv?'

DS Leyton squints up through the open driver's window. Skelgill scowls; he knows his sergeant is now taking the mickey.

'Save time if we divide and conquer, Leyton.' He jerks a thumb over his shoulder, indicating the wooded fellside that rises behind him. 'Besides, you haven't got the right shoes on for a yomp up here.'

DS Leyton grins.

'I must remember that excuse next time the Missus asks me to take the bins out.'

They neither of them look like they think this tactic would work.

Skelgill waves his GPS device, pressed into use for the second time this week. He has chosen what he considers the most direct route, and perhaps that most likely taken by the woman they believe to be Patricia Jackson, before she fell to an untimely death.

'You go and look at your latest molehills. If you're done first, find a café and send us a text – I'll meet you there.'

DS Leyton taps the steering wheel with both hands.

'Sure you don't want me to come back and park here, Guv?'

Skelgill frowns. His sergeant's car is squeezed against an open gateway beside the main A591 Ambleside-to-Windermere trunk road. Like many such Lakeland routes, it is comparatively narrow, snaking, and busy in both directions.

'Nay – it's not a good spot to wait. I'll come back down Skelghyll Lane – that makes a beeline for the town.'

DS Leyton looks like he expects some punchline – that this is a phrase Skelgill uses as a foible – the ignoring of private property, claiming anywhere he wants to go as his own.

When no further explanation is forthcoming, he acquiesces, and shoves the car into gear.

'As you like it, Guv. I'll go and find the nighthawker's latest handiwork. Picking on the Romans, now – what did they ever do to deserve that?'

'Take the first left in about a third of a mile.'

'Roger.'

DS Leyton pulls away rapidly, not worrying too much about other motorists and getting hooted from behind by a delivery driver.

Skelgill turns to face the trees. He cannot remember the last time he visited the wood with which he shares a name. It was, he thinks, a mountain rescue fund-raising event, from Ambleside to the pub at Town Head at Troutbeck, that involved running the full length of the impossibly narrow Skelghyll Lane, itself two miles of the five, and which cuts through the woodland as it traverses the fellside. That he has come at all, at this juncture, owes itself to an earlier call from his colleague, alerted to another incident of illicit excavation, this time at the Roman fort of Galava, in the adjacent town of Ambleside; thus there was an opportunity to 'kill two birds with one stone'.

The first portion is a semi-ornamental woodland garden of dark pines and vivid rhododendrons, in the guardianship of the National Trust, but this merges into wilder native habitat, and Skelgill follows the course of the small stream, Stencher Beck, in order to keep his bearings. He has the GPS merely as a back-up; he thinks he knows the spot he is looking for, beneath the bridge where the lane crosses overhead.

To enter an English oak woodland on a spring morning, especially those moist places found in the damper west, is not so far from the experience of a tropical rainforest. Ivy rises. Ancient plants, ferns, lichens, liverworts and mosses drape the boughs, their chlorophylls a complete spectrum of green in their own right. The air is heavy, damp, warm to the skin; with its tang of leaf mould, wood mulch, and invisible floating fungal spores; its bouquet of sweet, sickly honeysuckle and fresh wild hyacinth, the latter a sapphire blur that washes down the fellside between the old trunks like glacial meltwater. There are butterflies, orange tips that tumble tirelessly in search of a mate or jack-by-the-hedge; and speckled woods, that settle to sun themselves where shafts of light fall on bramble foliage. Birds abound. Unseen, but strident, an invisible choir too populous to list in its entirety; flycatchers, finches, thrushes and tits, jay, cuckoo, treecreeper and more. Underfoot, the peaty going is forgiving; place a steadying palm against the crocodile skin of an oak, and feel its irresolute antiquity.

Who needs virtual reality when there is multidimensional actuality?

All five senses stimulated, such is the overload that he notices everything, and yet notices nothing.

Stencher Beck is busy with recent rain. Not exactly a waterfall, but a cascade of white over the slick black rocks that is no less attractive to the eye, and soothing on the ear.

As he ascends, the sides of the gill close in and become increasingly mossy, too steep for most trees but the odd tenacious rowan.

Skelgill checks his GPS. The reading tells him he is within a few yards of the spot where the woman was discovered. Overhead, spanning what is a precipitous cliff, cloven by the water, is the rudimentary packhorse bridge that carries Skelghyll Lane. He squints; the oaks almost converge, but there is a strip of canopy missing that corresponds to the line of the beck, and the sky is a bright, dazzling blue.

He clambers among the wet rocks, to a position virtually beneath the bridge; it is something of a trolls' cave.

There is a gently sloping slab.

This was the place.

It was not a case he investigated.

How much thought was devoted to the position of the body? Would it be possible to come to rest naturally here? Just out of sight, she had not been found for two days, and only then by a botanist seeking a rare liverwort. The post mortem concluded that death would have been instantaneous – it eliminated any possibility that the injured woman had crawled.

He is pondering this point when the sound of a sharp female voice penetrates the background rush of the water. He is about to step out when something comes clattering down – a small rock or pebble or similar – he shies away and instinctively calls out.

'Below!'

It is one of the urgent mountaineering cries, usually uttered when the lead needs to warn their climbing partner that loose debris is coming fast under the force of gravity – but Skelgill does not rest upon niceties, and his bellowed retort is edged with anger.

Now, more cautiously, he leans out.

Silhouetted against the sky he sees a head and shoulders, topped by a wide-brimmed hat. Then a second figure appears, the impression shorter and stouter than the first, and a more modest bush hat. In the fleeting moment he can discern little of the faces. The first perhaps the older, more noble and chiselled; the second rounded, rosy-cheeked, alarmed.

'Chuffin' 'eck!'

It is the second that exclaims – and she retreats from sight and there is the impression of the first woman being tugged back out of view. Skelgill thinks he hears the voice fading away, the words, "Chop, chop –"

Hands on hips, he stares for ten seconds or so, but they do not reappear.

'Hallo!'

Though he hails them, it is to no avail.

Another pause, longer, and he eventually takes the strain off his neck.

Immediately he notices a small silver tin, embossed with blue graphics lying at an angle in a crevice of the rock. Indeed he recognises it. Kendal mint cake. In brand new condition, apart from one dented corner, still sealed, by the look of it, it must have been what fell.

He picks it up and grins wryly. There is some irony in being brained by a tin of the stuff. It would make a decent anecdote in the pub; indeed, he is tempted to fashion one accordingly. Although, when he thinks about it, that scenario must have happened multiple times in the whole history of the famous mountaineering confectionery.

He pockets the tin. He'll take it up and restore it to its owner. He backtracks a little before he can find a route that does not involve an exposed scramble. The gill – the gully – is certainly dangerous at this point. In the event he emerges onto what is an unmetalled stretch of Skelghyll Lane about fifty feet from the bridge. Of the women, there is no sign. But the wooded track curves away steeply in both directions, and while they could not have got far, he is not surprised they are out of sight. He wonders if they have scarpered, rather like naughty schoolchildren, embarrassed by their misdemeanour. Perhaps he ought to have been more circumspect, but his survival instincts had trumped decorum.

There is a silver lining. He slaps his back pocket. Finders keepers.

The parapet of the bridge is low in his estimation. It is not one where the elbows can comfortably be rested and one's centre of gravity remain chiefly on the feet. A backpack would provide extra ballast, but no luggage was found with the body, of course.

He reflects on this point.

If the woman had removed her pack and toppled over, and was not visible below, the wrong kind of passer-by might easily have been tempted to 'chore' it, as the local dialect goes. Could she have taken it off in order to get a photograph? But then would not a camera or phone have been found with the body? According to the reports there was nothing, above or below. And nothing left in a guest house.

The post mortem showed no signs of intoxication by drink or drugs; the clothes were of good quality and condition; the woman was no 'down-and-out' and the headlong nature of the fall did not suggest a suicide leap. The mere anonymity of this spot seems to him to rule that out; hardly any locals know of it, never mind a visiting American.

There are lots of imponderables crowding the waiting room marked 'sixth sense'. The time has not yet come to let them in.

Skelgill realises he is humming along to the tune of the 'Lambeth Walk' – and then the music penetrates his consciousness;

it is his mobile phone. He has a signal, and DS Leyton is calling.

'Leyton.'

'Alright, Guv. I could do with a hand if you're nearly done.'

'Aye?'

Skelgill sounds unenthusiastic.

'I reckon I might have the nighthawker bang to rights.'

'What are you talking about, Leyton?'

'I had a butcher's at the fort. Another flippin' hole in the ground. Not much I could do. I was just driving off to look for a caff and there's this geezer with a metal detector – swinging it about, bold as brass!'

'What, in the fort?'

'Nah – he was working his way along the verge. I've detained him for questioning – I've got him waiting at one of the picnic tables. Thing is, he's started to baffle me with local geography. I thought he wouldn't be able to pull the wool over your eyes.'

Skelgill casts about. He has seen what there is to see. He agrees to DS Leyton's request, and hangs up.

He wonders which way the two women went. If it was towards Ambleside, he expects he will overtake them.

*

The first thing Skelgill notices is the backpack and camping equipment propped up against the picnic bench. To his trained eye it looks like pukka gear. There is also a metal detector. And, finally, a middle-aged man of trim build and about his own height who rises to offer his hand.

DS Leyton introduces him as Derek Shaw.

Skelgill realises that he has no preconception of what a nighthawker will look like, but if he had, he feels this would not be it. He is respectable looking, and seemingly cooperative. Skelgill hears a Yorkshire accent.

DS Leyton passes over his notebook. Skelgill squints cursorily, but he does take in that the man is fifty-four, has an address in York, and is employed as Head Curator of Antiquities, Castle Museum in the same city. There are contact details, including a mobile number, which he assumes DS Leyton has already tested for accuracy.

The man waits patiently. Perhaps there is an occupational hazard about metal detecting that puts one under regular scrutiny of this sort. There is an assumption of raiding the public heritage. Yet without them a good deal of history would be unknown. Rather like fishermen. Without anglers the biology of most waters would remain a mystery, and conservation projects could never be designed. Perhaps Skelgill senses a kindred spirit.

He looks stern, however, as he hands back the notebook and addresses DS Leyton.

'Where are we up to?'

DS Leyton turns to the man, but he does not require prompting.

'Inspector – Sergeant Leyton was asking about my whereabouts on Tuesday night. As you can see – I'm camping – wild camping in places. I'm travelling on foot and by public transport. On Tuesday I got the train down from Maryport where I'd visited the Senhouse Roman Museum and fort. I pitched the tent on the cliffs just below St Bees lighthouse. Next morning I caught the eight o'clock train from St Bees to Ravenglass. I've since made my way via Eskdale and Langdale.'

Skelgill gestures towards the man's gear.

'What do you reckon to the Saunders?'

DS Leyton looks a little bewildered, but the man seems to take the question in his stride.

'Aye, well – there's lighter tents now – but it still takes some beating. That's the Spacepacker – it's got four exits, so you can always find the lee. I've had it for donkey's years – swear by it.'

Skelgill appears content with the response.

DS Leyton might reasonably think Skelgill has become distracted by his personal interest, but Skelgill's question serves a purpose; moreover, it buys a little time in which he reviews the geography. DS Leyton is trying to establish if the man could have been responsible for the digging that occurred at Castlerigg on Tuesday night. Without a car – or an accomplice – Keswick to St Bees would not be a feasible journey in the early hours, when no buses or trains run. It is twenty-five miles on foot, across several challenging ranges of fells.

'Do you have your rail ticket, sir?'

The man regards Skelgill apologetically.

'I'm afraid I recall diligently placing it in the bin on the platform at Ravenglass.' But now he raises an index finger, as though to test the wind. 'However, I did have a temporary travelling companion. In fact I made something of an acquaintance of her. The next day – Thursday – I chummed her on the train to Dalegarth near Boot. I left her at Hardknott fort – she was coming this way – I returned to my pitch at Ravenglass.'

The detectives remain silent, and perhaps Derek Shaw imagines a degree of heightened suspicion, for he qualifies his statement.

'Nothing untoward, mind. She was an elderly lady. Aged around seventy, I should say – but if you could contact her, she'd no doubt be able to confirm my account. She stayed at the Walls Inn at Ravenglass on Wednesday night. They would have her details – she's called Dorothy. I didn't ask her surname – but that should be enough. We also had afternoon tea in the café garden overlooking the foreshore. And we had a shared interest in The Times crossword.'

Skelgill can see that DS Leyton is looking somewhat frustrated. But logistically the man's story stacks up, and it seems his 'alibi' can easily be verified. Skelgill signals an end to the interrogation with the nature of his next question.

'Mr Shaw – perhaps before you go you could come and look at the damage. Give us your opinion. I reckon your kit will be safe here for a couple of minutes.'

The man takes a pace forward.

'Willingly. There's nothing I'd like to see more than this sort of thing punished. Personally, I would only ever detect where I have permission, or if it were a professional project. Gives me a bad name.' He makes a circular gesture to indicate his present predicament, by way of illustration. *'Quod erat demonstrandum.'*

Having no answer to the Latin, and muttering some Anglo-Saxon under his breath, DS Leyton turns and lumbers towards the Roman earthworks.

When they reach the offending hole, he assumes a stance that hints that he would still hope that the man might make a last-minute confession.

But Derek Shaw rubs the stubble of his chin with the fingers of his right hand.

'To be honest, that doesn't look like the work of a detectorist – a nighthawker or otherwise. It's too deep, for a start. Most detectors can't reach much more than eight inches, especially in highly mineralised soil like this glacial outwash.' Then he glances about. 'Also, notice the location. It's at the centre of a cross drawn from the corners of what would have been the praetorium.'

But DS Leyton is not prepared to concede total defeat. The hole is almost identical to that found at Castlerigg. And perhaps there is something in the position. While 'one hole' could have been an abandoned interment, 'two holes' points to excavation.

'What would anyone expect to dig up here? This place is Roman, right? The last one we found was Stone Age.'

Derek Shaw stares reflectively at the hole. He shakes his head.

'Could it be to do with geocaching?'

'What's that?'

DS Leyton glances at his superior to see that he is nodding.

The man explains.

'It's an organised outdoor activity. You join online and use a smartphone or GPS device to locate hidden treasure boxes placed by other members. The fun is in the hide-and-seek. You sign the logbook and put it back for the next person. You might swap over some of the trinkets. They say kids love it – keeps them occupied for hours. Gets them out of doors. I believe the National Trust encourages it.'

DS Leyton's ears have pricked up a little.

Derek Shaw elaborates.

'You can see why folk might pick ancient sites – it adds a bit of drama and jeopardy to the game. And since you use GPS you can do it at night as well, so long as you're in safe surroundings. However, you're not really meant actually to bury your box – more conceal it under brushwood or loose rocks.'

Skelgill again is nodding. English Heritage would certainly not want digging to take place at any of their properties. He turns and begins to move away. This is an investigative cul-de-sac; his intuition pulls in another direction.

The others drift after him. He only half-listens as DS Leyton, seemingly a little less accusative, makes a stab at conversation.

'Where does your metal detecting take you to next, sir?'

The man seems to bear no grudges for being hauled in by the police.

'I'm actually surveying some of the Roman routes across the north of England – for an exhibition we're planning. I'm aiming to pick up High Street – there's a good deal of conjecture over whether it really is of Roman origin, or just an ancient trackway. It's something I was telling the American lady about, as she has an interest in history. She was meeting a chap who's a bit of a Roman buff – at Little Langdale, I think she said.'

Skelgill has wheeled around.

The two men following look a little startled.

'The American lady?'

Skelgill's tone is flat; but in that quality DS Leyton recognises underlying interest.

Derek Shaw, however, takes the question at face value.

'Aye – did I not say? The woman I met at Ravenglass – Dorothy – she's an American. It should make her all the easier to track down.' He grins somewhat wryly. 'If you still feel the need to do so.'

*

'You alright, Guvnor?'

Skelgill is staring after Derek Shaw. He has zipped away his metal detector and hauled on his heavy pack, and is heading north, towards the centre of Ambleside.

'Aye.'

DS Leyton has grown used to Skelgill's idiosyncrasies when it comes to sharing ideas (namely, that he rarely does), albeit frustrating when said ideas are attached to information that might help a fellow officer. Skelgill would argue that he has only the same information as everyone else, and that it is not his fault if they process it differently. Progress can be further stalled, in that he may not process it at all. A sign that this latter response is presently gaining the upper hand can be gleaned in Skelgill's pensive expression, his front teeth protruding, giving his craggy countenance a decidedly shrewish cast. Some undercurrent is rocking his boat, and he is wrestling with the dilemma of whether to ride it out, or take some positive action.

It seems the latter prevails.

'Tell you what, Leyton. You must have stuff on today. You get back.'

DS Leyton is unprepared for such consideration.

'Well – now you mention it, Guv – the Missus wasn't exactly cock-a-hoop when I cleared off. I think we've got gymnastics club, football training, a birthday party and a double sleepover.'

Skelgill is staring at DS Leyton blankly; it might be his ongoing state of distraction, or simply that he is uncomprehending of such parental obligations.

'But what about you, Guv? You ain't got no wheels.'

Skelgill's gaze seems to re-focus upon his colleague.

'I'll get Jones to come down. She's usually at a loose end on a Saturday afternoon.'

DS Leyton doubts this is the case, but there is a gift horse not to be looked in the mouth. Grab the reins and go.

And Skelgill extends his offer.

'Your detector bloke's alibi seems legit. But Jones and me – we'll check it out.'

12. PAPER CHASE

Ravenglass – 3.12 p.m., Saturday 23rd May

'What are you thinking, Guv?'

'Eh?'

Skelgill is staring at the waterfall known as Birker Force, visible from the unclassified road through Eskdale as a prominent mare's tail, and still flowing well, despite today's blue skies. He appears baffled that she seems to be asking him about that particular feature.

He has been reworking a recent pub conversation. Birker Force has brought to mind its source, Low Birker Tarn, beyond sight over the ridge from which the water spills. Pub conversations are not like others, in that after about half a gallon of real ale per capita irrational conjecture and even the supernatural are admitted as reasonable points of view. Skelgill had enjoined with an angling clique that was debating the origins of trout and schelly in tarns (small corrie lakes) that have only a waterfall as an outflow (and therefore as a sole means of ingress for fish). Thus, "dropped by a careless osprey", "eggs stuck to a duck's feathers", "picked up by a tornado" and even "tunnelled up through snow" were assigned equal merit alongside Skelgill's more prosaic "stocked by human hand". He frowns. They have just passed Hardknott fort, and surely it would have dawned on the efficient Romans to take advantage of captive waters to secure their food supplies.

DS Jones, having collected an impatient-looking Skelgill from outside a café, hitherto has been concentrating on the task in hand. The road between Ambleside and Eskdale is probably the most challenging route in England, closed to all vehicles in winter conditions, and in places treacherous even on a good dry day. Thus she has refrained from questioning their purpose in any detail

– beyond accepting that they are going to check out an alibi for DS Leyton's putative nighthawker.

It is to her evident surprise, therefore, that Skelgill, rather like Birker Force, spills forth with a piece of information that has her resuming the grip on the steering wheel that she employed on the descent of Hardknott Pass.

'This woman – elderly. Backpacker. She's American.'

'Really?'

'Leyton's Shaw character says she's interested in history. Reckons she was meeting a chap, a "Roman buff" he called him.'

There is a definite tremor in the trajectory of the car.

'Meeting him at Ravenglass?'

'Little Langdale.'

DS Jones glances sharply at Skelgill. They have passed through Little Langdale. But Skelgill offers no explanation; it seems he means to start at the beginning.

And, while he is not one for wild and random theorising, there can be little doubt in his manner that these small confetti of facts, were they to be on a paperchase, indicate a direction of travel that is congruent with their findings to date. Now he slides back into his seat and begins to relate more of DS Leyton's and then his own encounter with Derek Shaw, and of precisely what he said about the woman called Dorothy.

Having listened bright-eyed, ostensibly concentrating upon the still-narrow lane that will bring them to Ravenglass, DS Jones reprises what she has learned.

'Let me get this straight. This man Derek Shaw told you that an elderly American woman was supposed to be meeting another male, a historian. And this is the same Derek Shaw that is a museum curator researching Roman settlements and communications. From York.'

DS Jones manages to keep all hints of irony from her tone, when some sort of disbelief or even exasperation might be reasonable. However, it is apparent to Skelgill that his partner is champing at the bit, and working hard to rein in her natural inclination to cut to the chase, to forge possibilities and conclusions.

'Aye.'

'You didn't happen to ask him whether he knew of Professor Felix Stowe-Upland?'

There is a long pause. Skelgill folds his arms.

'Happen I'm not quite as daft as I'm cabbage looking.'

After a few moments he turns to see that his colleague's lips are pursed; she begins to nod.

Skelgill pre-empts any further surmise.

'Have you eaten?'

Now she flashes him a confused look.

'Pardon?'

'Dinner – tea – whatever.'

'Oh – well, I grabbed a sandwich when you called. I was at the gym this morning, so I was starving. I ate it in the car'

She indicates with her left hand a wrapper lying in the footwell behind her seat. Skelgill stares at it critically.

'There's a café at Ravenglass. Nice views across the estuary. Served half-decent custard fritters last time I was there.'

'Oh, when was that?'

Skelgill clears his throat.

'Must be seven years past.'

*

Skelgill notices his reflection and rubs from his couple of days' stubble what might be remnant crumbs of batter. He has paused to look at a framed press photograph of an amateur costume drama, an alfresco event that looks like it was staged some decades ago at the Roman bath house.

In any event, there is no room for him at the inn's cramped reception, at the far end of the same corridor where an armchair has been placed inside an open door and blocked off from the rest of a small room by what constitutes the reception desk. DS Jones has taken a seat opposite a bald man of about forty whom Skelgill can only glimpse whenever he leans forward. He wears a black waistcoat over an open-necked white shirt with the cuffs rolled back and is most distinctive for his prodigiously tattooed forearms.

He sounds friendly enough, and relatively local going by his accent, maybe Barrow, Skelgill thinks.

DS Jones is explaining that they are trying to get in touch with a guest of Wednesday night; she provides a brief description: a single woman, perhaps late sixties or early seventies, American. First name, Dorothy.

The man must swivel in his chair, and Skelgill can hear the clicks of what sounds like an old-fangled keyboard. It would be in keeping with the hotel, whose interior looks a good generation behind the times, within a neglected shell that must date from the Victorian era, possibly even Georgian.

'Wednesday night, you say, love?' There are more volleys of tapping, interspersed by tutting and humming. And finally a flourish of clicks, a little finale. 'Computer says ... no American Dorothy.'

Skelgill can see that DS Jones tenses, probably because she feels the pressure of his eavesdropping (when he is pretending not to). Various thoughts must be running through her mind, including that he has conveyed false information provided by Derek Shaw. Skelgill is inclined to intervene, but DS Jones quickly adjusts her approach.

'Would she necessarily be in the computer?'

There is a pause. Skelgill hears more movement and a thump which turns out to be a large bound ledger being placed unceremoniously upon the desk. Then the sound of pages turning.

DS Jones sits patiently, motionless.

Eventually, a triumphant exclamation.

'Softly, softly, catchee monkey!'

The hotel manager turns the ledger one hundred and eighty degrees and raps upon the open page with tattooed knuckles.

'She must have walked up. Come on spec. We're not full this time of year.'

Now Skelgill approaches and cranes over his colleague's shoulder. The great tome is a traditional visitors' book. There are finely ruled columns for date of arrival, name, address, and vehicle registration number. It is nearing its end, and contains years of records, by the look of it. About a dozen entries from the bottom of the list, in black ink in a careful hand, small well-formed letters yet also flowing, dated Wednesday, are the words: "D. K. Baum, St Francisville, Louisiana, USA."

The last column is for room number, and a "7" has been inserted in an untidy hand in smudged blue ink.

DS Jones speaks as she copies down the information into her notebook.

'If she left a forwarding address, where would it be?'

The manager casts about the poky office somewhat haplessly.

'We don't have much call for that kind of thing.'

DS Jones looks up.

'Can you describe her?'

'I weren't here, love. I work Fridays to Tuesdays.'

'What about staff members who may have spoken to her?'

The manager rises and refers to a handwritten chart pinned to a cork noticeboard.

'Might have been Eunice that checked her in.'

'Is she here today?'

'Give us a minute, love.'

The manager disappears from sight and in due course a somewhat overawed young girl who would not look out of place in a school uniform is produced. DS Jones quickly puts her at ease in a way that Skelgill certainly might not, and elicits from Eunice that she does indeed remember the "nice American lady".

'She asked if we had a twin room.'

DS Jones nods encouragingly.

'Did you think that was odd?'

'Well – she were on her own. You'd think you'd just want a single – to save money.'

'Did she mention if she was expecting anyone?'

The girl shakes her head. She is rather plain, and her face expressionless, but then a thought obviously strikes her and she blinks repeatedly.

'She had a backpack. She kept it on and carried it up herself when I showed her to the room.' Eunice falters a little nervously. 'Then she still gave us a tip.'

'*Hah!* Proves she was American, eh? You can always trust 'em.'

137

It is the manager, standing at the back, who chimes in with this observation. He sounds like he would welcome more transatlantic visitors on this basis.

DS Jones remains undistracted.

'Could we perhaps see the room – if it's free?'

The girl looks with unease at her superior – but he reaches into an open wall-cabinet and takes down a key from the hook marked "7". It appears that most rooms are presently unoccupied. He passes the key to the girl.

'Eunice'll show you up.'

The girl turns and leaves, but reappears twenty seconds later at the middle of the corridor, where there is another door beside which a staircase rises. DS Jones thanks the manager and she and Skelgill approach the waiting Eunice.

The room proves to be surprisingly large. Skelgill immediately makes for the bay window and begins to take in the scene. The front of the hotel faces west, and directly opposite, through a gap between properties and a cluster of Scots pine and sub-tropical palms is a partial view of the estuary, presently flooded by the tide, and looking like an inland lake bordered by distant dunes. To his left, the main street ("Main Street") runs for a couple of hundred yards, directly into the sea; there is a slipway, as he recalls it. To his right the view also includes a sliver of the coastline, and the railway upon a trestle bridge that crosses the merged triumvirate of rivers, the Irt, the Mite and the Esk. Diagonally across the road is a dilapidated Post Office, the paint of its window jambs flaking and several slate roof tiles lying cracked upon the pavement. He notes the wall-mounted GR post box, a testament to its antiquity. A lopsided sign behind the dusty glass of the door states, "Open".

Meanwhile DS Jones is looking about the room while Eunice stands apprehensively beside the door, rather like a housemaid in days gone by, trained to shrink against the wall when one of her 'betters' passes. She looks like she thinks she is in trouble. The room is sparsely furnished with unappealing items, utilitarian furniture that would look more apt in an office of twenty years ago. DS Jones pays particular attention to the night stands – inside a drawer of each there is a leather-bound Gideon's bible – and to a long multi-purpose wall cupboard that serves as vanity unit, writing desk and a place for the plug-in tray with tea and coffee making facilities. She picks up a hotel notepad and tilts it towards the light from the window, and hesitates for a moment over the envelopes held in a stationery dispenser.

But the room has been made ready for its next occupant. It is clean and impeccably neat; a sterile environment as far as an investigator is concerned.

DS Jones stands pensively – but when she takes a step backwards she notices beneath the writing desk a bin that is divided into three compartments, marked "paper", "plastic" and "waste".

She turns to Eunice.

'What happens to the recycling?'

The girl blinks several times in quick succession.

'It goes int' different coloured wheelie bins – they're at the back door, where the deliveries come.'

'What day are they emptied?'

'The binmen call on a Monday every fortnight.'

DS Jones turns to see that Skelgill, silhouetted against the daylight, is standing casually watching her, his hands in his pockets. But he seems to give a faint nod of his head.

*

'So, what were these – fishermen's cottages?'

'Nope.'

When no further explanation is forthcoming Skelgill digs in. Two can play at that game. The tiny Post Office is a book that can be judged by its cover. The theme of external dilapidation continues into a hoarder's chaos. It is almost impossible to discern what is for sale and what is waste – with recycling in mind, a skip might have been emptied in here. There is a just-navigable circuit around a central stack of boxes and heaps of papers, while on the right, upon entry, the postmaster crouches behind a counter, just visible in the shape of a worn black beanie hat pulled low to rheumy eyes and a round florid face, and the shoulders of an equally shabby black fleecy.

Skelgill remains out of sight between the left-hand wall and the central island. He loiters belligerently, and in time his silent procrastination eventually bears fruit.

'Find what you're looking for?'

'Nope.'

Skelgill still does not emerge into view.

'What are you, hotel inspectors?'

Skelgill is jolted. The man knows there are two of them. And he has made an interesting suggestion, when most casual observers might have assumed they were a couple looking for a room. From his low seat behind the counter, despite the grime-encrusted shop window he would have seen them enter the hotel. He might even have spied Skelgill looking out of the bay window above and to the right.

Skelgill takes an uncharacteristic course.

He rounds the island of debris to the counter and displays his warrant card.

The man is unmoved, but Skelgill has a sense of a mollusc subtly drawing in its soft parts.

'An elderly American woman stayed at the hotel on Wednesday night. Did she come in here?'

Now Skelgill detects a certain smugness; the man makes him wait before answering.

'She slept the night in the room you were inspecting a moment ago.'

Skelgill realises the man has a refined accent. He seems entirely unabashed about what might be construed as the act of a peeping Tom. But what else has he got to do, limpet-like down amidst the irregular rocks of what look like years of accumulated admin and junk mail and unsold and unopened stock.

'She bought a postcard.'

In an unprompted act, he points listlessly to a dispenser that displays more copies, an unbecoming photograph of the main street, looking south towards the slipway.

'And posted it?'

The man gives a hint of a nod, condescending, as if what else does Skelgill expect. But he does elaborate in a small way.

'Wednesday afternoon. I was waiting to close up.'

'What about the postage – was it for the UK or overseas?'

'One first-class stamp. Delivery next working day to any part of mainland Britain.' The post master's promotional rejoinder lacks conviction.

'Was she alone?'

There is the nod again. It is his affirmative alternative to the "nope".

Skelgill has no further questions. But he drifts away to browse, informed by a new perspective. He speaks over Debris Island.

'Did she buy owt else?'

'Nope.'

He knew it was coming.

There is a small shelf of confectionery and he wonders if he wants anything. His eye falls on a tin of Kendal mint cake, and he is reminded he has the identical brand, now transferred to the door pocket of DS Jones's car. He does not need another. On a shelf just above the floor is an untidy arrangement of half a dozen newspapers. He wonders if they are today's – then he notices the Westmorland Gazette and his eye is caught by a flash above the masthead that announces, "New Angling Section". He is just about to reach for the journal when he spots a familiar byline on the lead article – and he pulls back.

And at this moment he glimpses the athletic figure of his colleague pass the grimy shop window. She is looking for him.

He exits with brusque thanks that receive no acknowledgement.

It seems DS Jones is guessing that he has made for the slipway, but when she hears the door slam of the Post Office she turns, and then waits – for Skelgill signals he will catch her up. He can see that she is rocking on the balls of her feet. As he approaches, she raises a folded copy of The Times.

But as she makes to speak, Skelgill pre-empts her.

'She sent a postcard.'

'Oh – but –'

Skelgill is looking pleased with himself.

'To a UK address. Last thing on Wednesday.'

He steps past her.

'Keep moving. Walls have ears.'

DS Jones has to take a couple of skips to catch up.

She inhales again – but before she can get a word in he points out an ancient petrol pump that stands in front of a house that might once have been a small garage business.

'Look at that – it's still got the old price. One shilling and fivepence.' He stops to stare at it for a moment. 'What's that – 7p? Imagine, 7p a gallon. What's sixty-five sevens?"

Without waiting for an answer, he moves on, and continues to highlight features of the village street that reinforce the impression of a 1950s time capsule. The pavements are ill defined; plants in pots and shrubs grow randomly, with no demarcation of front gardens, and occasional vehicles are abandoned haphazardly. Most of the properties are run down, and it looks like Ravenglass, despite being officially inside the Lake District National Park, has slipped under the radar of the staycation boom.

DS Jones tries again – but Skelgill is now illuminating the paradox of the palms that thrive in this maritime microclimate – "they wouldn't last ten minutes five miles to the east" – and then suddenly they must take evasive action – for a quad bike with a bale of straw strapped to its front rack roars at them from behind, scattering house sparrows that scavenge grain which might have been spilled on an earlier trip.

Skelgill resumes walking rapidly towards the slipway, and anyone observing them could think that DS Jones is some sort of PA, or perhaps even a reporter, vainly trying to win his attention. He gestures without breaking stride at a heart-shaped piece of cardboard, hand-painted blue above, yellow below, tied with string to a cast-iron lamppost – and then, as the road dips, he halts at a large sign, five feet by three, screwed to the stone wall of the last building before the foreshore. It is headed in red print, "Warning Notices".

He squints knowledgeably.

'Eskmeals MOD firing range.'

Now he turns to scrutinise the estuary. Canute-like, his striding out is thwarted; the high tide is lapping just a foot away, and the sign for "England Coast Path low tide route" partially submerged.

'You'd think she'd have a mobile phone.'

DS Jones looks momentarily puzzled. Is he still referring to the postcard?

But she sees her opportunity. At the water's edge, he can go no further.

'I think she does have a mobile phone.'

She raises the newspaper, but holds it against her shoulder.

Skelgill puts his hands on his hips.

'There was no number in the visitors' book.'

'But there was no space for a phone number. That register is so old they probably hadn't been invented.'

He stares at her pensively.

DS Jones further takes advantage of the hiatus.

'I found her newspaper. Here.'

She brandishes her trophy.

'Look – it's the same handwriting as her entry in the visitors' book. See – she was doing the crossword. That fits with what Derek Shaw told you and DS Leyton.'

Skelgill frowns. Jotted in the margins are what look like attempts to unpick anagrams.

'She didn't make much of a job of it.'

DS Jones resists the urge to refer to the adage of the kettle and the pot and instead – somewhat pointedly – she puts a finger on a specific item and thrusts the paper in front of Skelgill's face.

'Read that.'

He sways back – but he has no choice other than to accede.

"Questions to ask Felix"

She has his attention. How many Felixes can there be? She moves her finger to the words beneath the note.

"1 – Rooms"

"2 – Money transfer"

"3 – Rose C"

Skelgill backs away, as if the effort of close-focusing has been painful. He steps right into the water; it laps almost to the ankles of his boots.

'Where did you get it?'

'It was in a plastic tub of newspapers for recycling. I'd initially thought she may have thrown away a note she had written, perhaps a letter that she rejected and started again – or purchase receipts – or an itinerary.'

Without warning Skelgill takes a stride towards her and puts out a hand against her cheek. For a moment they are both frozen like statues of some coastal art project, *"The Cockler Returns"*.

Just as abruptly he withdraws the hand and wheels away, turning towards the sea.

It is a few seconds before he speaks.

'I wouldn't have thought of that, lass.'

DS Jones's high cheekbones are highlighted more than usual by a flush of pink.

But she is quick to adapt; she raises the newspaper and points enthusiastically.

'This is also why I think she has a mobile. Look – there's a mobile number written at the bottom of the page. In the same handwriting.'

This time Skelgill accepts the invitation more willingly; he takes hold of the journal.

DS Jones is watching him carefully – there is a flicker of recognition in his eyes.

'That's Derek Shaw's number.'

'Are you certain?'

'Aye – Leyton wrote it in his notebook. He showed me. How many numbers end in three nines?'

Skelgill hands back the paper and now he takes a few paces along the shoreline.

Across the water towards the arc of dunes a gang of black-headed gulls are dive-bombing a seal. Their harsh cries speak of hunger. Perhaps it has a fish; a meal they would covet for themselves. Beneath the rays of the late afternoon sun their distinctive white forewings flash like rapiers.

Skelgill observes them broodingly.

Like the movement of the flock, there is another flurry of facts; more confetti.

DS Jones perhaps voices his fears.

'Guv – don't you think we ought to find Dorothy Baum? I mean – what if she is in some kind of danger?'

13. TROUBLE BREWING

Old Beck Tavern, Troutbeck – evening, Saturday 23rd May

From: Dorothy K. Baum
To: Professor Felix Stowe-Upland
Subject: Another day

Dear Felix, another eventful day! Although we have not come far, from Ambleside to upper Troutbeck, as you suggested. I estimate five miles, from my Ordnance Survey map, although it certainly felt more than that, as we followed some roller-coaster cross-country paths in places, and my exercise app tells me I have climbed over two hundred floors which I believe equates to over two thousand feet!

I should say straightaway that we have rooms at an absolutely delightful seventeenth-century coaching inn called the Old Beck Tavern – just in case you are in transit and able to pick up this message. Of course, I will expect you when I see you – although I must say I have begun to anticipate that you will surprise me, and I will round a corner of a path to find you sitting upon a rock beside a stream smoking your pipe (or am I thinking of a leprechaun?), or scaling the walls of some ancient ruin halfway up the fellside, examining it for its Roman credentials!

You will note that I say 'we' – I have followed your advice – Cathy and I have journeyed together to Troutbeck. I had wanted to book ahead. But Cathy was confident – and indeed we did pass several B&Bs displaying vacancies signs – although it is good to have the option of an evening meal as well as the "Full English" – which, I must say, sustains one throughout the day with little need of a packed lunch – and which Cathy seems to feel it is her duty to demolish, trimmings and all.

The inn is traditional, with its beams, oak furniture and exposed stone walls. And what a lovely settlement is Troutbeck, strung out along the winding, rising lane pressed close by old converted slate barns and farmhouses and white-painted cottages that are hardly touched, as if time has stood still – I was inspired with thoughts of Rose Cottage.

Our walk was accompanied by the sound of playful lambs and joyous birdsong – the weather today has returned to glorious; it made me realise I missed the best of Eskdale and Langdale under Thursday's cloud – perhaps we will return there one day, and travel around to see Wasdale – I would like to retrace my steps and relive some of my adventures in your jovial company.

I say jovial because despite the sunshine Cathy can be something of a gloomster; she seems determined that the rain will return. She says the silver lining is that her waterfalls will come to life – although there seems to be plenty of water draining from the fells.

And you were quite right about there being some interest along this route for Cathy, and she quite readily fell in with my proposals. It seems she means to paint Aira Force, the main goal of her trip – she says the most dramatic waterfall in the Lakes – and that she can reach it by coming this way. Perhaps you can advise me of that.

Our first episode this morning concerned a waterfall, and I must say it was rather awkward – although I have begun to gather that Cathy does not go in for embarrassment, and perhaps this character trait of hers has its uses!

We had followed Skelghyll Lane from its origin in Ambleside – how impossibly narrow, I cannot imagine trying to drive even a small British car along there, never mind backing up when you meet a flock of sheep coming the other way! After a time the tarmac crumbled into a stony track and we entered woodland, and in due course reached the bridge over Stencher Beck – just as you said, there was something of a waterfall – not so much a direct drop, but a cascade down a steep rock face. It seemed that not a soul was about, just us and the birdsong, and the rush of the water and hum of insects, with sunlight filtering in golden-green shafts through the leafy branches.

I had expected Cathy to want to dwell, to absorb the 'artistic vibe' – but I suppose that is not her style, and she was content to lean over the bridge and take a couple of photographs. I must admit, I am not sure how one paints a waterfall from directly overhead, but no doubt Cathy has her methods. And she uses a camera primitive even by my limited knowledge of modern technology – the type that still takes an actual roll of film. She has no cell phone – she says her family would only pester her – and when she saw me framing a shot, she offered to take one of me, so that I could send it to you.

Coming along the high street in Ambleside we had stopped off at a candy store. I had noticed in the window a display of Kendal mint cake and it gave me the idea to buy a tin for you. Cathy had seemed a little peeved (I wondered if she was offended that I didn't offer to buy her a tin) – but now at the bridge she suggested I hold it up for the picture. So I retrieved it from my backpack and posed on the parapet of the bridge. I must admit, I felt a little silly – although, as I say, Cathy does not seem to notice these things.

But then it happened.

I think she was having difficulty with my cell, and managed to switch off the camera app before she even began. She stepped towards me squinting at the screen and stumbled over a protruding stone – perhaps I reached out instinctively to break her fall – I have quick reactions – but in the melee I dropped the little tin of Kendal mint cake ... and it almost landed upon a poor man's head!

Yes – there was another hillwalker below, at the foot of the waterfall. I know it was just a small tin, but at thirty feet it could be quite a dangerous missile. The man shouted something – he was justifiably annoyed – and I was about to apologize profusely. But Cathy took one look and dragged me away, and before I knew it we were both heaving on our packs and literally jogging off like paratroopers who had just ambushed an enemy! I repeat, the poor man – I cannot imagine what he must have thought.

The whole thing happened before I knew it and suddenly it seemed too late to go back – and by now you will not be surprised to hear that, no sooner than we had our breath back, Cathy was on to a different subject, as though the incident had never taken place! But I will be mortified if we cross paths with the fellow again. I remember as a child, with a friend, being hollered at by a farmer for running through a field of young corn – and later that morning having to pass him along the track, and to say hello, pretending it wasn't me.

I should add that I still have your gift – I had bought two tins of mint cake; the other one for fuel.

Upon which note, Cathy, despite her eccentricities, is very much a creature of habit, and she likes her cup of tea, "Builders Brew", she calls it. She carries a tiny but powerful portable gas stove and insists on a stop no later than midday, and another in the afternoon. I must admit, having allowed myself to become a little dehydrated on my trek over the Hardknott and Wrynose Passes, I can see there is some merit in the discipline. My only objection would be that she boils up the tea bag and milk together, and produces a concoction that is unlike any tea I have ever tasted! She uses stream water without compunction – but I suppose the boiling kills off any germs. I just couldn't help noticing the number of sheep on the fellsides above! Yes, Cathy can be rather down to earth.

Not long after our flight from the bridge we had stopped for refreshments alongside the stream that runs down the wooded gully described on the Ordnance Survey map as High Skelghyll. You mentioned this in your email last evening and Cathy was keen to explore and find the waterfall. We had calculated that if we headed north we could link up the series of green lanes, Skelghyll Lane, Hundreds Road and Robin Lane, making a route that would bring us to Troutbeck without having to use even a minor road.

I was still working my way through my first mug of Builders Brew. Cathy had managed two, and unsurprisingly decided she needed to answer the call of nature. She headed up into the trees. After about five minutes, however, she had not returned. I called out a couple of times but there was no reply. I did notice that she had taken her camera – I assumed in case the waterfall was close by. But ten minutes passed, and became twenty. At thirty minutes

I grew concerned. The stretch of woodland can only be a quarter of a mile, at most. Could she have turned an ankle – or worse – I was thinking of the poor man under the bridge – had she slipped on a wet rock and knocked herself unconscious?

Clearly, there was no point in calling her. As I say, she does not carry a cell phone. And, besides, I had no signal. To summon help I would need to find the nearest farm.

I decided the only thing to do was to investigate. We had not seen any other walkers, so I felt our backpacks were safe and I had on my belt-bag, and I set off to follow the same route into the trees that I saw her take. I picked my way carefully up beside the stream. The gully became increasingly steep, and dark in places. I came to something of a waterfall – though not enough to enthuse Cathy, I thought. There was a fall of large boulders that I'm not sure I could have scaled. I pondered. She could have been out of sight beyond them. But I figured I would see better if I scrambled up at the side and looked down.

I was just about to do so when I heard sounds directly above. A sudden disturbance, a scrabbling of stones and the rustle of undergrowth. But when I reached the top – nothing. And looking down into the gill – nothing. And certainly no Cathy. At this point I considered I could not go on indefinitely. I was a little worried about our possessions. And I figured there was just the chance that she had doubled back along the edge of the trees, and we had missed one another. Finally, I did not want to become lost myself – so I retraced my route beside the stream.

And – sure enough – when I emerged from the trees – there she was with yet another mug of her Builder's Brew!

Now you might think this is a non-story – but here is the remarkable part. In her peculiar style, rather than apologize for disappearing for so long, or even explain what she had been doing, she simply looked up at me and said, "Did you see it?"

"The waterfall?" I replied.

"The Ambleside Cat," was her retort. She sounded quite indignant.

I asked what did she mean, and she said when she went into the trees she saw a black panther, and had followed it, trying (unsuccessfully) to get a photograph. She claimed she tracked it for a couple of hundred yards, but it disappeared among the rocks where it must have a lair. A daunting prospect, which I innocently stumbled into!

I did not quite know where to begin. I mentioned that I heard something moving in the vegetation above the waterfall and she pointed at me in the way she does. "That was it, Dorothy." You would think we had experienced the supernatural.

And then, before I knew it, we were talking about something else, and then back on the move.

It was only after I arrived here that I was able to search online. I was sure I had previously read that in Britain there are no large carnivores, but I suppose at the time I just thought, well, she had seen a mountain lion – or a cougar as we commonly call it – perhaps a black variant. But, no – I was right – there are no mountain lions – only the wildcat, which is hardly bigger than its domestic cousin (and restricted to the Scottish Highlands).

But there is an Ambleside Cat!

I am sure this is the stuff of legends and too much alcohol (and a trick of the moonlight on the walk home from the inn) – but you can find it online, "The Beast of Cumbria" – and it seems there are reports from across the county – including a recent sighting of it chasing a deer across the grounds of Galava!

At this point, dear Felix, it seems our stories converge!

Naturally, I am firmly in the camp of the sceptic; it is so easy to misidentify an animal, especially when there is a lack of perspective. However, I did hear something above me – so perhaps I was stalked by the beast!

Cathy seems to be in no doubt. When I put it to her, she gave short shrift to my suggestion that it must be the collective imagination at play. Luckily, I did not say "her" imagination!

So, there you have it – today's adventures in glorious technicolor! Apologies, but I have had time to spare before we meet for our pub meal – for which I have certainly developed an appetite.

Who knows what tomorrow will bring?

Yours in continued anticipation,

Dorothy.

From: Professor Felix Stowe-Upland
To: Dorothy K. Baum
Subject: Re: Another day

My dearest Dorothy, how remiss of me! I trust you will not think it is old age catching up with me – but I completely forgot that the weekend had arrived! There was I, bright-eyed and bushy-tailed, up with the lark and setting out to give my solicitor a jolly good ear-bashing … and the bus never came! Only when I mentioned my complaint to a passing dog walker was I met with the reply: "Saturday service – every hour". Never mind the bus – I could have walked – *but my solicitor was closed.* Mine and every other in the land.

Thus, I am stymied.

I apologise, from the bottom of my heart. When I think of you bravely making your own way across the fells I feel enormously guilty, but I hope you will understand. And, at risk of repeating myself, every step you take is a step nearer to our eventual meeting. I can only put my lapse down to the combined excitement at the prospect of seeing you (and all it entails) and the turmoil of the property transaction, with its twists and turns that seem designed to draw out the process to its most tortuous extremity. They do say that moving home is one of the most stressful moments of life (and divorce being another – and I suppose ours is a comparable situation of the inverse kind) – so there always was double trouble in store for yours truly – perhaps I did not quite anticipate its full potential for mental turmoil.

But, enough of me. *Ad astra per aspera!*

Old bean, I appreciate your patience and I am greatly cheered to hear of your successful (if a little eventful) progress – and, frankly, I am relieved that you are still with your temporary companion, Cathy. It does take a small weight off my shoulders to know that you are in good company; it sounds as though she knows the fells and is a competent outdoorswoman. Perhaps we should offer to buy some of her paintings for Rose Cottage? It would serve as a thank-you and a memento of your journey. I am sure they will be of a fine standard. I can just picture Stock Ghyll Force in the downstairs bathroom, and Aira Force in the ensuite. Somehow appropriate, don't you think? You could perhaps offer her a cash advance to secure the deal, and to show good faith.

I ought to have mentioned that the bridge over Stencher Beck could be Roman in origin. One of the great mysteries of High Street is just where did it go, exactly, after reaching its zenith? My own research findings suggest it forked. One branch remained aloft, over Ill Bell and Yoke, while the other descended alongside Trout Beck to veer to the west. In due course this spur became Skelghyll Lane, leading to Ambleside and, of course, Galava. It would not have been like the Romans to take the long way round, and continue all the way to the shores of Windermere before turning north. So, perhaps you can tick off another Roman feature from your list, despite a day in which the waterfall became the dominant theme.

Indeed, your friend's interest in waterfalls might well be propitious, for many ancient routes naturally followed the watercourses – there being the need, human and animal alike, to drink – so I do not think you will find much divergence between her interest and yours – or, should I say, *ours* – if only I were there to enjoy it.

On which note, please bear with me.

I suggest you stick to the plan. Ascend to the summit of High Street, and do not miss the view down into Blea Water, one of the Lake District's most spectacular tarns, with waterfalls to boot. Thence make for Hartsop – a good path which will put you there over Sunday night and into Monday morning. I ought to be able to communicate with you about a plan for meeting later in the day – assuming all goes well on Monday with "the transaction". As I mentioned, you could either return to walk more of High Street – or there would be the possibility of remaining in the dale, and heading along to Ullswater. Since you say that the good Cathy intends to visit Aira Force, it is perhaps a sight that you should see, especially as there is more rain in the forecast. When Aira Beck is in spate it really is a 'force' of nature!

My little joke, Dorothy – 'force' being derived from the Old Norse 'fors' – and 'foss' is the name for any waterfall in Norway to this day. The Romans, you will not be surprised to know, called it a 'cataracta' – another word gobbled up by our voracious modern English language.

But enough of all things etymological!

I shall leave you in peace and we shall communicate anon.

With my fondest regards and deepest respect,

Felix.

Dorothy feels her eyelids drooping.

Although she has restricted herself to just one glass of wine (Cathy had no difficulty in quaffing the rest of the bottle), the excitement of the day and perhaps the cumulative uncertainty has taken its toll – after all, it is four days now since she touched down at Heathrow – and she refrains from investing further emotional capital in attempting to read between the lines of Felix's latest missive.

In composing her preprandial email she had resolved to be only positive, and not express any disappointment at his non-arrival. The situation is what it is, and he would not want her to nag on. Nor does she wish to burden him with her anxieties and discomforts. Besides, it had occurred to her that it might be impractical to expedite legal and financial matters until the next business day. Perhaps Felix is dancing on the eggshells of a white lie or two – himself not wishing to be the bearer of bad news, which in fact she has already priced in to her expectations.

Meanwhile, she seems to have bottomed the 'Felix situation' with Cathy.

She had been obliged to admit last night that Felix was not about to arrive. Cathy had been surprisingly understanding, merely letting slip an expression of scorn – which Dorothy had interpreted as being aimed at the unreliable male race, rather than at her own gullibility. So, Cathy it was today – and Cathy it will be tomorrow. Notwithstanding that she is more than a little erratic in her behaviour. It was most odd at the bridge; her reaction had been quite childlike. But, once committed, Dorothy had become a partner in crime. Thankfully the fellow did not come their way.

She notes that Felix has made no specific reference to her little adventures – nothing at all about the 'Ambleside Cat'. Perhaps he found it too absurd to partake in speculation – she hopes she has not made a fool of herself.

But he did have a view about Cathy's interest in waterfalls, about her paintings – and about a visit to Aira Force. Over dinner Cathy had mentioned it once again, and that she will wait for tomorrow morning's weather forecast in order to time her arrival for it to be flowing at its most vigorous. Come to think of it, had Cathy not used the phrase "time *their* arrival" – as though she already assumes that Dorothy will accompany her?

Certainly Dorothy does not object in principle. She noticed there are leaflets in the reception area that confirm Aira Force is 'must-see' attraction. And there is something mesmeric about a waterfall. She had felt that, even when looking down into the modest cascade of Stencher Beck. There is the sensation of falling without actually doing it – a vicarious thrill.

Of course, before then Felix might have arrived and swept her off her feet! Back to Roman Roamin' as he calls his tailormade route from Ravenglass to Carlisle ... and on, via Hadrian's Wall ... to Rose Cottage.

She only hopes that Cathy will not be too offended when the time comes – albeit she will take a secret guilty pleasure in seeing Cathy's face, even if that is a small descent to her oft-tetchy companion's level.

14. FULL OF BEANS

Little Langdale – 7.27 a.m., Sunday 24th May

DS Jones would swear that Skelgill pops the last of a bread roll into his mouth as she enters the breakfast room of the Little Langdale B&B known as Wetherlam View – and certainly he swigs down the last from a teacup and wipes his mouth with his sleeve – and affects to be looking at the said view.

She crosses the carpeted floor and joins him at his table in the bay window. Beyond, the fells are dappled, their spring colours in places brighter than others, a moving patchwork the product of great white sheets of cumulus that billow on a washerwoman's breeze; heaven has hung out its laundry.

To her surprise, Skelgill comes clean.

'Just ordered a starter, while I was waiting for you.' He grins mischievously. 'It was either that, or do the crossword.'

Since he has no newspaper, it seems it was an easy decision to make.

DS Jones flashes him a smile that acknowledges the incorrigible. Her hair is damp and her sculpted features seem more prominent than usual in the morning sun; as she takes her seat her appearance draws Skelgill's scrutiny. He does not remark, however.

'It's a subject of endless fascination in the canteen – how you can eat and not put on weight.'

Skelgill frowns. He might note that while she has not said "eat so much" the qualification is implicit.

'Most folk are hungry most of the time – they just don't admit to it. Besides, they don't know what I get up to in my spare time.'

'I know what you get up to in your spare time – some of the time.'

Her response is quick if a little coy. There is an enigmatic sparkle in the deep pools of her large hazel eyes.

Skelgill is unrepentant.

'There you go, then – put in a word for us.'

DS Jones looks as though this might not be most auspicious.

'Well – I could.'

Skelgill now admits to some intrigue in the misapprehension.

'What – do they think I lie about watching the telly?'

'Do you – watch any TV?'

'Only when I'm asleep.' He grins. 'It's more efficient.'

DS Jones is about to enquire further when a short, sturdy, cheery lady whom she does not recognise appears with a large teapot. She smiles admiringly at DS Jones and plonks the item down between them, removing a matching pot that is evidently empty.

She appears to be in cahoots with Skelgill; she takes away his side plate with its telltale breadcrumbs and smear of brown sauce.

'How was that, me duck – filled a gap?'

She is not local – a characteristic shared among many in the B&B trade, who have been attracted to live out their dreams of a running a small business in England's jewel. She looks from one to the other, beaming.

'Full breakfast for you both?'

When she is gone, DS Jones pours out tea, first for Skelgill and then for herself. She seems to realise that it will silence Skelgill – to give her a moment to say her piece. Sure enough, he raises his cup.

She indicates to her mobile phone, which she has placed on the tablecloth, along with her electronic tablet.

'I know we need to talk about Dorothy Baum – and, by the way, I've been searching through the Facebook group – however, if she's there, she's using a different name. But on the subject of Facebook I have received a private message from Professor Felix Stowe-Upland – the imposter.'

Skelgill raises an eyebrow over his tea.

'I didn't know you'd got back to him.'

DS Jones looks a little apologetic.

'Sorry – I meant to say.' She does not need to be asked to elaborate. 'I'd prepared a short message – I intended to run through it with you yesterday – but then I wanted to time the transmission to correspond to daytime in Florida – I sent it at about one-thirty last night.'

Now Skelgill looks just a fraction guilty – that she was on duty at some point in the small hours.

Notwithstanding, his response is pragmatic.

'He's replied straightaway?'

'Well, yes – at least, first thing this morning – about fifteen minutes ago.'

Skelgill drains his latest cup.

'What did you say?'

'I just gave him a bit more biographical detail – following on from his offer of advice and his question about relatives. I said I have no one living here now. I said I'd love to come back after all these years – that it's on my bucket list to see the fort at Hardknott Pass. And that I'm just tying up the loose ends of my late husband's estate – but in the near future I'll be free. I said that my husband was half-Italian on his mother's side, and that we had a running argument – amicable – about which had more ancient Roman sites, Umbria or Cumbria, and that we'd one day take a trip to both to settle it.'

Skelgill is watching her closely, unblinking – but there is something in his expression that tells he understands what she is trying to do. However, he offers a caveat.

'Mind you don't over-egg the pudding. What was it that bloke said? *Softly, softly, catchee monkey.*'

She nods dutifully.

'I know – you're right – but I think it was okay. The personal facts make what I say sound authentic. His answer was immediately to offer to help about sites and routes. He also said he has some academic contacts in Italy, and he would be able to suggest an itinerary for me. He said he'd let me know. He asked when I thought I might travel. And – get this – also that he takes occasional guided tours, and suggests I might be able to join in with one if the timings coincided.'

For completeness, DS Jones points out the corollary.

'He's making no effort to close down the conversation – the opposite in fact.'

Skelgill remains phlegmatic

'It fits, Guv.'

Skelgill, in fact, does not need any persuading on this point. But the food arrives. It is an eye-popping sight. The "Full English" does what it says on the tin. Full plate. Fully belly. Full value. There is a tacit consensus to deal with the priority in hand.

Besides, DS Jones can tell that Skelgill has heard enough. In this respect, at least, it is time to move on from ingestion to digestion.

When their plates are cleared – DS Jones having transferred her second Cumberland sausage and a slice of fried bread with baked beans; a move that might be judged to have qualities both diplomatic and waist-preserving – she takes the initiative by returning to the subject of Dorothy Baum. The woman represents their more immediate quest, having established she lodged here alone in a twin room on Thursday night. It is a trail that is not exactly cold, but – as they sit, where she perhaps did – two days old. She left no mobile number, nor details of her next stop, other than that she was heading in the direction of Ambleside.

'The questions she wrote beside the crossword. I was thinking about them.'

'Aye.'

His retort, though flat, signifies a preparedness to hear her opinion. And that he regards the questions as worthy of deliberation.

'She wrote the word "rooms" – and Derek Shaw said she told him she was meeting a man.' (Skelgill eyes her coolly.) 'We know she booked a twin room here, and at Ravenglass – but stayed alone on each occasion. It seems she was expecting him at both places.' Now she plies Skelgill with a challenging expression. 'It seems to me that she was apprehensive about the sleeping arrangements.'

Skelgill looks away and his gaze follows a buzzard that is being escorted from the territory of a pair of agitated crows.

When he does not answer, DS Jones concludes her analysis.

'But not unwilling to share. Which surely says something about their relationship – about their degree of familiarity; and perhaps the balance of power.'

Skelgill looks back at his companion. A furrow in his brow speaks of his unease with the metaphysical. But a sideways nod suggests she should move on.

'Then she wrote "money transfer" – I mean, Guv – I really can't help putting two and two together here.'

Skelgill grins, but rather sardonically.

'Perhaps she's tapped him up for a loan. Friends with benefits, don't they call it?'

'Don't you think more likely it's the other way around?'

DS Jones has wasted no time with her rejoinder. It prompts a more considered answer from Skelgill.

'You've not heard from the FBI, I take it.'

By referring to the case of Patricia Jackson he has circumvented the discussion and jumped ahead several steps in the logic – but DS Jones seems content with this, despite that she shakes her head and has to disappoint him.

'They've committed to get back to me on Monday. I suppose it will be in the afternoon. I've also emailed them the details we have of Dorothy Baum – just in case it throws up a link. There must be a chance they can get a mobile number. And they ought to be able to track down her point of origin. Although we have no street address, St Francisville is just a small settlement.'

Skelgill nods.

'The third question – who is "Rose C"? Again, I searched through the Cumbrian Confederates Facebook group but I couldn't find anyone who might be a match. As an alternative, I thought – maybe she has a relative here – someone she intends to visit. Maybe stay over for a night.'

Skelgill is looking a little disinterested.

'Happen that's who she sent her postcard to.' Nevertheless, it is perhaps a shrewd comment. 'What's the real Prof's wife's name?'

This seems to DS Jones an uncharacteristically speculative leap – but she has the professor's notepaper in a flap in the jacket of her tablet.

'The initials are E. F. And no letter C to be seen.'

Skelgill shrugs. 'It must be him that made me think of that – he was into his roses, wasn't he?'

DS Jones nods pensively. Now she sees where his subconscious made the connection.

'Judging by what we know, she's finding accommodation as she goes. So far she's been heading east. Do you think she would have stayed in Ambleside on Friday night?'

Skelgill seems reluctant to commit.

'Maybe. If she's visiting Roman sites.'

Rather abstractedly DS Jones surveys the vista beyond the window. Her eyes narrow as she turns towards the morning sun.

'I can't help thinking of the parallel with Patricia Jackson.'

But when she looks for agreement Skelgill appears less willing to join up the dots.

'All we've got there is she was found near Ambleside'

DS Jones leans forward, placing her palms on the tablecloth.

'American, Guv – elderly, travelling alone – her passport recovered from High Street.'

Skelgill looks rather pained.

'Which suggests she was coming the other way. Never made it to Ambleside.'

It is a fair point, but DS Jones is not finished.

'It doesn't negate the Roman history aspect. We know she was at least tentatively connected to the fake Professor Felix Stowe-Upland. And, frankly, Dorothy Baum seems to be meeting him.'

Delivered without vehemence, her argument is convincing, and Skelgill is obliged to recognise that there are almost too many coincidences. But then, here he is – if proof of interest were needed – investigating on a Sunday morning. How he spends some of his spare time.

'We need to catch her up.'

DS Jones sits back.

'Do you think we should issue an alert?'

Skelgill's reaction is illuminating – for it is clear that he thinks there would be a risk in doing so, but that he is conflicted, all the same. That he regards it as showing their hand means he also considers there is someone to whom he does not wish to reveal it. That there is a person (or persons) to worry about. After a moment, he nods.

'Not public. Not yet. Local police and emergency services. But we might get on her tail today.'

DS Jones does not demur – whatever she might have had planned for the day of rest.

She muses.

'I wonder what route she would take. It's likely that by now she has moved on from Ambleside.'

Skelgill points to the notepaper.

'Why don't we ask the expert?'

DS Jones glances up in surprise.

'The real Professor? Right now?'

'Why not?'

She does not have on her watch – but she turns her head to see that the time on Skelgill's right wrist is hovering around eight. Not that early – but perhaps for many on a Sunday morning.

'Okay.'

They have the breakfast room to themselves, and she switches her mobile phone to speaker and taps in the number, and slides the handset between them. It is answered promptly; a mature woman's voice, fine and clear with a light Yorkshire accent, who does not sound like she has been roused from slumber.

'Hello, Ampleforth 2403.'

'Dr Stowe-Upland?'

'Yes?'

'I'm sorry to disturb you, madam. This is DS Jones from Cumbria CID. My colleague and I met with your husband on Friday.'

'Ah, yes – Felix mentioned it.'

'There's just a quick question I would like to ask him, if it's convenient.'

The woman draws breath.

'Ah – that's a pity. He isn't here.'

'When are you expecting him back?'

'I'm afraid he didn't say. He has been asked to stand in at a conference for a former colleague who has fallen ill. He left in a hurry yesterday for London – was it yesterday, now? Yes – *Saturday* – while I was at the new garden centre in Thirsk. He left me a scribbled note. It just said he would be gone for a few days.'

DS Jones pauses to think.

'If I recall correctly, I think he said he has no mobile phone?'

'That's right, we neither of us have one.'

'Where is he staying?'

'I honestly don't know. He could be lodging with a colleague, or in university accommodation – or he sometimes stays at the Athenaeum Club – I think he still has an associate membership. I'm afraid he didn't even leave any details of the conference – or for whom he is filling in.'

DS Jones is looking intently at Skelgill.

'Is it like him to go off with little notice?'

It is a more intrusive question, but the woman does not seem to mind.

'Oh, yes – things crop up from time to time – especially since he has been retired – they tend not to be scheduled events, you see – just like this. Between you and me, he enjoys it. Unlike myself, he misses the cut and thrust of academia.'

DS Jones senses that the conversation has run its course.

'Okay. Thank you. He has my number. Would you mind asking him to call me if he contacts you?'

'Certainly.'

'Sorry to trouble you so early on a Sunday.'

'Oh – I was up – I have to rise early to water the azaleas.'

When the call is ended the two detectives spend a moment looking at one another in silence. But Skelgill's expression warns against further speculation – in his unspoken vernacular, not to open up an unnecessary can of worms.

DS Jones understands.

'I'll put DC Watson onto it first thing tomorrow. Just for peace of mind I'd like to know where he is.'

Skelgill now offers a more constructive input.

'There's another Prof we can ask. Jim Hartley will have a pretty good idea of the route we're looking for. Where the interesting stops might be after Ambleside.'

DS Jones seems to have second thoughts.

'But what do you think?'

163

Skelgill cannot hide that he was half hoping she would ask him, and shifts in his seat into a more upright pose. But equally, he is inherently reluctant to speculate upon where Dorothy K. Baum might be. Every point has 360 degrees of the compass around it. She could have headed back west, taken the bus, walked to the railway station at Windermere. Stayed put, even.

However, he supplies an answer.

'She's been to Ravenglass, Hardknott, Ambleside. The next Roman fort that I know of is at Brougham – top end of High Street. By far the shortest route from Ambleside would be The Struggle. That takes you directly to the top of Kirkstone Pass and a footpath along St Raven's Edge to High Street summit. You know – near the Kirkstone Pass Inn?'

'The one in the middle of nowhere?'

Skelgill grins.

'Aye, since 1496 – they must have got summat right.'

DS Jones is forced to concede.

'How long would that take – to reach High Street?'

Skelgill shrugs.

'You could do it in a morning. It's probably a six-mile walk. Three thousand foot of ascent.'

'And then where for accommodation?'

Now Skelgill ponders for a moment; his expression clouds, and DS Jones can see that he is passing his mind's eye over his mental map of the fells.

'It'd be too far to cover the whole of High Street in a day – for an older lady. It looks like she's doing seven or eight miles, at a push. You'd have to drop down to Haweswater in the east or Ullswater in the west. Unless you were wild camping – that'd be the ideal. Stay high.'

'It doesn't appear that she's wild camping.'

Skelgill shakes his head. But it does not escape his notice that Derek Shaw was. He also told DS Leyton that he was aiming to pick up High Street.

DS Jones is evidently having parallel thoughts. And, rather like DS Leyton, her suspicions have plainly been aroused by the obvious circumstantial facts (in DS Leyton's case, that a man with a metal detector and a camp shovel was found near a freshly dug hole at an ancient site).

'Guv – what I said earlier. About Derek Shaw being a Roman historian from York. These feel like connections that we can't ignore. He met Dorothy Baum. He mentioned High Street.'

'Who says I'm ignoring them?'

His retort is amenable, despite that his words suggest a defensive reaction.

DS Jones tries again.

'We have his mobile number.' She raises a palm in anticipation of an objection; she offers fresh logic. 'I get why you didn't want to mention the Professor, but we could call to confirm that his alibi has checked out, and thank him for his cooperation. Then we say that Dorothy Baum left a personal item at Ravenglass – some travel notes that she made. We'd like to reunite them, but she didn't leave details of her itinerary – and can he help?'

Skelgill seems pleased by the minor subterfuge, and his partner's ingenuity.

But the fisherman in him is resistant. To hoy too much ground bait into a swim is counterproductive; the fish instinctively move away from a disturbance, no matter how innocent or indeed beneficial the act might be. You spook your quarry.

He stares across the landscape; its detailed tapestry of shapes and colours is becoming more defined as the sun climbs in the southeast.

'Reckon we should keep our powder dry, just for a bit.'

DS Jones is content, but has other thoughts to share.

'Guv, it seems to me that Dorothy Baum has a mobile phone. And yet she chose to let him write down his number. It's interesting.'

'Aye.'

This is an 'aye' that suggests Skelgill has not the faintest idea of what she is implying, but is not about to admit it.

She understands.

'When a random guy is trying to get your number, he offers his.'

This has Skelgill's antennae twitching. He glares interrogatively.

She quickly elaborates.

'Like now – I could just say, I'll give you my number.' She holds up her phone and makes to type into the keypad. 'What's yours?'

'What? You know it.'

She grins. 'Yes – but if I didn't – you would have to give it to me now in order for me to call, so that your phone captures mine. Mine captures yours.'

Skelgill stays silent.

'Surely Dorothy Baum had her phone with her at the time. But it looks to me like she avoided giving out her number. I just wonder why that might be.'

But Skelgill's suspicions have been propelled firmly down another track.

'So, when do random guys try to get your number?'

'What?' She laughs, but perhaps a little disingenuously. 'Oh – I'm talking generally – it's one of those things unequally distributed between the sexes.'

Skelgill remains looking discontented.

DS Jones moves to defuse the awkward moment, for she is also a little amused. She reaches over the table and places a hand on his sleeve.

'Besides – I would make anyone show me their bank balance first.'

A tad reluctantly, he acknowledges the joke.

'Just as well you haven't asked to see mine.'

She is about to reply when her phone does ring.

Skelgill nebs.

'That's Leyton.'

She answers the call on speaker.

'Emma – sorry to bother you early on a Sunday, girl – I'm trying to track down the Guvnor. His flamin' phone's off – surprise, surprise. Reckon he must be out on Bass Lake.'

DS Jones simultaneously grins and winces and is wondering what her colleague might say next. As quickly as she can she gets in a rejoinder.

'He's here – you're on speaker!'

DS Leyton makes an unintelligible strangled sound in his nose and throat and then proceeds as though nothing has passed.

'Morning, Guv – something to bounce off've you.'

Skelgill grimaces.

'Leyton, haven't you got your family geocaching expedition to organise?'

DS Leyton chuckles.

'Thing is, Guv – you ain't so wide of the mark. The nighthawker's struck again. This time at the Iron Age fort near Pooley Bridge. And a witness description that fits the Shaw geezer. I thought I'd better drop down and have a butcher's – in case he's still knocking about.'

There is no suggestion in DS Leyton's tone that he is hoping to be told either not to bother, or indeed that Skelgill might offer to take up the assignment – but it is precisely the latter that comes to pass.

'Nay, leave it, Leyton, we'll have a deek. We'll be coming up that way, later.'

'*Up*, Guv?'

'Aye, we're in the Langdales.'

There is a pause.

'Of course you are.'

'And, Leyton –'

'Guv?'

'First thing Monday – check out his back story.'

'Right you are, Guv.'

15. CLOUDY BLUE

High Street – 2.08 p.m., Sunday 24th May

Dorothy wonders if she is getting used to the weather cycles. The pattern of clearing – and, as it is now, clouding seems to be repeating itself. A day that dawned with more blue than white has gradually become a sky of tumbled greys. As they have ascended, it feels like the cloud base has crept lower to meet them.

Earlier, Cathy had produced a rather pessimistic aphorism. "If you can't see the tops, it's raining. If you can, it's going to rain."

Thankfully, so far, neither has come to pass, but Dorothy supposes there is something in what Cathy says. Like no smoke without fire, there can be no rain without cloud. And the cloud does seem to be working its way up to something. Perhaps it is the next warm front. Dorothy is reminded of Derek. His adage was more positive. "There's no such thing as bad weather, only the wrong clothes" – which he had attributed to the hardy Scots. She wonders where Derek is now. She remembers his kindness in carrying her pack. She could do with that at this moment. It is not that she is defeated, but the going is tough. Remember, Dorothy, that's when the tough get going.

Leaving their lodgings at Troutbeck Cathy had seemed in high spirits – even by her idiosyncratic standards – she had appeared for breakfast at seven-thirty on the dot and was most animated. Her movements were fidgety and her manners even more random than usual. Still standing, she had drunk a whole glass of orange juice in one swallow and belched loudly, like a contestant quaffing a yard of ale. Perhaps she was celebrating a good night's sleep. Dorothy's had been less fortunate, despite a comfortable bed. She had slept fitfully and dreamt of being lost in the fells above Wastwater, where sleek black Cumbrian rhinoceroses stalked her in the mist – one had charged at her and to escape she was forced to jump from a precipice into the plunge pool of a waterfall, a leap of faith that it would be deep enough. The icy water woke her to a cold sweat. After that, she wonders if she actually got back to sleep proper.

But Cathy's mood seems to have darkened with the skies. Perhaps she has sore feet. Dorothy is thankful she broke in her own boots with plenty of walking practice before she came. Cathy's are more like trail shoes; they do not have ankle support, and look a couple of sizes too large. Nevertheless, she has been going at a keen lick. Since their regulation mid-morning stop for Builder's Brew – at Hagg Bridge, whence a tributary of Trout Beck has funnelled them up Hagg Gill – Cathy has pulled ahead by several hundred yards, and has not waited for Dorothy to catch up. Instead she marches relentlessly, despite her stocky and unathletic figure that seems ill-suited for mountaineering. Dorothy is glad at least of her own rangier frame, although she could do without the backpack. For her part, Cathy seems to manage with a remarkably small pack. Then there is her age; Cathy has not volunteered the figure, but there must be close on a generation between them.

All these things have conspired to make the last hour an uncomfortable experience for Dorothy. But the end is in sight. Even though it isn't, literally speaking – a phenomenon to which she is becoming accustomed. The sigmoidal curvature of most fells is such that their summits are hidden to the climber by a succession of bluffs; only the true 'pikes' really stand out.

The punishing rising traverse across the flank of what Dorothy's map tells her is Park Fell, fifteen hundred feet of unyielding ascent, has a gradient she estimates to be on a par with the worst of Hardknott Pass. But that was a tarmac road with a firm verge and this is a stony path, broken at times, boggy in places, requiring constant vigilance. That the fellsides have closed in all around and are not at their most visually auspicious passes Dorothy by, as this is a small battle for survival. She wonders again why Cathy is so remorseless in pushing on. Derek at least would have walked alongside her – on their route together she noticed he never took a step ahead, always adjusting so that she was able to dictate the pace.

The day is not hot but the overcast conditions create a draining humidity, a closeness unlike the cosseting subtropical warmth she is accustomed to; suffocating, pressing, insidious. And, while there is a breeze, little of it reaches the narrow dale. Dorothy's back is sticky, and sweat trickles from her saturated hatband. Once again she is becoming dehydrated, but gaining no cooling benefit from the process. What little water she has left in her canteen she wants to preserve, because she doubts there will be any to be found on the High Street ridge.

Her mouth is dry and her lips feel cracked. But she does not want to show weakness. Perhaps Cathy's tactic is to grind it out, to get this unpleasant haul over with, to drag her to the summit where they can celebrate with a mug of Builder's Brew. From there, it will all be on the flat.

But that is another thing.

They have not agreed upon a course of action. When Dorothy had raised it, Cathy had cut her off with "let's see the lie of the land" – meaning, Dorothy understood, they should get the climb to High Street under their belts and evaluate how they felt. There is some merit in this method – it is all too easy to make plans down in the dale, before fatigue sets in and the conditions deteriorate. Although, at least the weather's current progress towards rain seems to be as pedestrian as her own.

But the contours do begin to relent. The top of the "S" is flattening off.

Dorothy stops for a moment to look back. The view south is magnificent, and she wants to take a photograph for Felix – once on the plateau this telescopic vista to a distant sliver of Windermere will surely disappear.

But a cry comes from ahead and above.

Cathy is urging her on, beckoning frantically as if there is some danger in stopping; perhaps she is right, a loss of momentum now will be hard to recover, when their goal is tantalisingly within their grasp.

Indeed, as Dorothy falls in and Cathy turns, beyond her Dorothy can see the emerging summit cairn. But instead of heading directly for it, Cathy is veering to the right – to the east.

She pauses to see what Dorothy is doing, and again signals that she should follow her.

Despite that they are short of the cairn, Cathy now begins to give up altitude – but quite soon she halts and takes off her pack. As Dorothy approaches she appears to be fishing for her camera.

And now Dorothy sees why.

And she remembers what Felix had told her. "Don't miss the view down into Blea Water".

Of course, this is Blea Water Crag.

Beneath them, an almost sheer drop of a thousand feet, and a teardrop of a tarn, a mountain pool that must be only a few hundred yards across, nestled in the deep corrie like a dark sapphire in its setting. The surface of the tarn is mirror-flat, the corrie lies in the lee of any breeze. Into the still, silent ether a raven launches itself from a ledge with a resounding croak; they have encroached upon its territory. The great bird cuts through the air, a diminishing silhouette. Its descent seems interminable. Dorothy sways a little. After an hour staring at the ground under her feet – the sudden sensation that the ground has been snatched away is vertiginous, at once exhilarating and terrifying.

'The waterfalls are further round. We need to follow this sheep track. Leave your pack.'

Much of the rock face is obscured. Dorothy cannot see a waterfall, although there is the distant splash of water, its origin almost impossible to place – but if she had to guess she would say it comes from much lower down.

She is not sure she wants to go.

But she is glad to take off her backpack.

'Chop, chop, Dorothy – we've not got all day.'

Cathy sets off, picking her way along a narrow trod that descends diagonally and disappears beyond a crag. Dorothy does not follow. Cathy seems sure-footed; she is on a mission with her camera; she does not wait for Dorothy. Dorothy can imagine her muttering, "It's your loss, Dorothy."

Dorothy lowers herself onto the tussocky mat grass that forms a thick carpet where little else will grow; evidently it is the one thing that sheep will not eat. She brings up her knees and wraps her arms around her shins. Sometimes, to photograph a scene is to eschew its intrinsic worth; the camera renders the insider an outsider. The camera might never lie, but neither does it tell the whole truth. No machine has yet been invented that can replicate a million external stimuli and their billion internal responses.

And then ... another stimulus and response.

A firm hand grasps Dorothy's shoulder.

Dorothy, froglike, lurches forwards.

'Yikes!'

'Oh – my word!'

'Dorothy – it *is* you!'

'Derek!'

Dorothy, now facing him in the manner of a sprinter on all fours, makes a kind of hop; she is perilously close to the cliff.

Derek Shaw reaches out a hand to haul her to her feet.

'Sorry to creep up on you – you were so near the edge – and you seemed to be in such a trance – I honestly thought I might make you jump – and, well –'

'You did.'

Dorothy is smiling.

However, she puts a palm to her breastbone, as though to quell her beating heart.

Now Derek Shaw seems a little lost for words.

He indicates with a nod of his head.

'It's a heck of a view, though. Blea Water. It means dark blue in Old Norse.'

Dorothy steps alongside him, and they both admire the dramatic vista.

'Clear blue water.'

There is the suggestion that she appreciates the dangerous nature of the void.

'Perhaps we should move back?' He jerks a thumb over his shoulder. 'Have you been up to the cairn?'

Dorothy glances instead to the point where Cathy disappeared from sight; but there is no trace of her.

'Oh, well – I, er – I should –'

Derek Shaw seems keen to make amends for his clumsy

entrance.

'You know, I thought – there can only be one cowboy hat like that in Cumbria – and the way you were battering up Scot Rake – I said to myself it must be the intrepid Dorothy, solo explorer.'

Dorothy realises he must think she is alone; they were so far apart that perhaps he did not see Cathy. But something else puzzles her.

'Derek – when you saw me – where were you?'

Now he points roughly back in the direction from which Dorothy has come, but not to the broad cleft where she had climbed Scot Rake, as he has called it, instead to the higher ground to the left.

'I've been surveying the ridge. Some say that High Street actually continued over Froswick, Ill Bell and Yoke.' He bites at the side of his lower lip as he stares at the landscape. 'Frankly, the modern school of thought is more doubtful. There's no concrete evidence that this ever was a Roman road.'

Dorothy regards him a little pensively. It is not the first time that Derek's position has been at odds with that of Felix. But it would seem churlish to point it out at this unusual juncture; besides, Derek is so good-natured in all his ways.

Instead she gestures towards him.

'But you don't have your detector?'

He chuckles.

'So I'm not likely to add to the concrete.'

Now he steps close in a reassuring way. He takes a careful hold of her upper arm. He indicates with his free hand down into the corrie.

'See – the brighter green speck in the patch of bracken just above the tarn?'

Dorothy strains her eyes and endeavours to follow his direction. Perhaps she can see what he means.

Derek Shaw elaborates.

'Base camp. I'll be staying there tonight – no point lugging kit up and down.'

His grip on her arm seems to tighten a little, perhaps at the thought.

Dorothy is about to ask a question when out of the corner of her eye she catches a flash of colour. It is the cerise top that Cathy is wearing.

Derek Shaw follows her gaze.

Cathy has appeared from around the outcrop and is standing stock still. She must be fifty yards off, and out of earshot.

'Cathy.'

Dorothy has said the name before she knows it. And perhaps her tone reveals a slight guilt on her part. She blurts out a further explanation.

'She's photographing the waterfalls.'

Derek Shaw squints, his expression becoming a little incredulous, but he does not offer an opinion.

For Cathy's part, even at a distance it is plain that she is annoyed.

In fact, more than annoyed. In her large plain face with its startled eyes there are hints – Dorothy is sure – of alarm, of distaste – and of jealousy.

'Looks like I'm persona non grata.'

It seems Derek Shaw's reading of the situation is astute. Dorothy notes he has subtly shifted away from her.

'No – no – not at all, Derek. She's only –'

But Derek Shaw indicates to his wristwatch.

'I think I should make myself scarce – I've got a bucketload to fit in before dusk.'

He takes a couple of paces backwards – and Dorothy is sure he is waiting for her to gainsay the suggestion and insist he stay. But Cathy calls out her name – just an insistent "Dorothy!" and nothing else – and he smiles understandingly.

'If it's waterfalls you're after – Aira Force – not to be missed.' He raises a palm. 'Until we meet again.'

He turns and marches away in the direction of the summit cairn.

For the first time, Dorothy feels genuinely irked by Cathy. Her foibles to date she has tolerated; they have been of no lasting significance, water off a duck's back. But now her rudeness has impinged upon someone else, and it has reflected badly upon

Dorothy, never mind that she would have liked Derek to remain longer.

But there is a shadow that clouds her reproach for Cathy. She is surprised by Derek's willingness to retreat. Was he more offended than he had revealed?

And then a thought strikes her.

Does Derek think that Cathy is her partner – the 'friend' she had told him she was eagerly awaiting? Did he jump to conclusions and decide that now he would be cramping their style if he tagged along with them?

Of course, it would make sense – here they are, on the Roman Roamin' route. Did she describe that to Derek? She cannot remember, now. When she thinks about it, the offbeat name is the sort of thing that Cathy would have come up with. At least – one small mercy – he has not actually had to meet her 'up close and personal', as the saying goes.

Now Cathy is approaching.

Dorothy has a good mind to give her a dressing down. But before she can compose a diplomatic form of words (which Cathy would certainly not take the trouble to do, were the boot on the other foot), Cathy regales her with a complaint of her own.

'You have to watch out for strangers, Dorothy. You're not in America now. You can't just shoot people you don't like.'

Cathy's logic is disorienting and before Dorothy can muster a rejoinder her companion is casting more aspersions.

'I didn't like the look of him for one minute. He seemed dodgy – the way he was eyeing you up. He's probably watching us now, hidden in the heather.' She glares across the fellside; it suits her argument that there is no sign of Derek Shaw. 'People are always out for themselves – act like they'll help – give you directions or make you a cup of tea – but really they want something from you.'

Dorothy is thinking this is all unfounded nonsense – and that it is a shame if it is Cathy's outlook.

However, she offers a rather limp counter.

'He was being friendly. He was admiring our progress.'

'That's what they all say.'

Cathy's manner is categorical, as if this is a widely known truth.

Perhaps she deems that Dorothy, as a foreigner, can be excused for her naivety.

But now Dorothy decides she will not tell Cathy that she is acquainted with Derek – that he is a perfect gentleman – nor that she knows where he is camping.

Cathy bends with an involuntary groan and pushes her camera into her backpack.

'And you've missed your chance with the waterfalls.' She seems additionally displeased.

'Did you get your photo?'

'It doesn't matter. We need to put a shift in before it rains. We'll get the bus.'

Dorothy is nonplussed. A bus seems a far cry from their present location – never mind the abrupt about turn. And a bus, even if they can find one – to where?

Moreover, it seems that Cathy is about to skip what has been the obligatory Builder's Brew. She hauls on her pack.

As she moves away, Dorothy enters a small protest.

'Wait – I'm going to the cairn. I can't come all this way and not touch the top.'

Cathy glances over her shoulder; her scowl suggests she thinks it is a ridiculous notion.

'I'll walk slow – you can catch me up. We'll take the direct path to Kirkstone Pass.'

What Dorothy had called in her own mind the summit cairn (and Derek, too) is in fact a concrete surveying pillar. Rather disappointingly there is no plaque with information about the site or the route. But she appreciates the moment of calm, the separation from Cathy and the feelings of conflict that were growing inside her.

Now she wonders if Derek will come back this way; she is not actually sure where he went – perhaps he is surveying High Street to the north. She feels a little ashamed of what has happened – but still irritated that Cathy drove him off.

Then she has an idea.

She removes her backpack and from a side pocket brings out her reserve tin of Kendal mint cake.

She places it carefully on top of the pillar.

Walking, she uses the excuse of the small passage of time to keep her distance from Cathy. It gives her space to ponder further. Clearly, Cathy is jealous. That's what it is. She has hooked Dorothy, and now she is possessive of her. Perhaps this has happened before – and the person has moved on to a more desirable companion. Cathy's immature reaction, a childish mixture of fearmongering and bullying, reflects her fears.

Dorothy is not sure what she feels now about Cathy. And then there is Derek – it was heart-warming to see him, despite the shock of his silent approach over the soft grass. And she realises she has hardly paid a thought to Felix.

She plays devil's advocate with herself. Should she give any credence to Cathy's wild claims? That Derek is 'dodgy'? It would be wrong to say she does not harbour a tiny percentage of doubt about his credentials – it is only natural in the circumstances. But to admit such to Cathy would only be grist to her mill.

She wonders if she ought to shoulder some of the blame for the entanglement. It seems that Cathy did not get her photograph. Derek had looked dubious when she mentioned the waterfalls. After all, it was she, Dorothy who had, if not exactly dictated, then certainly suggested this part of the route – since they left Ambleside, really. It has hardly delivered Niagara for Cathy's camera or sketchbook. The sketchbook is yet to see the light of day.

She resolves to make it up to Cathy. She should raise Felix's suggestion of buying some of her paintings. Surely, to pander to her ego will put her in a better frame of mind.

And she looks with an ironic sense of optimism at the darkening skies. Maybe if it rains tonight it will cheer Cathy up – bring her waterfalls to life. She ought to have asked Derek; he knows his weather.

Cathy is waiting impatiently by the roadside as Dorothy comes down the last section of the path.

She sees that they are at the summit of what must be Kirkstone Pass.

The Kirkstone Pass Inn, the sole habitation in desolate

surroundings, long and low and uneven, looks lonely and deserted – although she notices that several cars are parked across the road in a rough gravel lot. Seated at a table close to the building, three men – thirsty walkers by the look of it – are knocking back pints of beer, and do not seem to notice the two women as they cross the road at a diagonal.

Cathy addresses her in a matter-of-fact manner, as though nothing of note has passed between them. But Dorothy thinks she detects an undertone of residual crossness.

'It's request stop. There'll be a bus along soon.'

How she can know this is unclear to Dorothy. And she wants to ask about their plan – certainly Cathy seems to have one – but she senses it might set her off again, and decides to wait until they are on the bus.

Occasional cars pass. It is the main Windermere-to-Ullswater route, wider than the single-track of her earlier experiences, but still a challenging winding pass of snaking switchbacks, comparatively narrow and bordered by unforgiving dry stone walls, if not quite the perilous gradient of Wrynose or Hardknott.

Dorothy finds herself looking at vehicles in the car park.

While they wait in silence she is reminded of the Wrynose incident. It is half-forgotten, so much has been happening.

And now she wonders – if she were shown a range of cars – could she identify the type that struck her the glancing blow?

She considers that one might almost be similar. But so many of these small British cars look alike. With the headlights and the mist, she never really saw the colour. This one is grey-green.

She did not mention the incident to Cathy – initially, at Little Langdale, having met her so soon after the event, and later for fear of evoking her wrath or her disdain – one never knows what one will get from Cathy, whether she would blame the driver or, equally likely, Dorothy for her incompetence.

And now Cathy makes a tetchy exclamation.

'Come on, Dorothy. The driver might not see us here. We'll move.'

She points to a layby, some fifty yards further along, as the pass begins to descend northwards.

Dorothy cannot see what is wrong with their present position – the local bus should surely notice them and be able to pull into the opening of the car park.

But she acquiesces. Cathy has her quirks, and she does not want to risk making her even more cranky.

16. SLIDING DOORS

Kirkstone Pass – 5.14 p.m., Sunday 24th May

'Sod's law.'

DS Jones murmurs a rueful acknowledgement – although it is perhaps as much in relief as in irony. The long green bus that has hindered their progress, too big for these roads really, has finally indicated to pull in – just when they have reached their destination.

Skelgill is not a relaxing passenger at the best of times and, in circumstances where he would overtake while a more cautious driver would not, his fidgeting can reach epic levels. DS Jones has tried to distract him with small talk, without great success. And, when the bus might ordinarily have been expected to make regular stops, on this late and quiet Sunday afternoon there have been no takers. Skelgill's frustration had become compounded when a chapter of leather-clad bikers first roared past them and then, in tight formation, overtook the bus with a burst of acceleration not available to a car. DS Jones's inquiry as to the status of his own bike had only served to remind Skelgill that it is still with his cousin Mouse, suffering from an obscure carburetion malaise (according to Mouse, who he suspects is just using it while his own machine is in dry dock).

The bikers are nowhere to be seen as the Kirkstone Pass Inn heaves into sight and the bus driver indicates either that someone wishes to get out or – more likely it would seem at this time of day – climb aboard.

'Turn into the car park on the left.'

Having issued this instruction, Skelgill's attention is drawn to the right. Two men are seated at a picnic bench on the narrow verge outside the pub. A third approaches unsteadily. He bears three pints of tawny real ale in straight glasses. Skelgill can tell it is real ale, because the glasses are brim full, with no trace of a head. Like a passer-by drawn to pause to watch a golfer's putt, Skelgill is captivated. Clearly, the two seated share his interest (in their case more vested) in whether their companion will successfully deliver the beer. With his long fisherman's fingers, holding three pints at once is a feat that comes easily to Skelgill, but he has seen it go wrong on enough occasions to make this one worth watching. He rather guiltily admits to a tinge of disappointment when, unable to bear the risk any longer, the two seated lurch in tandem to rescue their pints from peril.

DS Jones, concentrating upon the manoeuvre, is oblivious to this little cameo, but she does catch a glimpse of two hikers as they board the now-stationary bus; if asked she might be able to replay that there was an unusual hat, and that the shorter one in the pink top seemed to jostle the other for primacy.

She parks judiciously. The parking area is extensive, it accommodates not just patrons of the inn, who spill out onto picnic tables and a second nearby alfresco area in their droves on a sunny Bank Holiday, but also outdoor types, perhaps most notably 'top-baggers' of whom Skelgill is regularly disparaging – in this case for capitalising on the pass which, at roughly fifteen hundred feet, takes a good bite out of the ascent. "How can you say you've climbed a fell when you've driven halfway up?"

But this afternoon there are few of any types. Just half a dozen cars, and she reverses into a wide gap between a navy-blue Defender with a white roof tent and a small greenish Fiat that has seen better days.

She notices that Skelgill is eyeing the drinkers – they are having a laugh and raising glasses – and she wonders if he will suggest a beverage and take advantage of not being the driver.

But he rolls out and stretches his spine, grimacing as he presses his knuckles into the small of his back, a largely subliminal act which she recognises as indicative of preparation for action.

When DS Jones had picked up a waiting Skelgill in Ambleside on Saturday afternoon he had been toting a small army surplus duffel bag and, slung on one shoulder, a more familiar canvas rucksack of medium size; she had deduced he had brought these in

DS Leyton's car.

The rucksack has not thus far been called into use – but now he ducks into the rear seat and hauls it out. It makes a clank as he drops it onto the ground in order to retie his bootlaces.

DS Jones is looking at the skies.

'Should I bring my waterproof?'

Skelgill cranes around. She can tell from his wry reaction that any answer would be of the 'bear and woods' variety and she too reaches into the car. However, she is torn about whether to put it on, hesitation which Skelgill notices.

'You'll want it off in five minutes.' He indicates with a jerk of his head. 'Shove it in the bag.'

There is a low wall at their rear and she makes to lift the rucksack on top for ease of access.

'Heavens! What have you got in here?'

Skelgill looks mildly sheepish.

'Essential supplies.'

DS Jones loosens the drawstring to reveal that the main culprit is Skelgill's Kelly kettle. She hears the sloshing of water; she knows from experience it serves about six mugs. There is also a fuel bottle, kindling, a rolled-up Angling Times and – tucked inside the chimney of the kettle – a packet of chocolate digestive biscuits.

She looks at him questioningly.

'There's a mash waiting for us at the top. So long as we can find a couple of sticks to rub together.'

She grins. In most circumstances she would characterise Skelgill as an 'eat the best first' type of person – an ingrained competitive expedient that probably comes with having three rapacious elder brothers – so it is always an interesting insight to see that he is capable of delayed gratification when an incentive has a role to play.

'Is it that hard a climb?'

But he quickly shakes his head.

'Nay – nowt to it – bit of a sting in the tail after Stony Cove Pike.'

She crams in her jacket and fastens the strap.

'I'll carry it up.'

Skelgill laughs. But he also seems offended. There is the impression that she would deprive him of something.

'I'll cut you a deal. You can carry it back. All the more reason to drink the lot.'

'How long do you think we'll be?'

'If I knew what we were looking for, you mean?'

His sarcastic tone is employed only partly in jest. He frowns, further hinting at self-reproach – that he is dragging her around like this. Earlier, having visited Ambleside and (re-visited, in his case) Galava, they had wandered rather aimlessly, like a couple of ill-informed tourists. Skelgill had come up with the 'needle-in-haystack' analogy, adding the rider that they had not yet found the haystack. Certainly – and this being more DS Jones's bag – they would benefit from a systematic approach, and to marshal corporate resources, which they cannot do until Monday morning.

But meanwhile time passes. Skelgill, scrutinising the short, sharp pull up to St Raven's Edge, remains pensive. He is reminded that he has never caught anything by standing on the bank and talking to himself. He has to row to a likely spot and start fishing in earnest. At least, by visiting High Street, they are walking the walk.

DS Jones breaks into his reverie.

'I'm happy to go quickly – I've missed the gym today.'

'You can't get this in the gym.'

He casts a hand loosely towards the fellside. He could be referring to the nature of the exercise, as much as the surroundings.

DS Jones smiles agreeably.

'Cold shower, optional.'

'So, we'd better get a shift on.'

She nods, and without the slightest hint of losing her balance, stretches her quads, one after the other.

Skelgill watches, half bemused, as she completes a small routine; but he waits, nonetheless, for her to finish before he sets off at a brisk pace.

In his wake, DS Jones as always is reminded of the unusual speed with which Skelgill covers rough terrain. She notices that it is not so much his pacing rate, though he does have a long stride, but that he rarely makes a misstep. He seems to know precisely where to plant his feet, as if – despite that every rocky path is unique – there is some underlying pattern of which he has an intuitive grasp. And it is not as if he even watches his step – much of the time he is looking about.

'What's the scenery like?'

Skelgill makes a somewhat disparaging murmur.

'Dull and dreary – according to Wainwright – but he was a bit black-and-white. I reckon he must have had corns when he was in this neck of the woods.'

She laughs. There is a certain irony in Skelgill's bemoaning of characteristics so familiar in his own repertoire; Skelgill and Wainwright being bedfellows in cantankerousness.

*

'Hardly dull and dreary, Guv.'

Skelgill, caught mid-dunk, has to consume the biscuit before he can respond.

'I reckon he was talking about the way up. He doesn't even describe an ascent of High Street from Kirkstone Pass.'

DS Jones, sitting cross-legged upon her cagoule, stares out across the vista. The sky might be overcast, but the sense of awe and grandeur is undiminished; they look out from Blea Water Crag. And she senses that – perhaps aside from being in his boat on Bass Lake – this kind of moment will rank high in Skelgill's times of contentment.

He seems in good spirits. After a day of drifting it obviously suits him to be doing something with a purpose, however oblique to their investigation. And, while it would tire most people, it rejuvenates him.

'You've been up here before, of course?'

Skelgill laughs.

'How many times, then?'

'Two score – three. I don't know. I'm not a ticker.'

'But you've climbed all the fells.'

She phrases the remark as a statement of the obvious.

'Aye.'

She ponders for a moment. Then she leans back on her elbows and tilts her head to the skies.

'If you could have a mountain named after you, which would it be?'

Skelgill does not seem surprised by this question, out of the blue though it is.

'Thing is – growing up where I did – and knowing about Wainwright – it's hard to see past Haystacks. But I doubt it would make most folk's top twenty.'

Before DS Jones can offer an opinion, he continues.

'I mean, Scafell Pike – obviously – highest mountain in England. But Scafell's got more character. Blencathra's got Sharp Edge. Skiddaw's got Bass Lake.' Skelgill leans forwards, and braces his arms around his knees. He is genuinely absorbed by the poser. 'I suppose it's between Haystacks and Skiddaw.'

'And if you had to choose?'

He gives an exasperated gasp.

'Haystacks, then.'

DS Jones now lies completely supine.

'Pike or salmon?'

'Come again?'

'Which would you choose?'

'What is this, Twenty Questions?'

'Pike or salmon?'

'Pike. Obviously. I reckon.'

DS Jones gives a small murmur of satisfaction – that he reveals some doubt.

'Fishing at dawn or fishing at dusk?'

He makes one attempt and then another to answer, but he is stymied.

DS Jones decides to move on.

'We'll come back to that. Wainwright or Ordnance Survey?'

Skelgill scowls fiercely.

'Come off it, lass.'

'If you had to pick?'

Skelgill shakes his head, his features severely conflicted.

'Another pass.'

DS Jones is smiling broadly.

'Tea or real ale?'

Now Skelgill resorts to an expletive.

She persists.

'Tea or real ale?'

'How can I answer that?'

'Try.'

'Pass, again.'

'Bacon roll or Cumberland sausage?'

Skelgill hits the heel of one hand against his temple.

'You'll ask me what sauce next.'

'Red or brown?'

'Red on bacon, brown on Cumberland.'

'That's cheating.'

She admits he has wriggled his way around this one – but she can sense he is unnerved by her perspicacity.

Still gazing skywards, she folds her arms.

'DS Leyton ... or DS Jones?'

Skelgill cranes around to look at her, but she keeps her gaze fixed determinedly; a mischievous smile at the corners of her mouth.

He knows she is half-teasing him; accordingly he finds a lighter response.

'If a bull were charging at me, I'd rather be standing behind Leyton – but I can think of a few occasions when you might have it.'

'Very diplomatic.'

Now Skelgill takes the initiative; though a tremor in his voice hints at some underlying uncertainty.

'Okay – so here's one back at you. DI Smart – or DI Skelgill?'

'Are we talking dress sense?'

Her quip is immediate.

Skelgill's features darken.

'Can we start with common sense?'

'Then it's no contest.'

Skelgill shakes his head.

'If you'd picked me for dress sense, I'd know you're winding me up.'

DS Jones rolls over onto her front and rises nimbly. She pirouettes and takes couple of paces to the edge of the escarpment.

'Dress sense can be acquired. Being a dickhead is for life.'

Skelgill – a little stunned by her colourful description – stares past her, down through the corrie, to the distant tail of Haweswater, some two thousand feet below their perch, and over a mile thence. Slowly, his eyes trace the line of the ridge back up from the lake, and his gaze comes to rest upon Blea Water Tarn. He is ninety-nine percent certain he is on the right side of his colleague's answer – but it is in his nature to harbour a small doubt.

'I always thought you reckoned Smart were –'

It is evident that he has halted mid-sentence – but not because he is stuck for words.

DS Jones turns to look at him.

'What is it, Guv?'

Skelgill's eyes have narrowed; there is a greenish gleam to the grey substrate of his irises.

'Derek Shaw.'

'Guv?'

He points, down into the corrie.

'About thirty yards above the tarn, dead centre. That's his tent. Saunders Spacepacker. You don't see many like that.'

DS Jones might not have Skelgill's instinct for the atypical but her vision lacks nothing in acuity.

'Ah. Is that him?'

'Where?'

'At about nine o'clock – at the water's edge – see, that cluster of rocks. There's someone sitting there.'

Skelgill finds the target, but does not immediately answer.

'He's not fishing – he looks like he's smoking.'

'A pipe?'

Their view, so distant and elevated, is like trying to observe from an aircraft.

'You could give him a ring.'

Skelgill's remark sounds offhand.

'Seriously?'

But now Skelgill yields to an ironic chuckle, as if he feels it would be unfair to perpetuate his little joke.

'Lass – if he's got a signal down there, I want the name of his service provider.'

She gets it. She smiles.

'Actually, you probably don't.'

'Aye.'

She waits for the humour of the exchange to dissipate.

'Guv. If he's down there now – and was in Ambleside yesterday – it seems unlikely he could have been metal-detecting at Dunmallet, don't you think?'

Skelgill looks like he never thought it was Derek Shaw in the first place. But he offers an explanation for the sake of completeness.

'There's nowt to stop him getting the bus some of the time. Seems to me he's dodging about.'

DS Jones nods reflectively.

'I suppose that's true.'

But her mind is working away – and she cannot contain herself.

'We only have his word that he went back to Ravenglass. He could have followed Dorothy Baum to Little Langdale, and then on towards Ambleside.'

'We don't even know for sure if she made it to Ambleside.'

She looks at him as though that would only support her point of view.

But Skelgill perfectly well understands the hypothesis with which she is toying. That Derek Shaw fits the profile of someone Dorothy Baum may have arranged to meet. That she has disappeared. That this might be repeating a pattern of a year ago, when the lone hiker who may be American passport holder Patricia Jackson met an inadequately explained fate between Ambleside and their present location.

He is obliged to resort to devil's advocacy. They cannot both speculate.

'Why draw attention to Dorothy Baum in the first place? And what's he doing, sticking around?'

She reflects upon his questions.

'Well – like I said before – it could be a kind of hiding in plain sight. Or perhaps he just doesn't think we've got our eye on him.'

She sees that Skelgill is not particularly moved by conjecture, when evidence would be more convincing. She shifts to an aspect that is more tangible.

'How did you get on when you visited Skelghyll Wood?' She gestures around and down into the corrie. 'Is it en route to here?'

Skelgill makes a face. Though occasionally tempted when asked for directions to use the apocryphal reply, "You can't get there from here", in the fells it is a maxim that almost never applies on foot, provided there is a willingness for some circuity. In the first place he had considered the twelve miles between Skelghyll Wood and the fox's earth to be rather too far to draw any conclusions. Here there is a similar disconnect. If from Galava at Ambleside the next stop is the summit of High Street, a route taking in Skelghyll Wood would not make sense. Unless – and it comes back to expert advice – there is some other Roman attraction he does not know of – or, just some other attraction.

'Guv?'

Delayed by the conundrum, he opts to reply to the first part of her inquiry.

'Above where she was found – it's an accident waiting to happen. A low bridge and a steep drop. Easy enough to slip in the wet, if you leaned over.' While DS Jones is absorbing his words, he adds a postscript. 'Have we looked up what the weather was doing?'

She regards him inquisitively.

'I'll find out.'

He nods. He is reminded now that he has not given much thought to his visit to the wood and the bridge over Stencher Beck. DS Leyton's distress call, his animated sergeant believing he had netted his putative nighthawker, had pulled him away – subsequently, Derek Shaw's (seemingly inadvertent) revelations had put him on the trail of Dorothy Baum. But now DS Jones diverts him from further reflection.

'Do you think we should go down and speak to him?'

Skelgill makes a sound of protest.

'How much exercise do you want?'

She rows back a little. She knows the suggestion is almost impractical. Beneath lowering skies and hints of rain they could end up returning in the dark.

'I just feel we shouldn't lose track of him.'

Skelgill gives a shrug; he seems to recognise it is a fair point, but that he is resigned to some risk.

'I don't reckon he's trying to give us the slip. Let see what Leyton comes up with.'

Nonetheless, he stares down a little anxiously into the corrie. It is true to say that Dorothy Baum and Derek Shaw could have both been in Ambleside on Saturday. But one thing is for sure, they are not together now. The Saunders might be a legendary backpacking tent, but at best it is a one-man-and-his-dog affair. In fact, when he thinks back to his last broken night in his own prized model, he is tempted to add the rider, "Cancel the dog".

He rolls forwards and springs to his feet. He collects their tin mugs and stuffs them into his rucksack.

'So, you've not climbed High Street before?'

'To the summit, you mean? No.'

Skelgill suddenly breaks into a trot.

'Race you to the trig point.'

Despite his false start, he is overhauled halfway to the finishing line – claiming the disadvantage of his burden.

DS Jones mollifies him by explaining that she sprinted for the District – and anything beyond 100m and he would leave her trailing. Skelgill is not so sure, but he plainly does not want to admit it.

Facing him, DS Jones has stopped short of the summit. And now he pushes past – it seems to cheat and win the race. But he has seen something.

On top of the surveying pillar is a tin of Kendal mint cake, identical to the one he collected at Skelghyll Wood.

'What is it, Guv?'

He displays his find.

'The act of a good Samaritan. Calories for the needy fellwalker. At this rate, I shan't have to buy any for months.'

DS Jones watches evenly as he slips the tin into his bag.
'Is this a regular thing?'
But Skelgill grins wryly and hands her the rucksack.
'Your turn. All downhill from here.'

17. LEADEN SKIES

Rattlebeck Guest House, Glenridding – 8.14 a.m., Monday 25th May

From: Professor Felix Stowe-Upland
To: Dorothy K. Baum
Subject: One last push

My dearest Dorothy, apologies for such an early missive, I expect you are tucked up in bed at the charming hamlet of Hartsop; perhaps you will wake to the gentle patter of rain upon the slates; for if the weather report that I just checked is correct you are in for a couple of days' worth, and it appears the precipitation will get heavier before it eases. With this in mind and with your enjoyment to the fore (especially since some of our time has been cruelly snatched from us by circumstances beyond our control – *in gremio deorum*), I believe we ought to travel what remains of my Roman Roamin' route together – and that we do so in the best possible conditions. To traipse through the fells in persistent rain and beneath cloud that shrouds much of their beauty is not the best way. We should feel the sun on our faces and a song in our hearts, and picnic beside babbling becks to the accompaniment of the lark; and to be free to make detours at leisure to find those minor points of historical interest that a head-down rush to escape the elements militates against. Even good conversation becomes damped, literally!

Of course, I cannot predict what today will bring. I hope to have news at the first hour of business that your generous lending of the second tranche has been successfully processed and placed in secure deposit. Thereupon the property transaction will complete its designated course, so that I may sign and seal the deal and set sail for Cumbria! Naturally, I shall keep you fully abreast of developments. In the meantime, my suggestion is that you venture no further than Glenridding – I estimate just three miles from your present location – and which, if the conditions are adverse, may be reached by public transport. There is a wide choice of accommodation, from a budget-priced bunkhouse to a rather splendid spa hotel. Glenridding itself is an ideal base for various attractions – such as boating on the lake, the climbing of Helvellyn, and – as we have previously discussed – visiting Aira Force, which is certainly something not to be missed in the prevailing climate. My suggestion, you see, is that I meet you at Glenridding – I hope by this evening – but failing that, tomorrow, and that we stay one or two nights more, to ride out the storm, so to speak.

Then, when the sun has his hat on – *faenum faciunt!* – we set off in joyful pursuit of all things Roman, with Rose Cottage beckoning on the horizon!

I shall leave off now for that one last push, to gird my loins for the day's battles with bureaucracy, to strap on the sword that is the nemesis of red tape ... and leave you to your breakfast, after which perhaps this message will find you replete.

As ever, your most humble servant and most faithful friend,
Felix.

P.S. Did you have any success in pre-ordering paintings from your good friend and companion Cathy?

Dorothy has read, bleary eyed.

Now she leans back against the soft pillows and lets her handset drop onto the eiderdown.

Despite that it is after eight she feels as though she could easily drift back to sleep.

Her first thought always with an email from Felix is to scan through, should there be something to which she must make an urgent reply. But in this case there is nothing. Indeed, not only is he right about the weather – she can hear the rain – but he has in fact been uncannily prophetic about her location.

Yesterday evening she and Cathy boarded the northbound bus advertising its final destination as Penrith. The journey began with a somewhat stomach-churning descent of the winding Kirkstone Pass, eventually levelling out to skirt the small and charming

Brothers Water (an impression promptly tarnished by Cathy, who with macabre glee informed her it was renamed in the nineteenth century after the drowning of two teenage brothers); and on into a valley bottom of narrow paddocks, entering a wooded gorge of sorts; until the sudden appearance of the very tip toe of Ullswater, one of the 'great' lakes of the district, and famed of course for Wordsworth's inspirational daffodils.

"Here's our stop, Dorothy. Chop, chop."

Cathy had declaimed in a tone of annoyance, as if in her sightseeing Dorothy was abrogating some responsibility for their progress, despite that she had no idea – and did not feel like asking – what indeed was Cathy's plan.

"Our stop" proved to be Glenridding.

It is a small settlement, at first sight in nature and appearance resembling an alpine ski village, Dorothy thought. Like many it is strung along the main thoroughfare, with shops for grocery supplies for self-caterers and campers, outdoor equipment, gift outlets and cafés and hotels advertising their bars. There is, moreover, a substantial (by Lakeland standards) public green area, with a shady parking lot and picnic benches, some beneath the trees and others upon a grassy strip beside a small but vigorous stream – Glenridding Beck – that rushes down an artificially straightened channel directly from Helvellyn, on the other side of which there is a single row of properties. At this time the rain was not yet falling, and there were plenty of fellow hikers defiantly devouring ice creams at the picnic tables.

Across the main road the airy green impression is continued by the grounds of the spa hotel that Felix has mentioned – the Ullswater Host – the magnificent old building itself set back closer to the shore of the lake.

Upon their alighting Cathy seemed for a moment perplexed – rather oddly, since she had been so definitive about this being their stop. Was she making it up as she went along?

"Fish and chips, it is."

Cathy's announcement was intoned as though they had discussed the matter, and that she endorsed Dorothy's suggestion – when in fact any conversation must have taken place entirely inside her own head. She marched away without further explanation – and led a bemused Dorothy to join a queue of holidaymakers at a catering van that was parked in the designated area. Hungry, thirsty, and too tired to object, Dorothy went along without protest – and British street food fish and chips was, after all, one of those things she has been wanting to experience. She drew the line, however, at the unappetising-looking green goo that Cathy ordered, poured over her meal, referred to as "mushy peas".

She did accept the fish-and-chip man's suggestion of "salt 'n' vinegar".

They ate at one of the picnic benches alongside Glenridding Beck. Dorothy was pleasantly surprised by the piping hot fare. Cathy must have been even more hungry than she; she wolfed down her meal in two minutes; Dorothy was glad they were not facing one another.

"They've got vacancies."

This had been Cathy's next proclamation. Wiping her mouth (not entirely satisfactorily) upon her scrunched up newspaper wrapper, she rose and, leaving Dorothy to continue eating at her more modest rate, hitched on her backpack and, rounding the stream by the bridge, strode to a property about halfway along the terrace. Certainly there was a board advertising it as a B&B ('Rattlebeck House', as it has turned out), but quite how the eagle-eyed Cathy had seen a small 'Vacancies' sign in a front window baffled Dorothy.

But before Dorothy had even finished her fish supper, Cathy was shambling back towards her, now without her backpack.

"Chop, chop, Dorothy – the woman wants her tea."

Cathy was still in a somewhat recalcitrant mood, so Dorothy rather reluctantly wrapped up her uneaten portion and deposited the parcel in a nearby litter bin; meanwhile Cathy had set off again.

Dorothy followed some distance behind. When she reached Rattlebeck House there was no sign of Cathy, but the front door was ajar so she tentatively knocked and entered. Again, in the hallway, there was no trace of Cathy or her rucksack.

But within a few moments a woman of about her own age appeared. She greeted Dorothy in a friendly and relaxed manner that betrayed no hint that she was being held back from her evening meal.

"You're the lady that's looking for a room?"

It seemed a slightly curious question – but before Dorothy could begin to respond or engage in some sort of dialogue she was led up the stairs to the top floor, and a cosy room beneath the eaves. Perhaps there was something about the small sanctuary, the respite from Cathy, the rest-inducing effect of the heavy meal, disturbed nights, the day's hard walking, and simply the accumulation of tiredness that rendered her more exhausted that she appreciated. Dorothy let the woman's kind instructions wash over her, and as soon as she was left alone undressed and got into bed. It could only have been seven-thirty p.m.

Felix's alert has woken her from the best night's sleep of her trip, rhinoceros-free.

She is, however, a little surprised that Cathy has not been to see her. That is not like Cathy.

A small thought strikes her. Perhaps Cathy has gone.

She decides, however, not to dwell on this – if she is honest, it would be a relief.

She also determines that she does not need to send an immediate reply to Felix.

She thinks about Derek, out there in his tent in the rain, beside Blea Water.

She ponders Felix's mention of the spa hotel.

But principally, to her surprise, she realises she is famished – and she can smell fried bacon.

When there is no sign of Cathy at breakfast Dorothy again wonders if she has departed. Perhaps she did not even stay here last night. But Dorothy is late – it is last orders and the other tables have been cleared – so Cathy may already have eaten.

But, no!

Here she is.

Bizarrely, it seems to Dorothy, Cathy enters, limping with the aid of a furled green umbrella she had noticed in a stand in the hallway.

'Cathy, what's wrong?'

Cathy gingerly lowers herself into the seat opposite Dorothy.
'Sciatica.'

'But what has happened? You seemed fine yesterday.'

'It comes on when I don't walk at my natural pace.'

She glowers at Dorothy and if her aim is to make her feel responsible, she succeeds. Dorothy recalls one point when Cathy had rather callously called back, "Keep up, Dorothy Dawdle". She wonders if she has been more of an impediment than she is aware. But then if Cathy has a problem with neuralgia, it surely owes much to her injurious deportment.

In typical Cathy fashion, she brushes the matter aside. Without asking she helps herself to tea and a slice of toast from the rack that has been supplied to Dorothy.

And, despite her suffering, Cathy still manages to order the Full English.

'Nothing a morning's rest won't fix.'

Cathy returns to the subject of her ailment now they have finished eating, a process that has been conducted in mutual silence. Dorothy has been unsure of her ground, and has not wanted to antagonise her companion. In Cathy's case it has seemed largely down to hunger – she has cleared her plate without pausing for breath.

'What do you have in mind, Cathy?'

'I'll lie up – get a late checkout. We'll see what the weather's like. Push on.'

She makes no reference to Dorothy's immediate wishes. Indeed, she does not seem to care about Dorothy being bored or otherwise. But why would Dorothy be surprised? Cathy behaves like a teenager yet to undergo the invisible transition from egotism to empathy.

If Felix is right about the weather – and Dorothy has no reason to doubt him – there is little immediate prospect of it brightening up. There is also Felix's suggestion of dropping anchor.

Dorothy reaches a decision.

'I think I will take a stroll around the village – I noticed a gift shop on the corner. Perhaps I can pick up some local souvenirs.'

'Fine.' Cathy is staring at her. Her fixed expression of alarm could equally well conceal contempt as it could suspicion. 'They're all a rip-off.'

*

Dorothy has got no further than the window of the corner shop when she experiences an inexplicable pang of what feels like sympathy for Cathy. Clearly, the woman is emotionally compromised, and is unable to express herself in a way that wins the esteem of others. That she may have been in pain for much of yesterday certainly explains her erratic behaviour and irascible manners; no wonder she wanted to get off the fells and onto the bus; and, to her credit, she never actually complained; she just took out her discomfort in being more than usually crochety. Dorothy reproaches herself for not asking how she was.

Now she amends her decision.

She will book both a twin room and a single room – the latter for Cathy – at the Ullswater Host Spa Hotel. She will move them, and it will be her treat. And Felix will no doubt be pleased, too – surely he was hinting that he would like to stay there.

She will spring this on Cathy – she will return from her morning jaunt and deliver the good news.

She knows that Cathy would not spend the money – even if she can afford it. But she – Dorothy – has plenty of money. And it would be the last of Kooky Cathy. One expensive night to buy her off.

Feeling only a little guilty, Dorothy crosses the road and within a minute is at reception. Five more minutes and the transaction is completed. The hotel staff seem pleased that there is to be an American guest; Dorothy accepts a tour of the spa, a glimpse at the outdoor seating areas on the lakeshore, and the restaurant, bar and public rooms. All in all, it is a satisfactory visit.

But when she emerges from the driveway and is crossing the main road, Dorothy receives a shock. She has pulled down her hat; the steady rain is still falling. The sound of a large vehicle close at hand makes her realise she did not check properly – look *right*, Dorothy! It is a bus, just like the one on which they arrived, heading in the opposite direction.

But the shock is not the proximity of the bus, another near miss – but that a little further along the road, past the gift shop, a distinctive figure, small and stout, partly concealed beneath a green umbrella, with an unmistakeable shambling gait, hurries across the road ahead of the bus.

Cathy?

The bus halts for a few seconds.

Then it indicates and pulls away.

At the stop, there is no one.

The person – *was it Cathy?* – must have boarded.

Dorothy, who has halted, resumes walking. She reaches the little junction and crosses to the gift shop and then crosses again to the bus stop. She does not quite understand why – because she does not really expect there to be some tangible essence that will confirm her fleeting impression.

She reads the sign affixed to the post. Buses here for Windermere via Kirkstone Pass.

Her first inclination is to return to Rattlebeck House – where surely she will find Cathy resting up in her room. But some deeper instinct says no – and she continues walking in the direction taken by the bus.

In less than a minute she is roused from what are not exactly thoughts – more deep mullings – when her eyes fall upon a brown tourist information sign marked "Steamers".

There is a turn to her left, towards the shore. A roadway for cars and a separate sidewalk, which Dorothy follows.

After a short distance a pierhead comes into sight. A boat is moored – a traditional steamer with a massive red angled funnel which she learns from an information board is now diesel powered but which dates from 1877. The craft circumnavigates the lake, berthing at nearby Aira Force, Pooley Bridge in the north, Howtown on the eastern shore and here at Glenridding in the south. About a dozen people have braved the rain and are above deck, waiting for departure. Dorothy enters the pavilion and buys a ticket. She is informed she should hurry if she wishes to make this service.

The pontoon is manned by a cheerful looking man in his fifties, large and white-bearded, and something of a ringer for Santa Claus in his red waterproof jacket, and black over-trousers and wellington boots. The damp boards are slippery and he extends a hand to Dorothy, which she gracefully accepts.

'Sure tha'll be alreet, love?'

It seems he harbours doubts about a single senior lady.

'Should I worry?'

He regards her with genuine concern.

'Just wouldn't want you falling overboard – folk tend to panic – drown before they can be helped.'

Dorothy returns his gaze, her expression sincere.

'I once swam across the Spree at midnight – close to the Reichstag? Under Stasi gunfire.'

There is a considerable pause.

The man slaps his thigh.

'*Ha-ha-ha-ha!* Aye – of course you did! You Yanks – you crack us up. On you go, then, love.'

Dorothy senses his eyes tracking her progress. He thinks she's batty. Undeterred, she makes her way to the prow and a young couple close up to create space for her to sit. She bows her head in thanks; they might wonder at her smile.

'The scenery is marvellous, don't you think?'

For a moment they seem surprised – perhaps by her American accent. The man casts a hand skywards.

'There's nowhere more beautiful than England on a summer's day.'

His inflexion makes clear that he is being ironic – that he refers to the inclement weather. But the girl gives him a nudge with her elbow.

'Hey – wha' aboot Scotland!'

It is clear that she hails from north of the border.

'I *only* said there's nowhere *more* beautiful.'

They see that Dorothy is paying interest to their private conflict. The man now addresses Dorothy in an informative way.

'It's more like Scotland today.'

It is plain he means the rain, and that he is further ribbing his partner.

> She rolls her eyes at Dorothy.
> Dorothy acknowledges with a raised eyebrow.
> 'It's a day for visiting waterfalls.'

*

From: Dorothy K. Baum
To: Professor Felix Stowe-Upland
Subject: Re: One last push

Dear Felix, I was about to begin with, "It is almost 2 p.m. here" – but of course it is almost 2 p.m. there, as well! Old habits die hard.

I ought to begin by crediting you with what feels like a degree of telepathy. Yesterday evening we came straight by public transport from Kirkstone Pass to Glenridding, where Cathy homed in on accommodation. I have just returned from a morning – rather damp, as you foresaw – exploring our environs. I have not attempted to scale Helvellyn (although I saw a good number of hikers setting off in that direction), past our B&B and up beside the stream that is running with ever-growing vigour from the fells.

I am assuming that the financial and legal transactions have not yet reached completion; otherwise you would by now have sent me a further message; naturally I am on tenterhooks as we near the final push, as you call it – and at least I can inform you of what plans I have made in anticipation of your arrival.

You mentioned the spa hotel – the Ullswater Host – and I am delighted to say I have acted upon this and have made us a reservation for the next two nights. It is a grand palace in such a small settlement, both traditional and modern. The views across the lake are spectacular, and the menu mouth-watering. I feel it will be a well-deserved break – in which I include myself, if you will forgive a moment's self-indulgence – as small B&Bs are not always the most relaxing places to stay; one is always under the feet of the proprietor, however welcoming they may be.

Of course, the extra luxury does not come cheap – and the

benefit of B&Bs is the excellent value they offer – but do not worry, this will be my treat.

I should say that I have also booked a room for Cathy – but for tonight only. I am hoping she will take the hint and move on gracefully next morning. Although, as I reflect upon this likelihood, I feel that the phrase "Cathy left gracefully" is an oxymoron.

She appeared at breakfast this morning in an injured state, suffering from what she described as sciatica. I got the impression that she blamed me for her condition. She was not happy with me at all. However unreasonable that may be, I do feel a little responsible for her – after all, I am party to her having accompanied me thus far. I must confess, I have a faint suspicion that she will not be in her room when I call for her to leave. She has once or twice used an expression, "Now, Dorothy, don't be taking the huff" (as if I ever would!) – but I do wonder if she has, in her own words, "taken the huff" and left me.

We will see.

Notwithstanding, Cathy or no Cathy, I am looking forward to the warmth of the spa. This morning the rain has been incessant if not torrential, and it seems to have a way of defeating one's waterproofs, however good they are. The idea of a sauna, steam room and jacuzzi is sheer bliss. Can you believe, I saw teenagers swimming in Ullswater this morning, charging in from one of the little beaches and screaming in agony as they finally took the plunge. I would imagine there is a real risk of cold shock in these mountain water temperatures, and it is essential only to bathe where the bank is gently sloping. I will restrict myself to the heated infinity pool with a view of the lake! Hopefully, you will soon be there to join me – and if you are still troubled by your bad back I am sure you will benefit from the recuperative effects of the spa.

I had better sign off before we overstay our welcome here. I will pull together my belongings and collect my muddy boots from the hallway – and perhaps Cathy from her room.

Yours in anticipation,
Dorothy.

Dorothy has hardly finished pushing her personal effects into her backpack – with less care than usual, since she will be unpacking again in just a few minutes' time – when she hears a message alert. She checks her handset. It is Felix.

From: Professor Felix Stowe-Upland
To: Dorothy K. Baum
Subject: Re: One last push

Dorothy, may I briefly trouble you to confirm the latest financial transaction from your end, at the earliest opportunity. I appreciate it will be around 8 a.m. in your home part of the United States – perhaps a little too early at this moment – but I am informed by my lawyers that the funds have not yet cleared, and perhaps there is some problem that you can untangle.
I cross my fingers!
Felix.

Dorothy has hardly had time to reflect upon this short missive when her door opens.
'Cathy!'
The woman half enters, wearing her waterproof jacket and backpack.
'Don't sound so surprised. Are we getting a shift on, Dorothy?'
Before she can reply, Cathy, seeing her mobile phone, makes a further inquiry.
'Bad news?'
Her tone suggests that she would be proved correct if it were, and that it would serve Dorothy right.
Dorothy steels herself to be polite.
'No – not at all. But something I should attend to shortly. On the contrary, I have what I hope will be good news for you. I have booked us into the Ullswater Host – the luxury spa hotel just across the way. It will be my treat – a thank you, since it may be our last night together.'
Dorothy might have guessed that Cathy's reaction would not be conventional, and that words of appreciation were unlikely to

figure.

'I've not got no bathers.'

Dorothy hauls on her backpack.

'That will not be a problem. For a start, they will supply dressing gowns. And they have a shop – they sell swimwear and goggles and suchlike. I will gladly purchase a swimsuit for you on my account.'

Dorothy can see that Cathy is processing something. She presses home the advantages of her plan.

'You're right, we should go. Check-in was from two o'clock. With all those facilities we should not waste precious time. The spa will have massage and physiotherapy, which may help alleviate your sciatica.'

Cathy turns towards the door.

'It's sorted itself.'

Dorothy shakes her head and follows her ungrateful companion, wondering why she allowed herself to imagine Cathy might respond otherwise. Although, she notes, Cathy has not actually demurred, either to her proposal or the suggestion that it will be their final night together; perhaps she is getting somewhere.

Outside, in typical fashion, Cathy has not waited for Dorothy and has set off ahead, her hood raised against the rain; but at the corner shop she halts and gazes in at the window. Dorothy comes alongside her. There are crafts – pottery, jewellery and woollen items, much of these themed to Herdwick sheep – but also paintings by local artists.

Dorothy decides to throw more mud at the great wall that is Cathy's impenetrable obduracy. The offer to purchase some of Cathy's paintings. She decides to make it seem like her idea – as though it is something personal. At the same time, it is a further chance to reiterate her understanding that they will soon part company.

'I want to remember our time together. I wondered if I could buy from you a couple of your artworks from this trip – when you finally paint them. I can give you a deposit.'

She sees that Cathy glowers. Her small, wideset eyes seem to be scanning the works on display, without dwelling upon any one.

Dorothy adjusts her offer.

'Or even the full amount. I was thinking of the waterfall in Skelghyll Wood – and perhaps Aira Force?'

Cathy turns to look at her.

'They'd be a thousand each.'

She casts a sly glance at Dorothy's belt-bag.

Despite her best efforts, Dorothy finds herself responding in a way that must give a clue to her thoughts.

'I only have US dollars, I'm afraid.' She utters a nervous laugh. 'But I guess we can agree on a fair exchange rate.'

Surely even Cathy would read into her reaction that Dorothy has baulked at the suggested price. When before their very eyes are excellent original works – priced modestly, hardly one over a hundred pounds – Cathy has the audacity to ask ten times that! And she has the distinct feeling that Cathy's output will be of the painting-by-numbers variety.

But there is a more unnerving aspect. Has Cathy suspected all along what she carries in her belt-bag? She has an avaricious streak – it shows even when they have food placed before them. Could she have sneaked a look when Dorothy's guard was down? Is part of the explanation for her ingratitude that she is jealous – that by comparison Dorothy is wealthy – that she can afford to book them into the Ullswater Host, despite that Cathy herself is the beneficiary?

Dorothy for once takes the lead and steps away from the window and looks to cross the road, remembering to check first to the right.

Unexpectedly, Cathy hurries to reach her shoulder.

She points in the direction that Dorothy had taken earlier.

'The steamer's along there. It's like a ferry. We'll catch it to Aira Force in the morning – if you want your painting. That's the next stop. Then we'll cross the lake to Howtown and get back on your Roman route. High Street.'

Not for the first time, Dorothy finds herself bamboozled.

Has Cathy completely ignored her none-too-subtle hints? It is as though she has entirely dismissed the idea that Felix will come or even that he exists. Has she convinced herself that he is just some figment of Dorothy's imagination, a story that she has invented so as not to appear alone? It seems impossible to Dorothy, but perhaps it is exactly the sort of thing that Cathy would make up – the way her mind works. And therefore she is not particularly troubled by Dorothy's perceived fantasy. She is Dorothy's companion and that is that. In a sense, this is a practical approach, if inconsiderate of Dorothy's feelings.

Dorothy walks on in silent contemplation.

Clearly, Cathy has no plans to relinquish her stewardship.

'I'll tell you what, Dorothy. If this rain keeps up, you'll be chuffed that you came this way – wait till you see the waterfall.'

18. ANGLING

Police Headquarters – 2.38 p.m., Monday 25th May

'Are you free, Guv?'

Unusually, DS Jones has found Skelgill's door closed. She has had to knock. DS Leyton looks around from his regular seat beside the filing cabinet.

Skelgill inclines his head towards DS Leyton.

'We were just about to ring you.'

There is the suggestion that DS Leyton has some news to convey.

'Oh – sure – I –'

She stands poised on the balls of her feet. She is a little breathless as if she has come in haste. There is a flush on her cheeks. She has an uncharacteristically untidy bundle that she has evidently scooped up – wallet files, loose papers, her electronic tablet and her mobile phone.

Skelgill detects her heightened vital signs.

'What is it?'

She glances at DS Leyton and then back at Skelgill.

'The FBI have got back to me – about Patricia Jackson.'

Now another jerk of the head from Skelgill. This time that she should take a seat.

She understands she has the floor.

She unloads her material on the corner of Skelgill's desk and extracts her tablet. She locates the message to which she has referred.

She looks up.

'They're taking it seriously.'

She has her colleagues' attention, and she knows not to dwell. Economically, she relays the intelligence.

'They've confirmed the ID. They managed to obtain a reliable

DNA sample. It's a match with our profile. The woman who died last May at Skelghyll Wood was definitely Patricia Carolyn Jackson. It was her passport that was in the foxhole on High Street.'

Skelgill – at the point where DS Jones has uttered the word "match" – has made a brief face of what could be described as having survived a near miss. While he has been steadfast and collected without openly committing to the hypothesis, it is a reaction revealing of the fact that they have taken a flyer, and that their entire investigation, tentative at first but gradually gathering scope, scale and momentum, has been predicated on the assumption that this was the case. Like a game of snakes and ladders, the more upwards progress they have made, the more their jeopardy has increased. Had the Skelghyll Wood body remained unidentified, and Patricia Jackson ruled out, they would slither ignominiously back to square one. Instead, the home square is just around the corner. A couple more successful throws of the dice is all it might take.

DS Leyton suspects that DS Jones has more to tell.

'When you say they're taking it seriously, what do you mean?'

She nods quickly in accord, recognising that she has not explained this point – of course the FBI would not do any differently – and so there must be some extra factor.

'Well, they haven't indicated why. But they are clearly looking into this more deeply – beyond our request. Obviously, I supplied them with an initial report, which I have been updating, including – as I mentioned –' (she pauses to glance at Skelgill) 'what we have learned about Dorothy Baum. I don't know how much they have uncovered, but they have provided one startling piece of information.'

There is a momentary delay as she looks for the specific point on her screen.

'In May last year, six days before Patricia Jackson travelled to the UK, she transferred sixty-four thousand dollars to an offshore bank account. In the British Virgin Islands.'

She looks up to see that her colleagues are wrestling with this fact and its possible implications. DS Leyton perhaps speaks for them both.

'In that case – *hah* – the sixty-four-thousand-dollar question – whose account?'

DS Jones bites at her bottom lip.

'They either don't know – or, for the moment, can't say. But they state they do not believe that she was the beneficiary. It was someone else's account. They also understand the sum represented all of her available funds.'

'Highway robbery.'

It is Skelgill who utters this phrase, and his subordinates regard him expectantly. But he does not elucidate. It seems the image came to him unencumbered by trimmings.

DS Jones refers back to her tablet.

'There's another twist. Rather ironic this one, given that they have identified Patricia Jackson. They have been unable to find a Dorothy K. Baum. And I don't mean track her down – but trace her at all. There's no evidence that she exists.'

DS Leyton shifts in his seat as if he has received a sudden jolt. He raises a hand like a school pupil requesting permission to speak.

'Ah – that's partly where I come in, Emma. You see – I took a call from Border Control. I think they were probably trying to get hold of you.' Now he pulls at his necktie and collar as though the arrangement is troubling him. 'There's no record of a Dorothy K. Baum entering the UK. Our Dorothy must have come in on a different passport.'

DS Jones nods reflectively.

'The agent who has responded to me made the same point – that if they couldn't identify a Dorothy K. Baum then it might simply be a false name.' She hesitates for a moment before continuing. 'This might seem flippant – but she pointed out that Dorothy is the main character in *The Wonderful Wizard of Oz* – and that the author's surname was Baum.'

'*Hah!*' It is another exclamation from DS Leyton. 'Funny that – I only read it to the nippers a couple of weeks ago – bedtime story. Threw a bucket of water over the Wicked Witch of the West.' He chuckles introspectively. 'Reminded me of us lot – Dorothy, Tin Man, Scarecrow, dog –'

He notices Skelgill's disapproving glare – perhaps his superior is not enamoured by the suggestion that he might be one of the motley crew.

DS Leyton waves his hands as if the action will cancel the words from the air, and rises from his seat.

'Tell you what – I'll get us some cha – canteen brew, proper mugs.'

The suggestion meets Skelgill's grudging approval.

'Biscuits!'

But perhaps the door is closed too quickly for DS Leyton to have heard the supplementary order.

DS Jones resumes her deposition.

'The FBI have passed all the details to the local sheriff in St Francisville, the place that Dorothy Baum gave to the hotel at Ravenglass as her home address.'

Skelgill plies her with a frown.

'What's to say that's not made up?'

'I know, Guv.' DS Jones puts down her tablet and absently picks up her phone and, out of habit, opens the screen. 'It might also explain why I haven't been able to find her on Facebook – oh, wait a minute.'

For a moment she reads intently.

Skelgill waits in silence.

'The imposter professor – he's sent me a message. It's about Umbria – as he promised – that Assisi is a World Heritage Site; it has a Roman amphitheatre. Some other suggested sites.' Now she looks up. 'He says he's in Cumbria cataloguing ancient monuments – look at this.'

She turns the handset and reaches across to show it to Skelgill.

He glowers at the screen.

'That's the Kirk Stone.'

'Kirk Stone?'

Skelgill inhales – but checks himself.

It strikes DS Jones that perhaps if it were DS Leyton asking this question the word 'donnat' would now be rolled out. But it is not – one other small advantage she possesses over her long-suffering male colleague.

Skelgill has a second go.

'It's an erratic near the top of Kirkstone Pass. Pointed. Its shadow looks like a church steeple. Kirk means church.'

She nods; this much she knows. But there is a more salient point; and she does not wait to be asked.

'The message was sent just under an hour ago.'

Skelgill scrutinises the image more closely.

'Does it tell you when it was taken?'

DS Jones shakes her head.

'Not without getting it as an attachment. If it was taken on a phone the EXIF data could include the date and time – and GPS coordinates.

Skelgill stares out of the window; he narrows his eyes. Above the gently undulating horizon light-to-moderate rain percolates from an aluminium sky.

'Looks like today's weather.'

'I agree, Guv.'

They ponder in silence; undoubtedly, the prospect is just a little hair-raising that the person who masquerades as Professor Felix Stowe-Upland is in the vicinity.

After biding her time, DS Jones offers a suggestion.

'Guv – I think I should bait the hook.'

The allusion wins Skelgill's attention – but it is DS Leyton that provides a response as he backs into the office bearing a small round tray carrying three mugs.

'Didn't take the Guvnor long to get you onto fishing.'

Skelgill is scowling – until his sergeant produces a handful of wrapped biscuits from a trouser pocket.

DS Jones raises her eyebrows – but not in response to Skelgill's reaction to the biscuits – nor DS Leyton's sarcasm, nor even that he has mistaken the point. She turns to Skelgill.

'Remember when I joked about your bank account?'

'It *is* a joke.'

He grins at DS Leyton, who shrugs in the way of a fellow sufferer.

But DS Jones is not swayed from her course. She stares at Skelgill until he makes eye contact.

'Surely, this is catfishing?'

211

That she has used one angling metaphor is perhaps engaging, but two is perplexing. He makes to speak but she interrupts.

'You know what it means?'

'I know what a catfish is.'

It is clear he does not – at least, not in the context that she intends.

DS Leyton leans forward, as if he may have an idea – but, again, DS Jones interjects to pre-empt any conjecture.

'It refers to impersonating someone online – hiding behind a fake identity to trick another person out of information or money – under the guise of starting a relationship. Elderly widows are the most vulnerable.'

Skelgill is looking indignant.

'Why's it called catfishing?'

DS Jones realises she does not know; despite that the expression is the talk of the internet, and uncannily apposite. But she turns the tables.

'Actually, I thought you might be able to explain that.'

Skelgill makes a disparaging grunt.

'Catfish – not my bag. They stock them in artificial lakes. Monsters. Attract specimen-baggers. Might as well shoot yowes in-bye and call yourself a hunter.'

Clearly his attitude is unfavourable towards both the disciples of the species and their methods.

DS Jones has listened with interest; she shares her assessment.

'Maybe there's something in that – easy prey.'

DS Leyton wants clarification.

'Emma – so what you're saying is, this Patricia Jackson – she could have been taken for a ride – for her money?'

DS Jones regards him evenly.

'Looked at as part of the bigger picture – everything we know – yes, I am.'

'Why not pocket the cash and leave it at that? Why kill her?'

'I don't know. Maybe she came to get it back.'

'And now you're thinking this Dorothy is his next victim?'

DS Jones glances at Skelgill – but he does not seem to object to the emerging line of discussion.

'I'd say Dorothy could be his current victim.' She raises a hand and places her palm against her breastbone. 'And that he's angling for Cumberland Lass to be his next.'

Skelgill now reacts more strongly; there is alarm in his features, and a certain proprietorial cast in his grey-green eyes.

But DS Jones is undaunted.

'Guv – he's already showing a keen interest in me – my fake profile. I would call it the early stages of grooming. Obviously – he thinks I'm in the States, like the others. I've already suggested I'm a widow with resources. To come back to my point about baiting the hook, I think I should be a little more explicit – I'm talking financially.' She holds up her mobile phone. 'Maybe I can get him to tell us exactly where he is. Perhaps I can create a sense of urgency.'

The two men each regard her with a look of barely concealed helplessness – that there are just some things that females can do, that males will never understand. For her part, if DS Jones has a plan, she does not share it; instead, she stares pensively at the screen of her phone.

Skelgill, however, raises a related query.

'What about the actual prof – Stowe-Upland. Have we found him?'

His question might be a clue to his own train of thought. It is a salutary point – a reminder that they should not put all their eggs in one basket, however unequal the eggs.

DS Jones begins to shake her head. She retrieves a printed document from her pile, several pages held together by a staple.

'DC Watson gave me an update. So far she has been unable to track him down – there's nothing advertised – but of course he's a last-minute replacement for some other speaker – so his name is not appearing in any searches. Also, it's more likely to be a closed course or tutoring than a public event. As of noon today, his wife still hadn't heard from him. But she seemed to think that's quite normal – as she'd previously suggested. She pointed out that it was only on Saturday afternoon that he upped and left.'

DS Leyton seems rather wistfully to be contemplating such matrimonial latitude. Notwithstanding, he is alert to the underlying inferences.

'Could it just be him? The fake prof is the real prof? It would simplify things.'

DS Jones glances at Skelgill. Certainly, he shows no dissent – but she is less convinced.

'Other than his untimely disappearance – or timely, depending upon how you look at it – there's nothing evidentially to link him to the investigation.' She pauses for thought, however, and compresses her lips. She breathes silently through her nose, her sculpted features statuesque. 'But – well – we can't entirely rule him out.'

She does not dwell on this point, for there is more in the report. She turns the page.

'Unfortunately, DC Watson has also drawn a blank with Dorothy Baum. She's been contacting accommodation providers in Ambleside, but nothing so far.' She addresses Skelgill. 'Like you said, Guv – that always was going to be a needle in a haystack. And, of course, she could have registered under a different name – even if she did stay in the town. If her practice is walking up and paying cash, it avoids entering credit card details.'

'What about a booking in the prof's name? They could have met up.'

Of course, DS Jones would not have overlooked such an elementary point; but she replies patiently.

'We've been checking for that, too.'

DS Leyton decides to test something of a premature conclusion.

'So, she's disappeared into thin air.'

While the search based upon the premise that Dorothy Baum stayed in Ambleside is incomplete, the note of foreboding in his voice is valid. In their business, when someone has gone missing – a lone female – it is often for a very particular reason. And the now-confirmed fate of Patricia Jackson clouds their horizon.

Indeed, DS Jones harks back to this incident.

'DC Watson has reviewed the weather records. It was during a rainy spell when Patricia Jackson met her death.' She turns her gaze from Skelgill to DS Leyton. 'We were discussing the likelihood of her fall being an accident, due to the treacherous conditions.'

DS Leyton nods – but now he shifts in his seat and rubs his hands vigorously together as if to restore some circulation.

'Like to know what I've found?'

DS Jones looks a little apologetic – having thus far largely stolen the show. She nods enthusiastically.

'Please.'

'Derek Shaw.'

DS Leyton retracts his chin into his ample jowls as though, having cited the name of a likely felon, he is about to deliver a contradictory point.

'He's pukka alright – fits his description – but he ain't turned up for work this morning – and his office at York Castle Museum can't get hold of him. They were expecting him back today.'

Skelgill does not appear fazed.

'Leyton, a chap resembling him was alive and kicking at about half-six last night.' He glances at DS Jones for confirmation. 'Looked all set to kip beside Blea Water. I haven't seen another Saunders Spacepacker in donkey's years. Does he smoke a pipe?'

DS Leyton looks suddenly chastened, as though he has missed a key point. But he understands that Skelgill is conflating two rare characteristics that would be too much of a coincidence were the identification in doubt.

'I can find out easy enough, Guv. But if he's still camping it explains why he ain't at work. Don't suppose he'd have a phone signal, either.'

DS Leyton reaches for his mug, and takes a gulp – and then suddenly chokes, only just managing to replace the mug on the filing cabinet before he spills tea in a violent fit of coughing. DS Jones is out of her seat, preparing to slap him between the shoulder blades – but he makes a partial recovery, holding up his hands to wave her away, that assistance is unnecessary.

'I'm alright –' He wheezes the words. 'Thanks, girl.'

Skelgill seems largely entertained by the small cameo.

'I've told you before, Leyton – about thinking and speaking at the same time.'

215

'Yeah – very good, Guv – and there's me about to make my big revelation.'

Skelgill flaps a cursory hand.

'What's stopping you?'

'Right, Guv.' He glances at DS Jones, and then back at Skelgill. He clears his throat. 'Here's the thing. Derek Shaw was once charged with culpable homicide and assault to severe injury.'

He pauses to let his words sink in.

'In Scotland?'

It is Skelgill that recognises the Scots legal terms for manslaughter and grievous bodily harm, respectively.

'That's right, Guv. St Andrews, it was. He was nineteen at the time. Unanimous acquittal on the homicide and found not proven on the assault.' DS Leyton gives a little shake of his head, introspectively. 'There's that 'not proven' verdict again.'

But DS Jones wants to get to the heart of the matter.

'Who was the victim?'

Now DS Leyton inhales and releases the breath, vibrating his malleable lips in a gesture of frustration.

'Would you believe the Police Scotland computer's only gone and crashed. I don't know why they have to have their own.'

Skelgill makes a face that suggests he knows exactly why – but he does not elaborate.

DS Leyton continues.

'What I've got, that's just the top line from the National Crime Agency's database.'

Now Skelgill has a query.

'Any form since?'

DS Leyton shakes his head. He looks perhaps a tad disappointed.

'Not a sausage, Guv. Not even a speeding ticket. All the same, it's not every day you meet a geezer who's been up before the beak for an alleged killing. I've submitted a request for a detailed file report to be sent to me as soon as.'

This seems to be the end of the information exchange, and both DS Leyton and DS Jones regard Skelgill interrogatively, a small committee looking to their chairman for guidance, now that he has heard out their resolutions.

Holding his tea Skelgill rises to face the map pinned up behind his desk. By necessity, in covering the entire county of Cumbria, it lacks the detail of the large-scale Ordnance Survey maps which are his preferred reading, but the underlying features are all there. His eyes trace the pale blue ribbon that is Ullswater, jinking down between the massifs of Helvellyn to the west and High Street to the east. It is a while since he fished Ullswater; there are decent brownies to be had at this time of year, and always plenty of boats for hire at Glenridding. Then there is his latest twist on the traditional Peter Ross that he has been tying lately; as yet to break its duck.

He drinks, tipping back his head and emptying his mug.

'Leyton, I reckon you'd better find Derek Shaw. Jones – stick some maggots on that hook.'

19. FALLING

Ullswater – 10.12 a.m., Tuesday 26th May

'I can hear rain.'
'Aye, it's stotting down.'
'What are you doing, Guv?'
'The dog-walker's sick.'
'I see.'

What DS Jones cannot see is that Skelgill is in a boat, and has been so since considerably earlier. However, knowing him as she does, there would be a clue in his oblique reply. Moreover, that the rain is sufficiently audible to be picked up by the microphone of his mobile phone is a combination of its falling upon the becalmed lake surface and a tarpaulin stretched over the bow, beneath which Cleopatra the Bullboxer is curled up in a plastic crate (to which extent Skelgill can claim his doggy day-care role). That he is not in his own craft means he lacks his umbrella-holder contraption, and is instead bedecked in waterproofs – Tilley hat, Barbour jacket, waders; an impermeable but restrictive exoskeleton that has brought to his mind some hybrid of the Scarecrow and the Tin Man.

'Best time.'

His tone is decidedly defensive; he seems to have answered a charge she has not made.

'What's that?'

'Best time to come out – everyone else is indoors. Get the place to yourself.'

DS Jones murmurs agreement. But she has a more pressing point, and she drops any further pretence at tact.

'That aside – the fake professor has replied.'

'Aye.' Now he sounds like he is not fully paying attention.

'I'm saying I think I got a bite.'

'Me … too …'

He makes a small but exasperated expiration of breath.

'Pardon, Guv?'

'No – nowt – go on.'

DS Jones pauses for a moment – if she were with him she would be moving to make eye contact.

'In my message to him last night I said that I had to make an investment decision – the chance of buying a property 'here' in the States, from a distant relative. And that, if so, it might mean I couldn't travel to Europe until the autumn, or possibly next year. He replied that he's just developing a new guided route through Cumbria. He's calling it Roman Roamin'. He wants to give it a dry run before he fully advertises it – and has asked if I'd like to be a guinea pig. He wants to start in the next couple of weeks. He's even offered to reimburse me for my flights and pay for accommodation.'

'*Roman Roamin'?*'

The title seems to DS Jones to be the most trivial aspect of the response that she has succeeded in flushing out; but she understands that Skelgill has homed in on it as a way of buying time, to arrest some inner-headlong rush to a rash conclusion.

'I know – strangely twee – but there you are.'

All the time, Skelgill's eyes are scanning for a surface movement that is not rain-induced, a muscular swirl or an unnatural bulge; but it is second nature, and he can fish and think at the same time.

DS Jones has more to add.

'He's sent another photograph. I think it could be near live. It came through about a minute ago. He says it's a view of High Street – he explains about it being a Roman route – obviously, what we know.'

'Any identifying features?'

She gives a small hiss of frustration.

'To be honest, Guv – I don't even know if it is High Street. There's a long fellside with the top in cloud, and water in the foreground. I thought if I sent it, you might be able to identify the place – and, more to the point the angle from which it's been taken.'

Skelgill scowls at his handset.

'I've got no data signal.' He harrumphs. 'Miracle I've got any signal in this weather.'

DS Jones is thinking it is a miracle that he answered.

She inhales, presaging a suggestion.

'Where are you? I could just come and meet you.'

Skelgill is staring at the montane horizon. It is just discernible through the veil of the rain, a pale charcoal line drawn by the cloud base.

It takes him a moment to reply.

'I'll see you in half an hour. Glenridding, by the beck – there's picnic benches. Park beside the burger van.'

Skelgill has correctly assumed that his colleague is at her desk, and has made calculations accordingly. That he has now revealed his location seems slightly to trouble him, despite that DS Jones has long shed any illusions about where she might find Skelgill on duty. Afloat on Ullswater is not a regular place; then he is not a regular police officer.

Rather brusquely, he ends the call. But to keep his half of the bargain he needs to get a move on.

He boats his rod and turns the craft.

He rows fast and hard.

The traditional long wooden Lakeland boat cuts easily through the water, unlike his own more conventional rowing boat, which sacrifices rapidity for practicality.

He hears the throb of an engine. Across his right shoulder he glimpses the steamer.

He pulls to port, to take the wash head on.

As they cross, he gets a view of the larger boat; he contemplates the unfortunate tourists – he can just discern faces at the misted windows of the main cabin.

Ullswater at its best can bring a rush of emotion, a lump in throat, speechlessness, a tearing of the eyes – even for a battle-hardened old salt like him.

Any tears today are of the rain-induced variety.

Glenridding car park – 10.42 a.m.

A louder tapping on the window alerts Skelgill to more than just raindrops wishing to penetrate the shell of his car.

He reaches across to open the passenger door for DS Jones; his shooting brake, if it ever had central locking, does not now boast a functioning version.

"One less thing to go wrong," would be Skelgill's rejoinder.

His colleague drops quickly into the seat; opaque beads of water stream from her cagoule like a cascade of pearls suddenly shaken loose from a necklace.

For her part, she is glad not to have found him seated at one of the nearby picnic tables.

She exhales in relief, directing the expelled air to blow a drip from the tip of her nose.

Cleopatra, curled on a blanket on the back seat, opens an eye and beats out a welcome with her tail.

There is a clearing of a throat – and DS Jones realises that Skelgill is on a call; his phone is set to speaker in its cradle. It explains that he has not greeted her.

She recognises the voice as belonging to Professor Jim Hartley.

'Yes – as I was saying, Daniel – your little inquiry about Stowe-Upland – reminded me of that committee we served on. I decided I'd like to re-read a paper I'd submitted on the pre-Norman rural framework' (he gives a self-deprecating "ahem" here, acknowledging the obscure topic) 'and I came across a pamphlet he authored that struck a chord. I had completely forgotten he'd done some research up in our neck of the woods – I even put him up for a couple of nights. His work is entitled, *High Street – A Road To Nowhere*. He was arguing against its Roman provenance. I remember now putting up a token defence – it wasn't my specialism, of course. But I couldn't have that without some kind of a fight. It would be like me going down there and proclaiming that York Minster's not medieval after all, and that Queen Victoria had it built in the Gothic style.'

He laughs; it sounds like the notion appeals to him.

Skelgill makes an accommodating murmur of agreement.

'Anyway – I have the pamphlet here, if it's any use to you. And it's the least I can do in return, if you're sure about those flies? Four Ullswater brownies for three pounds, you say. I'm both envious and delighted for you, Daniel.'

'I was well taught, Jim.' Skelgill glances a little sheepishly at DS Jones. 'I'll drop off a box over the weekend, if not before.'

'Splendid. I shall look forward to seeing them. The "Bloody Peter Ross" has a killer ring to it!'

Skelgill raises his eyebrows – but he contrives to end the call, and does so successfully, without introducing the presence of DS Jones.

He must think her expression is censorious.

'Catch and release. Barbless hooks.' In support of his protest he lifts his Tilley hat from the dashboard and points to a small hand-tied fly hooked into the crown.

Unlike, say, a golfer, who might return from a round at any point on the emotional spectrum, from cloud nine to black as thunder (and perhaps more often the latter), DS Jones generally finds Skelgill in a predictable mood after fishing, calm and phlegmatic. It would appear that he considers the activity a success in its own right, irrespective of the outcome.

Nonetheless, she steers away from any suggestion that he ought to explain his actions.

'I take it you phoned Professor Hartley – he's not suddenly on our case?'

Skelgill shakes his head.

'I rang about dropping off some of these flies – now I know they work.' He gestures at his handset in its cradle. 'That were a complete coincidence.'

They sit in silence for a moment.

DS Jones can tell that the professor's intervention has come as – to keep the theme – a small fly in the ointment. She iterates her thoughts.

'Professor Stowe-Upland didn't think to mention it to us when we met him. It's not as though we didn't make clear our specific interest in Roman Cumbria.'

'Aye.'

The 'fly' is not one that can easily be picked out and discarded. But neither is it material to their immediate quandary. And DS Jones has a more tangible prospect at hand. She pulls her mobile phone from the inside map pocket of her jacket. She manipulates the image on the screen.

'Speaking of effective baits – the fake professor's latest photo.'

Skelgill takes the handset. He glances at it, and then switches on the ignition, and activates the fan and the wipers. His car is facing a low wall and pointing due east, and now he compares the small image with the actual cloud-shrouded backdrop. His features harden.

'We're more or less on the same bearing. I reckon this is taken from Glenridding pier.'

He hands back the phone and selects reverse with a regulation crunch.

'No need to strap in.'

He casts a somewhat longing look back at the catering van.

It takes under a minute to drive the short distance to the lakeside.

The rain is unrelenting; the generous parking area largely empty. Although there is a tourist coach.

There is no sign of the steamer.

Indeed, there seems to be no one about – until a movement catches Skelgill's eye.

Squashed into a narrow sentry box that guards the entrance to the main landing stage is a large bearded man in a red cagoule. He sits, doubled up, leaning over a soggy-looking copy of The Sun.

Skelgill has shed his restrictive outer fishing garb; now he rolls out another of his local words for heavy rain, "hoying" (accompanied by a less printable muttered adverb). To DS Jones's ear, this means it has gone up a notch from just plain "stotting". He reaches into the back for a lightweight waterproof that matches DS Jones's own black.

'Looks like he's our man.'

Cleopatra has already divined Skelgill's intentions, and is on her feet, champing at the bit. Skelgill loops a strand of baler twine through her collar, and she scrambles between the front seats lest he have a change of heart.

The dog seems to know whom is their object, and pulls ahead, straining at the leash.

The pier attendant eyes her with some consternation.

Indeed, the approaching trio must be hard to read: a fierce-looking dog; a rather fierce-looking man; a rather attractive younger woman.

Skelgill pre-empts at least one of his concerns.

'It's alreet – she's daft as a brush.'

The man makes an effort to stroke the dog – although he seems to be virtually jammed into his cubicle, and Skelgill keeps the twine taut, should his charge get any ideas about one of her trademark lunges. The man seems good natured, and perhaps Skelgill's local accent has put him at ease.

'Thou've missed t' boat, I'm afraid. We've only got the one running at the moment – it's quiet this time of day – and t' weather don't help any.'

Skelgill glances at DS Jones; she produces the necessary identification – but it is Skelgill that takes up their inquiry.

'It's a passenger, we're trying to find. An elderly woman, American. Possibly travelling alone.'

The man's keen dark eyes flash from one to the other of the detectives.

'Oh, aye? I reckon I might have seen her. She got the last sailing. I remember her because she took a trip yesterday, an' all. She wears one of those cowboy hats. Bit of a comedian, with it.'

The detectives exchange glances. Skelgill continues.

'Was she on her own?'

The man rubs pensively at his beard.

'Aye – yesterday. And I reckon today – she were a bit of a straggler – she made some joke about being trapped in the "restroom", as the Americans call it.' He grins shrewdly. 'Mind – you don't want to be caught short on board, right enough – there's a netty, but it's not a pleasant place.'

Skelgill looks like this is not an issue that would greatly trouble him.

'When did the boat leave?'

The attendant hesitates for a moment – his gaze dwells upon DS Jones, for no apparent reason; other than it is not unusual for males to be drawn by her striking looks.

'It were 10.15.' He seems to understand they will want more information. 'It'll not be back while 12.30. It's a scenic cruise, takes a bit longer than the regular sailing. Calls at Aira Force at 10.50.' He pulls at his sleeve to reveal a wristwatch. 'Few minutes time. Then Howtown at 11.15, Pooley Bridge at 11.40. Not everyone stays on, mind. Folk might get off to explore – there's some as use it as transport – crossing the lake – or saves you hiking the length of the lake. She had an open ticket – that I do know. She could come back on the same boat, or one later.'

Skelgill is listening carefully; he has always thought of the Ullswater steamers as pleasure boats, but in their own way – as the man points out – they double as a form of public transport. He has a question that may qualify this aspect.

'Did she have a full-size backpack?'

The man begins to shake his head, although it seems to be an act of racking his brains.

'Not as I recall. In fact – now you say it, she's got one of them – like, bum-bags, they call 'em. She was fiddling to fasten it up as she went aboard.' Now he muses over the image. 'I suppose it's tricky for a lady – using the loo, like.'

Skelgill moves on.

'Were there many other passengers?'

The man shakes his head.

'About thirty, I'd say. A quarter capacity.'

'Did you notice if there were any single males?'

The man looks a little troubled by the question; he puffs out his cheeks, as though this is a severe test of his powers of observation.

'You've picked a bad day. You see – folk were waiting int' pavilion for t' boat to arrive – then they came out in a line and got on as fast as they could – most of them went straight below deck.' He makes a guilty face and casts a glance out at the skies. 'I can't say I were being too pernickety, either.' He pats the breast of his waterproof jacket. 'I've got the day to survive. To keep dry.' He sighs, and then adds a rider. 'But to answer your question – there were a number of chaps, stands to reason – but I honestly couldn't say how they were configured. You never know these days, do you?'

When Skelgill does not immediately reply, DS Jones chips in.

'Can we contact the boat?'

The man makes a face as though he does not want to purvey more unsatisfactory news.

'You'd be best to ask Jean – at t' ticket desk.' He inclines his head in the direction of the pavilion.

It seems that this is as much as they can expect from him.

DS Jones indicates to Skelgill that she will inquire inside. They thank the man. Skelgill informs him that the rain is due to ease off around midday, although he does not appear convinced. Skelgill pulls back his hood, as if to reinforce his point. The man seems suddenly animated.

'Didn't thou row past, a while back?'

'I did, aye.'

'That's some lick thou were gaan.'

Skelgill grins.

'You should see me when I'm proper clemmed.'

The man chuckles.

'The café opens at eleven.'

It appears he means inside the pavilion.

'Don't tempt us, marra.'

Skelgill leads Cleopatra back to the car. Now she is desperate to get in; clearly they are departing, and she does not want to miss the action. DS Jones diverts to the booking office.

As she returns a couple of minutes later, Skelgill sees that she is trying to make a call – but without success, it appears. Once inside, she elaborates.

'They're waiting for their two-way radio to be fixed – apparently it hasn't worked this season. I've got the skipper's mobile number, but it's diverting. Must be the weather. However – a woman with an American accent bought a full open ticket, and no other.'

'Dorothy K. Baum, we presume.'

'Perhaps we should wait here, Guv? If she didn't have her luggage, it's probable that she'll come back – that she's still based in Glenridding. It looks like she's exploring the area, taking different stops and walks. At least we know she's currently in one piece.'

Skelgill rakes the fingers of both hands through his damp hair.

'She might be in one piece. But the fake prof was here, too.'

He scowls, and checks the time on the console.

'I don't want to go round the houses. But we can't sit here for the thick end of two hours.'

DS Jones grins wryly. He seems to be waiting for her cue. After a suitable hiatus, she obliges.

'There's always that burger van.'

Aira Force visitor attraction – 10.53 a.m.

Dorothy wonders if she can trust what Cathy has said.

Cathy's sciatica has returned, and she is perhaps in more pain than she is prepared to admit.

She has told Dorothy to go ahead, right from landing. She wants to take a couple of photos further round the shoreline – where Aira Beck runs into Ullswater – something about the gravel beds that give the stream its name.

But is she using her photography as excuse not to come at all?

They were the only ones to disembark. Now Dorothy thinks she must have given the impression that she was apprehensive. Cathy had rather scornfully said that she needn't worry – that there would be no one to watch her. As if Cathy thought Dorothy would be embarrassed by other walkers observing her slow progress on the climb to the waterfall.

But Cathy had also berated those absent visitors – scornful of their fair-weather attitude, that they didn't know what they were missing. And she had hobbled away, signing off with a disparaging: "Chop, chop, Dorothy – I'll soon catch you up."

The footpath from the pier meets the lakeside road at a bus stop. On the opposite side of the road is another bus stop, and an expanse of short grass beneath oaks, beyond which – behind a wall

– is the parking area; indicated by a brown tourist information sign that states tautologically, "Aira Force Waterfall".

Dorothy crosses the road and follows the path to the walkers' entrance. To her left, through the trees, a small lime-green tent catches her eye – but after the slightest hesitation she presses on. Though she thinks about what it would be like in all this rain. And whether the camper is dozing inside; she feels a nostalgia for the cosy drum of rain upon canvas. Now it beats out a tattoo on her hat. She recalls the words of the man at Carlisle railway station – that last year it only rained twice in Cumbria.

She smiles, ruefully. Much water has flowed under the bridge since she redeemed her tickets at left luggage.

And now she has a sudden sense of having forgotten something – but she is reminded that her pack is back at the hotel. She feels strange without it. She pats her belt-bag. It is secure, if a little unwieldy with her present attire. If anything, the outdoor gear is what will encumber her, not her lack of fitness or physical alacrity. Thanks to the rejuvenating spa she is well recovered – the aches and pains of the past week have been soothed away.

She passes through the gate into the car park. As Cathy had forecast it is largely deserted. There is hardly anyone here – despite that the falls must be at their best. It has now been raining continuously since Sunday evening.

She notices a log cabin visitor centre – it is gloomy, beneath the trees and in such cloudy conditions, and there are lights on inside and she can see some movement. But she decides she can come back to that. Better, given Cathy's mood, to make some progress.

A signboard shows a circular route, up one side of Aira Beck and down the other.

It says the loop takes about an hour, although these things are often conservative – designed for the likes of her!

Dorothy chooses to stay on the near bank, the west – presumably the most popular route. In fact, she does not see the alternative – perhaps they prefer to have visitors rotating in a one-way system at busy times. This is certainly not one of them.

The ascent at first is gradual, the ancient trees widely spaced and the ground beneath well-trodden, giving a cathedral-like feel, mystical and otherworldly.

But soon the gradient increases and the woodland closes in on the path, which begins to enter a gill, so that not only is there an incline as she moves forward, but also a slope from left to right.

The path winds and zigzags, crossing exposed tree roots and rocks, and puddles and rivulets. The persistent rain is, to a degree, intercepted by the canopy, but only to the extent that larger drops accumulate on the leaves and boughs and fall as little wetting bomblets.

There are the occasional strains of subdued birdsong; of species alien to Dorothy. Otherwise the sounds are of water – the pattering of the rain, above and all around, and occasional rushes of Aira Beck, somewhere down to her right.

As the path steepens Dorothy is glad that she is not doing this en route – although she supposes heavy packs can be deposited at the visitor centre and collected on the way back. She is reminded that Cathy's gear is also at the hotel. That has been a little awkward. It had been her hope that Cathy would take the hint, and pack and come with her rucksack, meaning to go on alone and leave Dorothy to return and await the arrival of Felix. But she has not managed to broach the subject: that this is where they go their separate ways. Cathy could stay on – but Dorothy is even more certain than before that she would not pay for the hotel out of her own pocket.

She had behaved rudely to other guests and staff, not only apparently ignorant of procedures and protocols, but also lacking in basic manners. As far as she could, Dorothy had maintained her distance; she did not want to be blamed for bringing her along, which of course she had done. Cathy had greedily gorged an expensive dinner, whilst unappreciative and complaining about the unfamiliar cuisine, and all the time drinking liberally from pricey bottles of wine intended to be savoured. Dorothy had opted for an early night. She had used the excuse of dehydration from the sauna, and thus a headache, and had retired leaving Cathy presumably to finish off the wine and with carte blanche to order liqueurs.

She had bragged to Dorothy at breakfast how she had taken a week's worth of toiletries from a cleaner's trolley on the landing outside her room; and she had made three visits to the hot buffet, saying, "Got to get your money's worth, Dorothy". Whose money's worth?

It would have helped if she had received a definitive message from Felix. Indeed, had he arrived and Cathy been confronted by the couple, it would have cast into sharp contrast her status as the odd one out. Although would Cathy even notice? But Felix's rather short and – if she is being honest with herself – terse, impatient and even a little bad-tempered missive concentrated upon the fact that her second tranche of funds had still not been cleared by close of business yesterday (despite that, as she had pointed out in her short reply, Louisiana banks are six hours behind, and there was still plenty of time). Felix had said his hands were tied. He hopes it will be sorted this morning.

There has been no word from him since yesterday evening. Dorothy has taken it upon herself to tell him that she was visiting Aira Force with Cathy. She did not wish to antagonise him any more than necessary. She has done what she needed to do, for the time being.

So she and Cathy will be returning to the hotel later. Subject to timings, they may be able to pick up a passing steamer. Or there is the bus – that convenient stop outside the car park. Come to that, they can walk. It is under three miles and there is a footpath along the lakeshore, part of the circumnavigational Ullswater Way.

Dorothy has neither caught nor crossed paths with anyone. She supposes most walkers would take the route in the same direction as she, so it would only be if she overtook (unlikely) or was overtaken (also unlikely, in that nobody seems to be around).

She hears a melancholy cry – a plaintive mewing – she believes it to be a bird of prey, lamenting its lot.

She wonders if Cathy will catch her up.

Glenridding car park – 10.55 a.m.

Within fifteen minutes of having left, Skelgill and DS Jones are parked once again at what Skelgill referred to as the burger van. It advertises its fare as fish and chips, but such is not a morning meal and now the aroma of frying bacon wafts through a small gap in Skelgill's lowered window.

There is a modest line of determined, evidently hungry, would-be patrons.

There is no shelter from the rain.

With time to spare, there is some attraction in waiting for the queue to dwindle.

Neither of them having volunteered, it is DS Jones that makes the first move.

'What will you have, Guv?'

But it might be a feint. Her wording does not commit her to an offer to brave the elements.

'Bacon roll.'

'Not bacon and sausage?'

There is the suggestion that she is inviting him to consume one of each; perhaps he suspects mischief at play.

'What, together?'

DS Jones chuckles.

'What sauce would you pick, then?'

Skelgill is genuinely stymied. He is unable to answer. While he is pondering, a group of four hikers join the queue and the lines in his brow deepen.

Then DS Leyton's ringtone intervenes.

Skelgill answers on speaker.

'Guv – I'd put out an alert in the Ullswater area – usual thing – visitor centres, farms with listed ancient monuments, castles and stately homes. We've had a report of a tent matching that geezer Shaw's – what do you call it, a Flycatcher?'

'Spacepacker.'

'Yeah – that was it.'

'Where?'

'Aira Force – is that how you say it? Between the bus stop and the car park, apparently.'

Skelgill takes a moment to decide what he thinks.

'Bit of an odd place. When was this?'

'I'm literally just off the blower from HQ. I thought I'd go down. I'm actually at Pooley Bridge already – I wanted to interview the woman who'd seen him at the weekend – but she ain't turned up.'

It seems DS Leyton has the bit between his teeth as far as Derek Shaw is concerned.

'Leyton – we'll meet you there in ten minutes.'

Aira Beck gill – 11.04 a.m.

Dorothy has made steady progress for the last fifteen minutes or so. If it is an hour's round trip, she estimates she must be about halfway up. There are small painted wooden arrows here and there, but no indication of distance covered.

She pauses at a view down into the wooded gill. The trees seem to be straining, competing for light, their boughs draped with mosses and other plants of the damp and shade, little nature reserves in their own right.

Dorothy is breathing heavily. It is an energy-sapping climb. The rocks and roots demand an uneven stride pattern. She is becoming hot and uncomfortable. Condensation is forming inside her waterproofs – she might almost question their worth in these conditions. In her heyday she would have bounded up in sportswear, and plunged into the lake afterwards – or perhaps found a waterfall to luxuriate beneath.

The physical demands of her ascent have rather militated against enjoying the surroundings – or even inward contemplation of her predicament.

Indeed, she wonders what, if anything, she has been thinking about.

What is for sure – and Cathy was right – there seems to be no one else here, no one to pity her brave efforts.

But more than once she has heard sounds she has not quite been able to place. Is it her own breathing and heartbeat, echoes of her own footfalls, splashes she makes in puddles and rivulets, disturbed birds – or even animals? Could there be sheep in the undergrowth?

Now that she has paused there are none of these noises – just the general background susurration of rain upon the canopy, drippings on the leaf litter, the tumbling beck below, somewhere out of sight.

But she does have a sense of being followed.

She is reminded of Cathy's black panther.

For a country with no large wild animals she has been dogged by fantastic beasts!

And there goes that mewing again.

She smiles grimly to herself.

Chop, chop, Dorothy.

Aira Force visitor attraction – 11.05 a.m.

Skelgill and DS Jones are first to arrive.

Skelgill immediately spies the tent – and, yes, it is the now-familiar lime-green Saunders Spacepacker – but he passes and slews into the car park entrance just past the spot.

'It's quiet here, Guv.'

Skelgill selects an empty bay close to the wall on their left.

'I'll have a deek – wait here. Keep your eyes peeled.'

For a moment DS Jones thinks he refers to the visitor centre – but as she watches he rounds the car and scales the wall. He intends to inspect the tent.

Quite soon the windows become fogged, and DS Jones turns to her mobile phone for a means of distraction; Skelgill is taking longer than she has anticipated. Perhaps he has found Derek Shaw hunkering down in his tent.

He causes her to jump when finally he returns. He must have gone around and used the vehicular entrance, for he comes from the rear, and even Cleopatra has not detected his approach. He yanks open the door and drops heavily into his seat.

'It's his tent, alreet.' The statement tells her there is no occupant. 'I recognise the rucksack. His metal detector's in there, as well.'

Skelgill hesitates to draw any conclusions from his findings.

'He could be in the visitor centre, Guv? It says there's a small café.'

Skelgill looks doubtful. The report received by DS Leyton is only of the tent, not its owner.

'Is it open?'

DS Jones holds up her phone.

'I don't know, but I've got onto their Wi-Fi – I read about the café on the log-in page.'

Skelgill shows only a vague interest; it is apparent to his colleague that he would rather be in one mode or the other; indecision does not sit easily with him; his preferred alternative is action – without having to think too hard about each move. Now he is becoming increasingly frustrated by their stop-start morning.

She explains what she has been doing.

'I was thinking that if I searched Facebook for "Cumbrian Roman trips" – that sort of thing – maybe someone will have posted something. If he's been doing this for a while. You know?'

He sniffs an agreement and wipes a drip from his nose with the sleeve of his jacket.

Then he looks at his wristwatch.

'What's keeping Leyton?'

He folds his arms and then unfolds them and grabs the steering wheel. He turns it a little in each direction repeatedly, as if he is checking the degree of play.

DS Jones has resumed her internet browsing.

Skelgill stares ahead; he might almost be imagining he is driving, picturing a road ahead in the opaque blur of rain and condensation.

DS Jones works her way through what might be an endless series of posts; occasionally there are sound effects as she clicks on a video clip.

Skelgill suddenly reacts like he has received a small electric shock.

His knuckles are white on the steering wheel.

'What's that?'

His voice is strained, his words terse.

DS Jones regards him with some alarm – the depth of his reaction is unmistakeable.

'Oh – er – it's a video of what seems to be a school trip – in May last year at Hardknott Pass Fort. The kids are all lined up on top of a wall. Do you want to see?'

'Play it again.'

'Sure.' She taps the screen. 'Hold on, it's just buffering.'

She reaches across and turns the handset so that Skelgill might better see – but instead he assumes a most peculiar pose, leaning forwards and pinching his eyes closed with the fingers of both hands. He looks pained, as if fighting a sudden migraine.

He remains motionless – and unseeing – as the video plays.

Before it finishes he starts getting out of the car.

In a flurry of limbs, Cleopatra scrambles after him; she knows something.

'Guv – what –?'

Skelgill ducks back in.

'Bring Leyton – the second he comes.'

He slams the door.

Then he begins to run.

DS Jones has to open her door and half hang out.

'Guv! Where to?'

Skelgill shouts a reply without looking back.

'The waterfall!'

Then abruptly he stops and rotates on his heel.

'Send Leyton up the east side of the beck. Tell him to radio for back-up.'

He turns and runs again.

The dog trots easily ahead; is this about to be the most fun she has had all day?

Aira Force – 11.29 a.m.

When Dorothy reaches her destination, she is relieved to be there first, to be alone.

The path follows the narrow, arched bridge, built in stone in the manner of an ancient packhorse bridge, although she has read this was constructed during the Victorian era, when the Lake District experienced its first mini-tourist boom, as those made wealthy by the Industrial Revolution began to spread their wings, and railways like ground ivy sent their tentacles creeping throughout Great Britain.

There is no tourist boom today.

Dorothy crosses the bridge; its continuation marks the start of the return path on the east side of Aira Beck. There is a natural rocky shelf that juts out over the waterfall, a better spot in fact for viewing, bordered by a single waist-high cast-iron railing – also antiquated, though it looks solid enough. Underfoot, the wet rock is slippery; it would be a dangerous spot were it not for the fence.

Here there is mist in the air, not the sort of condensation, of cloud, but of kinetic energy, of the pounding waterfall that like a great continuous piston makes its own steam, that rises from the plunge pool.

Dorothy is panting, though she cannot hear her own breathing, such is the noise.

She approaches the rail; she is uncomfortably hot and sweaty and she loosens her jacket and her belt-bag, and hitches up her damp hiking pants beneath her waterproof leggings. There is a metallic clink as she leans over the rail.

Is it worth all this?

The sight of the stream in spate, surging down into the black-sided chasm is dizzying, and seems to amplify the roar; it is literally deafening, all-enveloping, it makes her want to yield to the fatigue of the ascent, of the past week, of anxiety and doubt, strangeness and loneliness; to lean, to overbalance, to be gently drawn into that column of white water, its magnetic pull irresistible and final.

And then she feels the push.

At last.

20. LIFE FORCE

Aira Force – 11.30 a.m., Tuesday 26th May

Skelgill's lungs are bursting.
His heart is pounding.
He can barely think. All available oxygen is being diverted to the muscles.

But he knows the pieces have fallen into place.

The full picture, he'll recognise when he sees it.

And he has wits enough to marvel at the dog. What physiology has nature endowed upon these creatures that they can run uphill with impunity? He has appreciated it since boyhood, out on the fells, at the lambing gather with pal Jud Hope, accompanied by cur dogs that could range hither and thither, one minute far below them, foraging in a deep gill, the next silhouettes sprinting along the skyline, returning with hardly a pant, ready to go again.

Even Cleopatra, no Greyhound, possesses this quality. Moreover, rather like DS Leyton, she is good in a fight. And she would be loyal to the death.

Not that these eventualities loom for Skelgill; his only primitive urge is to get there – and even 'there' is not entirely clear – but instinct and subconscious have coalesced, a Big Bang in microcosm – and the blast has impelled him from the car park to – now – within striking distance of Aira Force.

He reaches the bridge.

Nobody.

But the dog knows otherwise.

She accelerates, out of sight, round and down.

Skelgill, slip-sliding, skids after her.

Then he sees it.

A hooded figure, a person possessed.

Stretching high, a rock raised over their head.

Lips twisted, spitting words of malice.

'Stop! Police!'

Skelgill might as well shout at passing lorries from the bridge over the M6 at junction forty. His entreaty is subsumed by the roar of the waterfall.

But the dog hears him.

No mention of Cleopatra.

And she is nearer, and faster, than Skelgill.

Death, too, is close at hand.

Fight it is.

The dog springs.

And then – a double-sound, that even Skelgill hears – a sharp, explosive report and a ringing ricochet.

The rock spins back over the aggressor's head.

The 'Canine Cannonball' delivers a debilitating head-butt.

Skelgill finishes the job with a ferocious shoulder charge.

But he does not stand on ceremony – there is still movement and he pinions the arms and pulls out his length of baler twine.

A hand falls on his shoulder.

DS Jones! The lass is even fitter than he thought.

'Jones – the rail! Over the rail!'

She hears enough and comprehends. And the dog is now pointing, her tail thrashing excitedly.

DS Jones takes one look over the precipice and drops prone to the ground.

She crawls forwards, dangerously unbalanced, and reaches down, out of Skelgill's sight.

He cannot let her act unaided.

How can she get any purchase – let alone not fall?

His captive immobilised, he lurches across.

He slides into a sitting position and grabs the waistband of DS Jones's hipster jeans, and braces the soles of his boots against an iron upright.

With a heave of his legs – straightening them like the action of rowing on a machine – he drags her backwards. The jeans come down a few inches, revealing skimpy briefs – but the denim holds – and now DS Jones gets one hand on the rail above her – and between them, in a bizarre tug of war, inch by inch, they haul first a bright yellow duplex webbing sling and then – after maybe four feet of material – over the edge appears a rain-washed countenance and a drenched head of grey hair.

What determination there is in those blue eyes.

She is not heavy. Now they pull her by the arms to safety – but only so far – for remarkably she is secured to the iron post. The climbing sling is held at the top by one locking carabiner and the bottom by a second, clipped into a sit-harness that she wears beneath her partially displaced nylon overtrousers.

Skelgill stares at the arrangement with alarm and wonderment.

Then the face – the distinctive chiselled features and noble bearing – that he last glimpsed peering over the bridge at Stencher Beck in Skelghyll Wood.

DS Jones hitches up her jeans – she flashes a wry glance at Skelgill.

She turns her attention to the elderly woman, leaning close in order to be heard.

'Dorothy?'

There is a moment's hesitation before the woman nods.

'We're the police. Cumbria CID. We've been trying to find you.'

The woman looks gratefully at DS Jones – and then turns her gaze to Skelgill.

'I've dropped something.'

She seems disturbed.

Skelgill edges closer, better to hear.

'Aye?'

She indicates towards the waterfall.

He looks with trepidation – as if he anticipates her answer.

'My hat.'

21. DOTTY

Aira Force parking area – 12.34 p.m., Tuesday 26th May

'Where are they taking him?'

DS Jones, gently chaperoning Dorothy K. Baum from the visitor cabin – a temporary police operations centre where a paramedic has checked her over – feels the woman falter in her stride. She looks across, following her charge's gaze. DS Leyton is feeding Derek Shaw into the back of a marked patrol car, taking care that he does not bang his head. Dorothy Baum stops completely – and for a moment she and the man make eye contact.

'We're based at Penrith. It's not far – just over ten miles.'

DS Jones waits patiently as the older woman watches the car pull away – the last in a small convoy of emergency vehicles that includes an ambulance. They have no need of sirens, but their blue lights strobe in a striking if unsynchronised display, unnaturally bright beneath the dense oak canopy and counterpane of cloud. The rain, however, has stopped.

When the woman does not speak – and seems diverted by some thought – DS Jones offers a prompt.

'We thought we'd take you to collect your belongings.'

Skelgill, gaining on them, overhears.

'First things first.'

DS Jones grins a little sheepishly.

'He means a cup of tea.'

Dorothy seems to perk up.

'I could murder a Builder's.'

She sees Skelgill's reaction and plainly approves that her vernacular has worked. For the first time since the rescue, she has a smile on her face.

Skelgill is thinking that the Yanks breed them tough.

They reach his car.

'All aboard.'

Glenridding car park – 12.46 p.m.

'I feel like someone has been trying to kill me for the past week.'

Skelgill raises an eyebrow. It is not a phrase even a man in his job hears every day.

'That's the conclusion we were coming to – we just didn't expect it to be a woman.'

He and Dorothy are seated at a picnic bench, opposite one another.

DS Jones is waiting in the queue at the burger van.

The sun makes a tentative peep through a rent in the cloud.

Skelgill squints pensively at the American. It is just sinking in that his team was not alone on the trail of the fake Felix.

Dorothy seems to understand his quandary.

'I suppose we have a lot of questions for one another.'

Skelgill makes a rueful face; perhaps he is wating for his colleague to return.

'That's some accent you've got.'

Dorothy smiles.

'I was just thinking the same.'

Skelgill grimaces, a mea culpa. But he engages with the subject matter.

'In a manner of speaking, it's what brought us to Aira Force.'

Now the bright blue eyes are penetrating.

'That's probably my first question, Inspector.'

Skelgill inclines his head in the direction of the burger van.

'My colleague was searching on Facebook – Roman trips. She played a video clip from last May – a bunch of schoolkids at Hardknott fort. I recognised a woman's voice in the background. She said, *"Come on, Patricia – chop, chop."'* Skelgill imitates the Lancashire accent.

The blue eyes are unblinking. Skelgill senses that, while they do not give much away, a whole gamut of emotions swirls behind them.

She asks the rational question.

'But how did you recognise the voice?'

'Stencher Beck – Skelghyll Wood.'

She hesitates, processing the information.

'That was you? My tin of mint cake.'

Skelgill affects another 'guilty as charged' look.

'We were revisiting an investigation. The death of one of your countrywomen, by the name of Patricia Jackson. It was where her body was found. It was originally believed she fell to her death.'

Now she is definitely repressing some powerful sentiment – Skelgill is not quite understanding why – unless it is the realisation that the same fate had been intended for her that day.

However, she muses calmly.

'And you are a Skelghyll.'

'With no 'h' and an 'i' – aye.'

'It feels as though it was meant to be.'

Skelgill shrugs.

'At that point – we didn't know you existed. I was inspecting the site because Patricia Jackson's passport had recently come to light. That same morning, my colleague DS Leyton picked up the chap Derek Shaw in Ambleside on an unrelated matter. He put us on to you – you were his alibi.'

Dorothy looks alarmed.

'Has he done something wrong?'

Skelgill regards her, perhaps a little guardedly.

'Not that I know of. Not lately –'

She seems shrewd enough not to push this further.

And now DS Jones returns, bearing a borrowed tray.

'Proper crockery, by special dispensation.'

She deals out steaming mugs of tea and bacon rolls on side plates. Finally, she dabs down two plastic squeezy bottles, one red, one brown.

'Dorothy – which sauce would you like?'

The woman looks at Skelgill.

'When in Rome?'

He hands her the red.

To say they are all hungry would be an understatement. There is a fourth bacon roll, which it might be deduced DS Jones has purchased for Skelgill. But, after a substantial bite of his own, he hands it down under the table, and then starts again on the spare. There is a brief moment of amused eye contact between the two females.

Then DS Jones remembers there is something she wants to say.

'By the way, Guv – over there. That greenish Fiat.' She has taken up a position beside Skelgill, and now she has to crane around. He follows suit. 'That's the car that we parked beside at Kirkstone Pass.'

When Skelgill turns back to the table, he realises Dorothy is staring past him.

'I saw it there, too. I also recognised it.'

'What do you mean?'

'I'm ninety-nine percent certain it's the car that ran me off the road in fog at Wrynose Pass. I saved myself by jumping down an embankment.'

She has the detectives' undivided attention.

'Her first attempt. Felix went to some lengths to convince me to go that way. The original plan had been to pass via Wastwater – which I so much wanted to see – but the weather took a turn for the worse; and, on my own, it made sense to follow the road. I was a sitting duck. Almost.'

DS Jones is already on her feet and has moved away a little, such that she can read the plate number of the car. She types it into her mobile phone and transmits a request for identification. She returns – and immediately she has a query for Dorothy.

'Were you with Cathy at all times after you met her?'

Dorothy shakes her head – and clearly she understands what DS Jones is getting at.

'Far from it. She could have been moving the car along from point to point – catching the bus – in fact I believe I saw her doing exactly that, here, yesterday morning. And at Ambleside she supposedly went off to visit the waterfall – but she could easily have returned to Little Langdale, and driven to Kirkstone Pass. Then a bus back.'

Skelgill shifts in his seat.

'She was keeping it handy, for a getaway.'

Dorothy nods.

'She was Felix – I told him about each of my stops. Particularly at the start – she knew exactly where I would be, and what my plans were.' She smiles absently. 'One way or another, she made most of my plans.'

There is a pensive silence; they each take the opportunity to eat. It is Skelgill that finally speaks.

'I've got two big questions.'

'The first?'

'What were you up to?'

Dorothy is about to reply, but checks herself.

'Is your second question, *why?*'

Skelgill nods.

'Patricia Carolyn Jackson. She's my sister. I *am* Dorothy – but not Baum.'

The silence that now ensues is one of respectfulness. In due course, Dorothy picks up her narrative.

'We lived separate, single lives – with no great deal of contact. We have never been especially close. And hundreds of miles apart – and, for long periods, thousands. But when she went away, for what proved to be the last time, she sent me a strange message – that she didn't want to talk about it, other than that she had met someone online – but that she would bring me up to date if everything worked out as she planned. Then I heard nothing. Through some contacts, I managed to find out that she had sold up and had travelled to England. There wasn't much to go on – but with our distant family roots in Cumbria I eventually came across her history on the group Facebook page. And that's where I discovered Felix – and that she had probably been interacting with him.'

She pauses and gazes reflectively into the distance, the true horizon of High Street taking form as the cloud base lifts imperceptibly and mist and rock become separated.

'Of course, I had no thought of there having been foul play. It was merely the one lifeline I had to Patricia. I developed a relationship with Felix.' She jerks her attention away from the skyline, and interrogates the detectives in turn. 'You see, I am growing old alone.'

DS Jones is watching with glistening eyes; Skelgill is stern but appreciative. Dorothy continues.

'The picture that Felix painted was very appealing. A good part of me – more than half – wanted it to be real. And if it were not – I was drawn anyway. It felt like a calling – that I should follow the road that stretched out before me.'

DS Jones leans forward.

'But you were suspicious – you came prepared.'

Dorothy lowers her gaze and shakes her head, almost in self-reproach, as if this were some failing of her character.

'I suppose … one's life experiences … they prepare you for things to be not as they seem, for disappointments, for dishonesty. So – yes – I hedged my bets. I set up an anonymous profile. When we began to correspond in earnest, I called myself Dorothy K. Baum.'

'You catfished the catfisher.'

Dorothy glances sharply at DS Jones.

'You might say I did. But my part was played with sincerity. I was the Dorothy K. Baum that believed she was here to start a new life with Professor Felix Stowe-Upland, to buy Rose Cottage together. Sure – deep down inside there was another me, the real Dorothy, analysing, asking what if? But with hindsight, had I not lived in character I would never have fooled Cathy. Imagine – there were times when I was defending Felix against Cathy's criticisms and she was he all along. And at other times I was not always most complimentary about her, in my messages to him!'

Dorothy gazes wide-eyed at her audience, as if she cannot quite believe what she is saying.

DS Jones goes again.

'When did you realise it was a woman – that it was Cathy?'

Dorothy lays her palms flat on the timber surface and leans forward; her eyes implore them to believe her.

'You know – I didn't.' She sits back, and contemplates for a moment, intertwining her slender fingers in a rhythmical motion. 'As the time to travel to England approached, I sensed that Felix was taking considerable lengths not to reveal himself to me. You would think he might have telephoned, for example – but he was content to do everything by electronic means – indeed email. Lately, I couldn't help noticing that some of Felix's emails came soon after conversations with Cathy. She was using Felix to steer a course that suited her best – that provided her with opportunities. She must have a smartphone. I thought it was odd that she claimed not to – although she is an extremely odd person. That is to say, if 'Cathy' is no less of an act than 'Felix'.

Dorothy pauses – as if this idea has come new to her in this time of self-enlightenment – but she visibly brushes aside the distraction with a shake of her head.

'I also let her know that I still had money in my account. Shortly after, Felix came up with a need for more, for the property transaction. All the time, the pennies were dropping – the possible explanation and motivation for what might have befallen Patricia. That the fantastical world of promises woven by Felix was just that – a fantasy designed to deceive. So, I played for time. I held back the funds. I thought it would force a mistake. I suppose it was something of an insurance policy for me. Felix also thought I had ten thousand dollars in my belt-bag.' Perhaps subconsciously, her hand moves to touch the item at her waist. 'I had begun to understand that Felix's time and opportunities for 'mishaps' were running out. Wrynose Pass. Skelghyll Wood, and High Skelghyll. Blea Water Crag.'

DS Jones cannot conceal her fascination.

'But you were expecting to be pushed – at Aira Force – you were prepared – your climbing harness, anchored to the railing.'

'I felt Aira Force would be the last big chance. The signals I was getting – everyone seemed to be saying that I mustn't miss the falls in the rain – that no one would be there because of the weather. I made a reconnaissance visit yesterday. I bought the climbing equipment in the shop, here in Glenridding. I told the assistant it was a gift for my granddaughter, who is my size! I thought if I was going to be pushed over, I ought to choose the best spot. I set the trap – I had to take it to the limit.'

The detectives are both shaking their heads.

DS Jones, in particular, is perplexed.

'But what were you going to do?'

Dorothy glances at Skelgill.

'I still had a couple of shots in my locker.'

Skelgill looks momentarily alarmed – but when DS Jones inhales, perhaps to press her inquiry, he throws in what might be considered a diversionary question.

'Why not just go to the police – in the States – here?'

Dorothy smiles coyly.

'I think I might have been told I was a dotty old lady playing at Miss Marple.'

DS Jones, an aficionado of the murder mystery genre, has a rebuttal to this argument.

'She was dotty – but ruthlessly effective.'

Perhaps it is the harsh adverb – but now Dorothy seems to row back a little from her position.

'You see – it was so tentative – really until it began to unfold around me, once I was here.' But she seems to feel she might have made a small faux pas. She presses her palms together in a gesture of supplication. 'Of course – I underestimated your fine British police – you, yourselves. You – you had it worked out, with only a fraction of the information at my disposal.'

Skelgill makes a tutting sound, an attempt at self-deprecation.

'Aye, one step behind, though. You led us a merry dance in the fells.'

Dorothy looks inquiringly from one officer to the other; DS Jones obliges.

'We couldn't find where you stayed after Ravenglass and Little Langdale. And in both of those places it appeared you were alone. Although Derek Shaw told us you were meeting a friend – and we found a reference to a 'Felix' on your discarded newspaper.'

Dorothy raises an eyebrow – it could be admiration of DS Jones's tradecraft – or, equally, self-admonition for her own lapse.

'I suspect Cathy had a range of accommodation booked in advance.' She half turns and points across her shoulder at the row of properties beyond Glenridding Beck. 'Over there, for instance – I think she was pre-booked into Rattlebeck Guest House –

anticipating that I would be lying at the foot of Blea Water Crag. At Ambleside, she also added a room for me – but in her name.'

Skelgill grunts.

'That's where we lost the trail.'

Dorothy regards him phlegmatically.

'At that stage it seems clear I wasn't supposed to get beyond Skelghyll Wood.'

Now Skelgill shakes his head resignedly.

'And I just thought you were a pair of eccentric hikers – chucking stuff off bridges. After that, we were looking for either a single woman or a male-female couple.'

Dorothy is nodding pensively.

'Cathy is wily. I had to get proof. For myself – that if she were willing to murder me – then it must have been her that killed Patricia. And, to come back to the question – I don't feel that I absolutely did know until she was wielding that boulder, shrieking, *"Die, Dorothy!"'*

She pauses, and then inhales as though to continue – but she sees that Skelgill is regarding her as though he is wrestling with the notion that some reciprocal arrangement had been in the offing.

In the event her poignant words silence all three of them, and they turn their attention to what remains of their bacon rolls. In short order, Skelgill is beginning to eye the lack of a queue at the burger van; a corresponding aura of restlessness emanates from beneath the picnic bench.

But a thought strikes Skelgill that causes him to make a little exclamation of guilt.

'We even shook down the real prof – Stowe-Upland – the chap whose profile she hijacked.' He glances at DS Jones. 'We'd better let him know. He'll be a witness to the impersonation.'

DS Jones nods, and is about to answer, but Dorothy interjects.

'And Derek – may I speak with him?'

'Aye – soon enough – we're just taking his statement.' Skelgill looks at her with a glint of amusement in his eye. 'Seems like you had one wing of a guardian angel there.'

But Dorothy is quick with a counter.

'And you, Inspector, were the other wing.'

Perhaps with a modicum of reluctance, Skelgill plays down the suggestion.

'If it weren't for my team, I'd still be scrattin' about in Skelghyll Wood.'

Dorothy looks generously upon DS Jones; but now her features harden.

'And what about Cathy?'

Skelgill hesitates to answer, and indeed inclines his head to indicate that he is passing the responsibility to DS Jones. She takes a moment to compose herself.

'Dorothy, with what you have told us – together with what we have witnessed – we have enough to press initial charges today – sufficient to hold her in custody. I'm just waiting for the doctor's all-clear to interview her this afternoon. We'd also like a formal statement from yourself.'

Dorothy bows her head cooperatively – but Skelgill notices that she flashes him just the faintest of glances – and he cannot help feeling that there is something she wants to tell him.

DS Jones, meanwhile, is prompted to check her mobile phone – and it seems the wires are hotting up.

'Ah – that's us.'

She looks at Skelgill for guidance.

But Skelgill is still regarding Dorothy with a degree of uncertainty.

'Guv?'

Skelgill drums the fingers of his left hand on the table surface; it seems he is torn.

Then he addresses his colleague.

'You head back – see what else you can find out, before we start. No point going in blind.'

DS Jones nods compliantly, although she does not look approving of the entirety of Skelgill's suggestion.

'What will you do, Guv?'

Skelgill turns to Dorothy.

'You wanted to see Wastwater?' She seems hesitant, and does not have a ready reply. He casts a hand skywards. 'Give it half an hour – the sun'll be cracking the cobbles.'

He rises and – trailed by his canine familiar – he stalks across to the burger van.

22. SO LONG

Wastwater – 3.03 p.m., Tuesday 26th May

'What a glorious sight.'

Skelgill cannot help but agree.

'Deepest lake in England – the bottom's below sea level. The screes are a famous feature. And that's Great Gable at the far end.'

'You must be proud of your heritage.'

'Keeps us daft country coppers happy while we're on duty.'

She looks at him reproachfully.

'You have proved yourself to be far from daft.'

Skelgill seems reluctant to bask in any praise.

'Small beer – compared to what you've done.'

Dorothy does not argue; but neither does she seem inclined towards a display of triumph.

'I wonder if Patricia saw this view.' She pauses, her gaze pensive, as Wasdale and its lake stretches out before them, colours, shadows and highlights coming to life in the sunshine, everywhere bright with the gloss of the recent rain. 'And I wonder why Cathy changed her mind.'

Skelgill tilts his head from side to side deliberatively.

'Happen it were just to get you interested – promised you the scenic route. From Wasdale Head to Boot, mind, it wouldn't have been much fun in the rain. Though it's do-able – there's an easy path, no need to go right over the tops.'

'She must have decided that an automobile accident was too good a chance to miss. Then when that did not succeed, she reverted to her tried-and-trusted method. Where there's a waterfall, there's a dangerous drop.'

'Sounds like that were a close shave at the Wrynose.'

Dorothy gives an ironic laugh.

'I suspect she actually believed she'd got me. I wonder what she thought when she found me at her B&B in Little Langdale. I'd never have guessed anything from her reaction.'

Skelgill murmurs his understanding; but he waits, and after a moment she picks up her thread.

'I should have put two and two together sooner. Felix would write to me – he frequently used Latin phrases – intended to embellish his classical persona, I suppose. But some of them were just plain nonsense – as if the writer had resorted to Google Translate. And there were flaws in several of the historical assumptions. I put the latter down to Derek being wrong – but plainly it was the other way around.'

They both gaze reflectively at the absorbing vista.

Skelgill is scouting for rises. Wastwater is known for its Arctic char.

Dorothy unfastens her seatbelt.

'Would you mind if I went out for a short while?'

'Be my guest. Take as long as you like. We can get back by the coast road and the A66 – it'll be a lot quicker.'

He watches as she leaves the car and walks, gracefully he thinks. She has dispensed with her waterproofs and of course the sit-harness, though she still wears her belt-bag over her hiking trousers. There is not a lot to her – and he is thankful for the fact, for there was a moment when he singlehandedly hauled the combined weight of Dorothy and DS Jones – but maybe only equivalent to one DS Leyton. Nevertheless, he had thrown caution to the wind as far as his recalcitrant spine was concerned; but all seems well.

He imagines that Dorothy is thinking about her sister. He hopes she did make it here. Notwithstanding that the spot is perennially voted the best view in Britain by quack Sunday newspaper travel correspondents, the more credible reviewer Alfred Wainwright waxed lyrical about the Wastwater Screes. Skelgill feels in the door pocket for Book Four, which he has consulted several times in the past week. But his hand falls on the tin of Kendal mint cake, his trophy from High Street summit.

He examines the tin – thinking he ought to return it (if indeed it had belonged to Dorothy). The traditional embossed design is partly obscured by a gaudy yellow promotional sticker. It tempts the prospective buyer to *"Make a Mint!"*. He extends his arm in order to read the small print. Squinting, inherently cynical of commercial enticements, his expression gradually changes, and by the time he has absorbed the message his jaw has dropped slightly open. He looks up – and stares unseeingly down the lake.

And then he starts – for his phone strikes up, a pleasantly melodic guitar riff that he seems unwilling to terminate.

But he accepts the call just before it diverts.

'Jones.'

'Guv – can you talk?'

She has a breathless note in her voice – intended to convey a sense of urgency.

'Aye – she's out by the lake.'

'Guv – where to begin.'

'Aye.'

Platitudes exchanged, DS Jones continues.

'Yes – we've unearthed a bucketload of evidence already. And there's feedback from the States – quite extraordinary.'

He waits as she inhales, necessary preparation to launch into an explanation.

'That car – the green Fiat – is registered to a woman called Lilith Marjory West at an address in Pendle, Lancashire. She lives alone, unmarried. Until three years ago she was a history teacher at a nearby school, when she was dismissed for some impropriety. She was also involved in local amateur dramatics. *She is the woman called Cathy.* We've already got photographic and fingerprint matches – a local unit has been to the property. To cut a long story short – they've found a drawer that contains passports, IDs, credit cards. It looks like she's been up to this for some time. I think it's her occupation.'

'Happen Dorothy's right – and Cathy is an act, an' all.'

DS Jones does not demur. But she has more facts to convey.

'One of the credit cards belonged to Patricia Jackson, issued by an American bank. DC Watson has interrogated the transactions – it was used last year at a small hotel at Pooley Bridge on what was probably the day after Patricia Jackson fell to her death. That explains the passport being at Arthur's Pike on High Street – the Cathy woman must have been heading north, and dropped it – just as you thought, Guv.'

Skelgill is nodding; DS Jones continues.

'If Cathy made the reservations, it explains why we couldn't trace Patricia Jackson at Ambleside. And Cathy must have removed her possessions after the fatal fall in Skelghyll Wood. My guess is that she enacted a very similar plan to that she tried on Dorothy – she befriended her and played on her loneliness and insecurity when Felix continued not to show up. I think we're going to have a lot on this woman, Guv. Clearly Dorothy and Patricia Jackson are not her first victims. I only hope it has been limited to fraud – and those who have been scammed have just been too embarrassed to come forward.'

Skelgill is now looking at Dorothy; she remains in a meditative pose.

'What about the FBI?'

'This is amazing, too. The local sheriff in St Francisville put two and two together and identified Dorothy. So, the FBI know who she is. Guv – she's got a classified file.'

'What does that mean?'

'Secret service.'

'What – now?'

'Oh, no – she has been long retired. They won't tell me too much. By my contact has given me an off-the-record briefing, on pain of death. Dorothy Jackson served in the United States military before being recruited by the CIA. She worked undercover in East Berlin during the height of the Cold War. She is a judo black-belt and won national medals for shooting when she was at college – and she achieved the Olympic sprint breast-stroke qualification time of her era. She speaks fluent German, Russian and Czech.'

'Explains how she can understand me.'

DS Jones cannot suppress a chuckle; Skelgill has a knack for dry understatement.

'It also explains how she has managed to do what she has done – to have the knowhow – and the spirit.'

But at this point Skelgill disagrees.

'You can't be taught guts – you know that, lass.'

There is perhaps a rare compliment here, sprinkled with introspection – but DS Jones argues her corner.

'What I mean, though, is how she managed to stay in character – almost to convince herself. She would have been trained in anti-interrogation techniques.'

Skelgill finds he is staring at Dorothy, sitting elfin on a large rock. To be sure, she is something of a dark horse. He watches as she reaches down, and a couple of times casually skims pebbles across the water. He notices she is left-handed. And then she adjusts her trousers, and rolls to one side, and rises, and in one smooth movement she throws something, far out across the surface. It glints in the sun as it spins, and Skelgill could swear to the bluish-purple tinge of gunmetal. And a modest splash; a pound, maybe a pound and a half, were it a lake trout.

She begins to stride briskly towards the car.

'Jones – she's coming back – I'll catch you later.'

He must seem disturbed, for a frown creases Dorothy's brow as she ducks into the passenger seat.

'Are you alright, Inspector? Was there something – I heard you got a call on your cell?'

'Aye – nay bother. Look – ' He realises he is still holding the tin of mint cake. 'I found this at High Street – the trig point. I reckon it's yourn.'

'Ah – yes – more good detective work.' She smiles, rather knowingly, it seems to Skelgill. 'I left it – I suppose it was a kind of goodwill message to Derek.'

Skelgill makes an apologetic face.

'Sorry about that.'

'Not at all – why don't you have it? You seem to be the mountaineer between the two of us.'

Skelgill grimaces.

'I've already got the one you nearly brained me with – it's in Sergeant Jones's car.'

Dorothy makes a sound of regret.

But there is a short silence; no conversation is far from recent peril.

Skelgill sticks his neck out.

'I see you're a cuddy wifter.'

'I beg your pardon?'

Her tone is ingenuous, if edged with just a hint of guardedness.

'A lefty's what you call it, I reckon.'

'Ah.'

She relaxes back into her seat and folds her arms. She gazes ahead.

'The deepest lake in England, you say.'

It is not so much a question as an answer, and Skelgill is pretty certain he understands. He reaches for the ignition. He clears his throat.

'We'll drive by Nether Wasdale. There's a store with a pillar box outside – send another postcard, if you want.'

There is perhaps a chuckle, a purr in Dorothy's throat.

'Touché, Inspector.'

Penrith railway station – 7.47 p.m.

'I reckon if we stand here, it'll be about right for your coach.'

Skelgill places Dorothy's rucksack carefully on the platform. He and DS Jones have accompanied her, despite her offer to walk alone the comparatively short distance from headquarters to the railway station. And they have assented to her request to continue with her journey; good weather is forecast and – out of the fells – there will be no problems in keeping in touch, to facilitate subsequent interviews.

Skelgill checks his watch against the station clock; the express from London is on time and due in three minutes.

His mobile phone strikes up. Dorothy is amused – the Lambeth Walk – she looks like she knows it, and is tempted to react to the irresistible strains of the tune.

'Leyton?'

Skelgill listens.

'Hold on, marra. We're just seeing Dorothy off.'

He turns to DS Jones.

'You might want to hear this.'

They excuse themselves to a distance out of earshot. Dorothy waits beside her luggage.

Skelgill engages the loudspeaker.

'What it is, Guv – I've got the gen on Derek Shaw. Just to remind you, he was charged with the English equivalent of manslaughter and GBH. He was aged nineteen at the time and a student at St Andrews University. He was walking back from a nightclub when he came across a woman being hassled at knifepoint by two geezers. They turned on him – but it seems he could handle himself. He sparked out the first lout and gave the other a right old pasting. The one he knocked out hit his head on the kerb and died in hospital three days later. The survivor claimed it was Shaw that had assaulted the woman, and that him and his mate came to her rescue. The prosecution tried to argue it was excessive force. The lady obviously testified in Shaw's favour. And the jury believed his story.'

Just as DS Leyton is finishing his account, Skelgill and DS Jones are distracted by what could seem like an eerie manifestation of mental projection – for Derek Shaw passes through the doors of the ticket office onto the platform. He carries his full pack, Saunders Spacepacker strapped on top, metal detector slung to one side, and notices the detectives, whom he acknowledges with a respectful bow of the head. Then he spies Dorothy waiting; she is facing away, watching for the train. He makes his way in her direction, but he pulls up short.

Skelgill's voice takes on a note of urgency.

'Leyton – I take it you've got his witness statement sorted – because he's just turned up at the station.'

'Oh, yeah, Guv – all hunky dory. He reckons he was keeping half an eye on Dorothy – as they seemed to be crossing paths – and he witnessed some strange behaviour by the Cathy woman. But nothing controversial as far as he's concerned. Truth be told, he seems a decent enough cove. Although I still can't get it out of my head that he was the one digging up the ancient monuments.'

Skelgill makes a strange exclamation that has DS Jones looking at him in alarm.

'Leyton, that reminds me – I've cracked your nighthawker case for you.'

'Really, Guv?'

'On your way home – stop at the garage and buy a tin of Kendal mint cake.'

'Say that again, Guv.'

'Mint cake, Leyton – silver tin with blue design. You want the one with a yellow sticker. Alreet?'

Skelgill rather peremptorily hangs up. But he has spied the Glasgow-bound express, silent in the distance, making its slow reptilian approach to Penrith, winding into sight around a bend in the track.

There is also the small matter of Derek and Dorothy.

Indeed, Derek Shaw, after standing for a few moments – perhaps uncertain of whether to approach, and hoping she might turn and notice him, begins to whistle the opening bars of "The Star-Spangled Banner".

The detectives watch on.

Dorothy turns.

'Derek!'

'I didn't recognise you without your hat.'

Dorothy flashes him a smile of resignation.

'I mislaid it at Aira Force. In the heat of battle.'

'But the flag was still there.'

They exchange a glance of the sort that carries unspoken words.

The train is nearing; the rails are humming, and they are all starting to hear the locomotive. Other waiting passengers begin to gather up their belongings and edge closer to the track.

Derek Shaw raises his voice.

'Where are you heading?'

'I intend to pick up Hadrian's Wall at Carlisle.'

The man holds out his hands.

'Me, too.'

Dorothy regards him with a twinkle in her eye.

'Perfect.'

'Carry your bag, madam?'

'You are ever the gentleman.'

Derek Shaw chuckles.

'Hey up – it's lighter than I remember – have you used all that ammunition?'

Dorothy flashes a glance at the detectives, whom she knows can overhear the exchange.

'I decided there was no further need for my climbing gear.'

Derek Shaw appears to think she is joking, but he plays along with it.

'Hadrian's Wall's fifteen feet high in places – but I can always give you a bunk up.'

But now any further conversation is drowned out by the arrival of the express.

The detectives watch on as the pair board and get themselves settled. As the train begins to move again, Dorothy waves from her seat.

When the last carriage has passed, it seems that DS Jones has been waiting to speak.

'Guv – just before I reached you – at the waterfall?'

'Aye?'

Skelgill's response has a ring of expectation about it.

'There was a sound – like a gunshot.'

Skelgill is watching the rear of the train as it diminishes in size, now rounding a bend in the northerly direction.

It takes him quite a few moments to answer.

'You did say she was in the CIA …'

He leaves any implication hanging; DS Jones is not quite ready to let it drop. She tries a more oblique tack.

'Do you think she still has active contacts here in the UK?'

Skelgill shrugs.

'Don't suppose she'd be allowed to tell us.'

DS Jones presses her point.

'But not Derek Shaw – you don't think?'

'Nay – not him.'

But Skelgill's negation carries a contradiction.

DS Jones gestures to the point on the platform from which the couple had embarked.

'Do you think they arranged this?'

Skelgill understands she means the apparently impromptu meeting. But he seems phlegmatic.

'It's what folk do.' There is perhaps a wistful note in his voice. 'Can't say I'd blame her – after a narrow scrape like that.'

DS Jones regards Skelgill pensively.

'Do you think she intended to take Cathy over the edge with her?'

Skelgill nods in a non-committal manner, but one that suggests he has certainly entertained this possibility.

'I don't know about that – but she nearly took you with her. Just as well your jeans held out.' He glances down mischievously. 'And I'm only saying this since you've said it to me – nice pants.'

She gives him a sharp jab in the midriff.

Skelgill flinches, and raises his hands in surrender.

'Just saying, lass – you'd be alreet if you were run over by a bus.'

Now she folds her arms and stares at him inscrutably.

'That could be *one* reason for wearing them.'

***

POSTSCRIPT

Article in the Westmorland Gazette, by Kendall Minto

POLICE SOLVE METAL-DETECTING MYSTERY. Just when it seemed a gang of ruthless nighthawkers had got away with desecrating archaeological sites across the county, DS Leyton of Cumbria Police, speaking exclusively to the Gazette, yesterday revealed the culprit. And the answer is … KENDAL MINT CAKE! Yes – and no need, dear reader, to point out the literal connection to yours truly; it has been mentioned once or twice over the years (despite that Minto is a good Scottish Borders name).

But I digress. Sergeant Leyton – a colleague of the highly regarded DS Emma Jones, with whom readers of this column will be familiar – has identified a most unexpected explanation. A well-known local brand of Kendal mint cake, to celebrate their centenary, came up with what has proved to be a rather unfortunate marketing campaign. *'Make a Mint'* involved the firm having ten specially minted commemorative gold coins secretly hidden at places of historic interest throughout the Lake District. Codes on the tins could be entered on the brand's website, in exchange for clues to likely locations. Unfortunately, the robust consumer response left the marketing team red-faced – as eager treasure-hunters set about ancient monuments with picks and shovels, in a race to unearth the valuable prizes!

Suffice to say, the National Trust and Historic England were not amused. However, there is a silver lining. The campaign has been a roaring success – sales have boomed and all excess profits have been pledged to the aforesaid charitable organisations. It seems there are no hard feelings. And how could a grudge be held when we have such a precious local product, one that has revived many a tired walker and been carried to the highest point on the planet? As a perspicacious Sergeant Leyton put it:

"Kendal mint cake to the Lakes, it's an institution – it's like pie and mash to London, or sprouts to Brussels."

Next in the series ...

TROUBLED WATERS

An attempted murder in the United States ... a tragic road death in a Cumbrian forest ... an old photograph stolen from an ancient coaching inn. Unrelated events – until a midnight drowning below Ouse Bridge exposes a connection. After two decades, has a killer returned to Cumbria to ply their trade? Does a suspect hide in plain sight among loose acquaintances? Who is truthful and who is lying? Skelgill must patiently circle ... until finally he picks up the scent.

'Murder at the Bridge' by Bruce Beckham is available from Amazon.

FREE BOOKS, NEW RELEASES, THE BEAUTIFUL LAKES ... AND MOUNTAINS OF CAKES

Sign up for Bruce Beckham's author newsletter

Thank you for getting this far!

If you have enjoyed your encounter with DI Skelgill there's a growing series of whodunits set in England's rugged and beautiful Lake District to get your teeth into.

My newsletter often features one of the back catalogue to download for free, along with details of new releases and special offers.

No Skelgill mystery would be complete without a café stop or two, and each month there's a traditional Cumbrian recipe – tried and tested by yours truly (aka *Bruce Bake 'em*).

To sign up, this is the link:

https://mailchi.mp/acd032704a3f/newsletter-sign-up

Your email address will be safely stored in the USA by Mailchimp, and will be used for no other purpose. You can unsubscribe at any time simply by clicking the link at the foot of the newsletter.

Thank you, again – best wishes and happy reading!

Bruce Beckham

Printed in Great Britain
by Amazon